Highness

A Lonely Heart Series Novel

Latrivia S. Nelson

Highness
RiverHouse Publishing, LLC
1509 Madison Avenue
Memphis, TN 38104

All **RiverHouse, LLC** Titles, Imprints and Distributed Lines are available at special quantity discounts for bulk purchases for sales promotions, premiums, fund-raising and educational or institutional use.

First RiverHouse, LLC Trade E-Book Printing 4-28-15

Report abuse to the FBI at www.fbi.gov.

www.latrivianelson.info

www.riverhousepublishingllc.com

ISBN 978-0-9962725-2-0

This book is dedicated to Bruce Welch, who taught me the meaning of love at first sight.

Acknowledgments

To my awesome team of beta readers from the Love Pub, Karen Moss, Michelle D. Jackson, Leonie Radway and Sheila Kehinde, I cannot thank you enough for your encouraging words and wonderful feedback and most importantly awesome eyes during this process. To my friends, fans and supporters, I love you all and truly hope that it entertains you.

Chapter 1

London, UK
Brixton

The sun seemed bright. *Too bright.*

Rolling over in the bed to cover his face from the glimmering rays, Michael suddenly realized that it was morning, or at least daytime. The exact hour was as questionable as…

Oh God, where was he? His body went rigid in its stillness. While not fully sure of the answer to his question, he was still grateful it was not somewhere public. He had done that once as a young man in his 20s, and made front page news.

His auditory functions kicked in first. Without opening his eyes, he listened carefully to his surroundings. Through the open window to the left of him, he could hear vehicles driving down the street in the distance and the echo of people talking outside. Based upon their dialect, they were poor, and at least one of them was drunk and furious over 20 quid.

The smell of the room was the next thing he noticed. It was a curious and unintentional mix of cheap perfume, curry, and marijuana, which meant he had either gone home with a young woman over 18 but and under 25 years of age or a cross-dressing, Indian man who would soon have the munchies.

As he moved into a groggy consciousness, vivid flashes of the night before clouded his mind.

All Michael could remember before blacking out the night before was walking into Boujis, a well-known West London club with his entourage, where he decided to forgo VIP, and proceed straight to the main bar where he was forced to take a hundred selfies with socialites, down shots of Whiskey with celebrities and dance with pretty half-naked locals to DJ Klaus. By all accounts, the same thing he did any Saturday that he could steal away from travels and work.

About ten Whiskey's and jelly body shots later, everything quickly and abruptly faded to black. The club began to swim. The music became louder. The strobe lights became dizzying and whatever he said after that, he should not be accountable for in a court of law.

Fast forwarding to early dawn, *which was the next flash of conscious poor decisions*, he vaguely recalled giggling girls undressing and fumbling with an edible condom in the dark, but who the girls were was as much of a mystery as what had truly happened afterward. Questions plagued him. Had he passed out cold or had he completed the deal?

There was only one way to find out.

Reluctantly, he finally opened the slits of his crystal blue eyes and focused.

There was a dirty blonde beside him on the bed, looking directly at him with a smile on her face – a sort of twisted smile. It was the kind a woman gave when she was proud of herself for her performance the night before. She was young, over 18 for sure but barely in her 20s. With a round face sprinkled with freckles and doe-like chocolate brown eyes, she gazed at him as if she was waiting for him to say something. *Approve of her performance, perhaps?*

Pity, he didn't remember the night before. And he didn't recognize her from Adam, but he did recognize his tailor-made Oxford, which she now wore and would probably ask to keep. Sure of this from multiple previous experiences, he made a mental note not to ask for it back this time.

"Good morning, love," she said, biting her pouty pink lips. From what he could tell, they were the most attractive things on her.

Michael blinked hard and stretched out his long body. "Good morning," he said at the same time covering up his mouth. *Ugh*. Morning breath. Only, he wasn't sure if it was his or hers.

Raising his head up slightly, he yawned again and checked out the room.

First glance revealed a small bedroom littered with piles of clothes, old fast food containers, and posters of rock bands.

"Good morning," another voice said from the other side of the large bed. He turned unenthusiastically and stared at a voluptuous mid-to-late 20s redhead, still very naked. Like a cat, she slinked up closer to him and rubbed down the center of his muscular back with the tips of her tiny fingers. Her blue eyes sparkled bright with promising mischief.

Now, he could understand how she had gotten him in bed, but the blonde must have been *value added*, like the coupons one gets in the bottom of a box after purchasing a very large piece of kitchenware.

He smiled back at the redhead, mirroring her knowing grin and then realized that he too was naked, only because at that moment, she was giving him a serious erection, or maybe it was just morning wood, though he dared not go to the loo in this place unless he was near an eruption.

Milky white, natural breasts pushed up towards his face as she wrapped her slender arms around his neck and hugged him tight, raking her nails through his tendrils of blonde hair. It was the manner in which she pulled him in that made him forget himself for the moment. She was warm and alluring, and something about her naked body reminded him of Christmas morning. He nuzzled his head into the side of her neck and smelled her scent - a mix of perfume and sex. Pushing her pelvis up against his erection, she started to slowly grind against him.

As if reading lines and following cues, the other blonde was on his back now, rubbing through his hair and kissing the back of his neck. He could feel her rigid nipples against him and her sex pushed up against his bottom.

Hmm. That felt good. A nice little early morning *ménage à trois*.

"Care to pick up where we left off?" the redhead asked in his ear as her legs parted just enough for him to feel the heat rush from her core.

What is your name? Michael thought to himself. For some reason, he'd really wanted to know, but was a little afraid to ask. In the past, when he had drank too much, he had promised women *like her* the world and when they discovered that he wasn't serious the morning after, they had become...angry.

"I'd love to pick up where we left off," Michael answered, feeling the blonde reach over him and run her small hands over his erection. "But first things first, ladies." He managed a small chuckle. "Where the hell am I?"

Both of the women giggled. "You're in our flat," the blonde said, biting his ear.

"Brixton," the redhead answered, being more specific. "Have you ever been to Brixton, your Highness?"

"No," he said, smile faint. *How in the hell did he get to Brixton last night?*

The redhead moved to kiss him, but he quickly pulled back. There was no denying that he was a freaky guy, but he had a thing about kissing strangers. *Not on the mouth.* It was way too personal for his taste. *A man had to have standards.*

"Maybe I can kiss something else for you?" the redhead said, slipping her hand over the blonde's hand around his shaft.

Temptation started to flood him again.

He closed his eyes and debated whether or not the impending threesome would be as fun sober. Sober meant that he'd remember it. Sober meant that he'd have to think about it later. But their heat was intoxicating as was their movements. He'd need some help to get out of this debacle, lest he find himself buried in between both of their thighs giving them a proper fucking.

Prayers answered, a loud knock on the front door interrupted his internal debate.

Arresting her progress for the moment, he held up her chin as she moved towards his throbbing penis. All three rose up and looked towards the open bedroom door. It was a clear view down the hall to the small living room, also covered in clothes and rickety furniture.

Goodness, did these women never tidy up?

"Who could that be?" the blonde asked the redhead, voice a lot less sexy suddenly.

"Don't know." the redhead shrugged.

Michael knew that knock without even seeing who was behind the door. He had heard it a hundred times before. With a cosmetic growl and internal relief, he pulled himself from the hold of the young women and stood up at the end of the bed.

On the floor were his clothes in a pile, right beside three used condoms, underwear, slacks, shirt, and wallet. Within seconds, he was dressed in all of it, and again another loud knock rang out at the front door. It was like a second warning shot in his ears, demanding his immediate attention.

"I'll get it," the redhead moaned, jumping out of bed. She walked towards the door naked, not bothering to cover herself.

With a gentle hand, Michael grabbed her softly by the fold of her long arm and smiled. "No need, love." He slipped on his black loafers without socks. "*That* would just be my wake-up call."

"Oh," she said, lips parting. She rubbed a hand down the side of his square jaw. "Well, when you have some time, make sure to come by again." A wicked smile crossed her lips. "We can all pick up where we left off. I would love to have you in my mouth again. The taste of you is delicious."

Unsure of how to reply, he looked over at the blonde still in bed and cleared his throat. "I'll make sure to remember that." Inwardly, he was praying that all of his DNA had gone either down the girls' throat or in the condoms. Otherwise, he might be in trouble.

The reality of his one-night stand sobered him completely up. Time to go...NOW.

Patting his pants for his keys, he looked down at his wrist to see the time.

Right. Of course, that wasn't there.

With a raised brow, he looked back up at them. "You girls haven't seen a Rolex around here by any chance, have you?" He had been through this a hundred times also, and he was certain that these girls were not amateurs. *A man wakes up, realizes where he is, and prepares to bolt out of the situation and in the midst of it forgets to check for all the valuables that he may or may not have voluntarily parted with the night before.*

The blonde gave a *jig's up* smile to her roommate and then turned, perfect naked bottom up in the air, to dig over in the corner by the bed. He enjoyed all five seconds of her searching for the said watch and also noticed that she bleached her woman parts. *Nice.* Too bad they didn't bleach anything else in their flat.

Pulling a Presidential Rolex from the pile of papers beside the nightstand, she got up from the bed; breasts exposed and passed it to him. The gold glimmered across her face as the sun's reflection hit it. "I wonder how that got there," she said, not bothering to hide her naughtiness.

"These things happen," he grinned. "Thank you," he said, slipping the watch on his wrist. With a sigh, he gave one last look around the closet of a room. Two beautiful girls. One shitty flat. One forgettable night. It was a shame that he'd done it all before. "You ladies have a wonderful..." He looked at his watch. "Afternoon." He dipped his head respectfully. "Thank you for your hospitality."

Walking through the messy apartment, past the pealed paint, over the stained carpet and through the woods, he arrived at the door covered in latches and bolts and worked his way through the locks. When he finally opened the door, his men were there patiently waiting for him.

"Your Royal Highness," his head guard Geoff said nodding at him. "It was getting late, sir. I apologize for interrupting, but her majesty the Queen requests your presence at Balmoral Castle at once. We are to put you on a private plane and get you there immediately, if not sooner." He had used her exact words.

Michael's stomach growled furiously. "You are to take me to get some breakfast immediately, Geoff. The queen can wait. Besides, I don't need two guesses to know what she wants."

Michael reached for his shades to cover his bloodshot eyes and ward off the hangover headache approaching, but realized that they must still be inside. And there was no way in hell that he was about to revisit Cinderella's stepsisters to get them back.

Closing the rickety door behind him quietly, he stuck his head over the iron banister and looked downstairs at the paparazzi waiting for him on the patchy lawn. *Great!*

"Is there any other way out of here?" he asked.

"No, sir. One way in and one way out," Geoff said disgusted by the very existence of the place. "They've been camped out all night," he said of the photographers. "They followed you here from the party. I think that your two lovely friends in there tipped them off."

Michael chuckled. "But of course they did. Well, let's get this over with," he said, running a hand through his blonde locks. He paused. "Did you happen to get the paper?"

"Yes, sir," Geoff said, passing it to him hesitantly. "You made the front page...again."

Michael opened it and gaffed at the picture of himself. Not one of his favorites. There in bold block letters it read, *PRINCE MICHAEL AND LADY THALIA ARE DONE. BREAKUP OF THE CENTURY*.

He snickered. "Always the bridesmaid, never the bride," he said with a huff.

Using the newspaper to cover his face, he followed his men down the rickety steps of Donovan Flats to the black Land Rover waiting for him in front of the complex. The flash was unbearable from the cameras. Reporters converged on him in an instant like killer bees on an animal in the wild.

"Prince Michael, how were they?" one reporter screamed.

"Did you do this to get back at Lady Thalia?" another reporter screamed.

"Did you know that those girls are sisters?" another reporter asked.

That question made Michael nearly stop. *Sisters? Really?* He looked back up at the flat and saw the two women looking out of their open window waving at him. He waved back in disbelief. He had never had sisters before – not intentionally and not at the same time. Now, he really was upset that he hadn't remembered anything.

Luckily, his guards shielded him from the reporters long enough for him to jump in the back of the SUV and as soon as Geoff jumped in the front of the car, the driver sped off.

The photographers kept snapping shots of him, and the reporters kept screaming even after they pulled off into the streets. He looked back and shook his head. *Who said being a prince was easy?*

Sinking down into the comfort of the leather, he closed his eyes. Thoughts of the day before and the reason behind his momentary lapse began to come back to him. Thalia. The breakup. The reality of a two-year investment down the drain. It all made him want to start drinking again.

"So. How bad is it, Geoff?" Michael asked, not really wanting to hear the answer.

"I have no idea, sir. From what I've gathered, Her Majesty is not pleased," Geoff said with a frown. "We tried to deter you from going home with those women last evening, but you were quite insistent."

"I'm sure that I was," Michael said. Grunting, he sat back up. "I'm a grown man. For goodness sake, I'm 31 years old. I'm a fucking dinosaur in some societies. I should not be summoned by my mother, because I've made the fucking paper." He slapped the newspaper on his knee. "I plan to tell her that as soon as I arrive."

Geoff was silent.

Michael looked out of his window at the passing building, none of which he recognized. *Dear God, what was he thinking last night?* This place looked like a war zone. "I need to get out of here. It's driving me crazy."

"You are only about 30 minutes from the plane, sir," Geoff reassured.

"No," Michael said, pinching the bridge of his nose. "I need to get out of Europe."

Chapter 2

Dipping the delicate bristled tip of her wooden brush in a beautiful, vibrant almost translucent purple oil paint, Hope Daniels carefully lifted it and stroked strategically across her wide linen canvass, adding the perfect accent to the face of her newest muse.

In an artistic trance, she stood for a moment feet planted before her work, critically assessing every detail. The toned ground, the acrylic definition, the lines, the angles, the depth, it all told a story for her. And if it told her a story for her, then it could speak to others, much like words on paper or lyrics to a song.

The melodic sounds of Billy Holiday played in the background among scented pumpkin spice candles and the warm glow of low-lit Tiffany lamps. Crystal vases full of colorful rose bouquets were strategically placed around her studio to add color and inspiration, along with piles of leather bound books written by Maya Angelo, Gandhi, Plato, Nicky Giovanni, and Langston Hughes.

It was her perfect place. Serene and calming, full of beauty and harmony, she had created a peaceful safe haven from the world where she could be alone with her thoughts and her art.

Doing a complete collection on the many faces of Black Royalty throughout the ages, she was working on the very last of 10 remarkable life-size paintings. For the last six months, she had toiled endlessly on her work, determined to present to the world with an authentic and diverse look at African kings and queens, who were beautiful, strong, and polarizing.

It had been a major undertaking, but her agent loved the concept and so did the potential buyers. This was only her fourth collection, but so far, she had been moderately successful in her career. Some serious players in the industry were looking at her, national publications had written articles on her, and art brokers were putting in their bids.

In a word, Hope had promise.

Only, for the moment, she also had a block.

This last painting had caused her the most agony of all 10. The previous nine, she had ripped through vigorously. However, much to her surprise, she had toiled over the face of Hannibal for weeks. The intensity in his pensive eyes was lacking, only because her creativity was starting to wean.

"I need to rest," she said aloud, setting her brush on the rustic vintage table across from her.

When she looked over at the tall grandfather clock in the far corner of the room, she saw that it was a little past 10 o'clock at night. It dawned on her right then that she hadn't talked to her boyfriend, Sean, since earlier in the day. Unfortunately, it was a common and selfish mistake that she made when she was in the middle of her work.

Her studio was an interior room of the large old house with no windows to give indication as to the time of day. The room, opulent and grand in nature, was originally built pre-Civil War as a library for Confederate Colonel James Taffy, a man with a penchant for privacy, Whiskey, and books. It was later discovered, however, that the lower room was also an entrance to part of the Underground Railroad. His dual and often misunderstood personality, had been the discussion of Hernando, Mississippi for over a century as well as her family, but that was a whole other story.

Normally, she would have pressed on through the night, burning the mid-night oil until the last of her work was completed or she spent the last of her energy, but tonight, she decided to stop her work and go and see him.

Picking up her pink I-phone, she dialed his cell, but it quickly went to voicemail.

A deep baritone with an extremely southern drawl came across the phone. "Hi, you've reached Sean Pritchard, I'm sorry that I missed your call. Leave me a message and I'll call you back as soon as I can. Thanks." The phone beeped, but she decided against a message at the last minute and hung up.

He had probably gone to sleep already considering it was a work night, but she'd never known him to complain in the past about an impromptu night cap. It had been days since they had made love and the last time that they had talked it had been about how rude his mother had been to her over dinner.

Sean was a momma's boy and the fifth of six well-groomed, genetically perfect Pritchard sons. However, his mother seemed to spoil him the most. When he had brought Hope home, for the first time over six months ago, to announce that they were dating, Mrs. Pritchard had nearly died at the dinner table, clutching her pearls while turning ghostly white.

Her precious baby boy had brought home a black girl and *an outcast at that*.

That Sunday had been one of the longest of Hope's adult life, outside of the day that she had lost Grandma Pearl. In all the years that she had lived in the sleepy town of Hernando, Mississippi, she had never come into contact with blatant racism, which outsiders would have found hard to believe. But she found that while it was no longer polite to suggest the back door or another drinking fountain, people still kept to their own here. And as long as one kept to his or her own, they need not worry.

Momma Pearl referred to it as *polite racism*, if there was such a thing, but Hope called it what it truly was... fragrant bullshit.

"It was understood in my day," Sean's mother had explained at that very unfortunate one and only dinner. "No matter the times, people have to protect their own family lines. I mean, would you want your line washed out? When God said to be fruitful and multiply, he meant along the color lines...why else would He have made the races. It's just common sense."

This trip down memory lane led quickly into a conversation by Hope, which included informing the old woman of the rulers of Africa – Kings and Queens who could buy and sell her ass with a single coin. Going on and on for over 20 minutes, Hope gave a brief but very detail explanation of how Africans were a proud people and blacks in the United States had nothing to be ashamed about, especially considering their survival of the middle passage, tyranny and slavery, despite their origins as the first humans, the most powerful and richest rulers and the first architects of civilization. Jaws dropped all around the dinner table, all except Sean, who sat with his mouth covered and his head down. He knew Hope and knew her mind, but he thought she'd have more discretion when it came to sharing her thoughts on race. When she was certain that she had made her point, she ended the conversation by saying, "So you see, in their day, you would not have been asked to sit at their table or even their presence. It's all relative really."

Obviously, the conversation had not gone over well, and she was never invited back to dinner, but she and Sean had continued the relationship despite the disapproval of his mother.

Since that evening, however, things had gotten a bit tense. Sean had become distant. Where he used to invite her out with he and his other colleagues from the law firm, he now found a reason to always cancel and spend the night with her alone. She hated to say that it was because he was ashamed of her, but sometimes, the doubt crept into the back of her mind.

Hope knew that he was trying, but the work on her project was due in three months and she wanted it to be perfect, much as he was about his case load. The overall strain of their situation was souring a once sweet love affair, and she had to do something about it. And for her, that was to give him a little more attention. Tonight, she could have some spearmint tea, eat some cookies, and keep her focus on the painting until she broke through her creative block, but instead, she opted to stop her work and go surprise him. She was certain that he'd be happy to see her, and happy for a late night romp before bed.

Stepping out of her denim overalls covering her pink leggings and long white t-shirt, she grabbed her keys from the counter in the kitchen and headed out into the drizzling rain to see him.

Hernando was nice this time of year. Wind blew up her long black hair as soon as she closed the door. Stepping out onto the wrap around wooden porch, she closed and locked the large door behind her. Even with the moon hidden from the sky because of the clouds, the night still looked beautiful. Her house was perched up on a tall hill with two acres of a well-manicured lawn and tall oak trees surrounding her.

Dashing out to her grandmother's black 1979 Chevy pickup, she darted through the thick drops of rain with her hands covering her head and jumped into the pristine all black leather interior of the vehicle.

She loved this old antique truck more than any other vehicle on the planet. It had been Grandpa Solomon's prize possession, but when he passed, he had left it to Grandma Pearl, and when she passed, she had left it to her. It was one of many very important family heirlooms that she treasured, which was why she was berating herself for not parking it in the barn today instead of leaving it out in the driveway.

As soon as she slipped the key in the ignition and turned, B.B. King blasted through the stereo. According to the music legend, the thrill was gone, but Hope was quite giddy about her late night booty call.

When Hope arrived at Sean's home, near the center of the newly developed portion of town, all of his lights in his renovated one-story brick bungalow were turned off and his BMW was parked in the driveway. By all accounts, just as she had expected, he was out for the night.

Not wanting to wake him up by shining her lights on the house with her monster of a truck, she parked on the street in front of the house and jumped back out in the rain and ran to the open porch.

She and Sean had not gotten to the point in their relationship where she had a key to his home or he had a key to hers, but he had shown her in case of emergencies, where he placed the extra one. Running her hands down into the fern hanging on the porch near the door, she felt for the Ole Miss key ring with the house key attached.

As quietly as she could, she slipped the key into the lock and pushed the large wooden door open.

Closing the front door behind her, she tiptoed through the old cottage-style home, passed his perfect little brown leather sectional in the living room, the flat screen television against the wall, the neatly displayed law degree from Ole Miss, and the many pictures of he and his brothers and father during their famous fishing trips, through the small dining room complete with a petite oval dark oak table and finally down the small hall into the master bedroom on the left.

A zinger of excitement coursed through her veins at the thought of surprising him. He always said that he would like for her to be more spontaneous, and she knew that he meant so about their sex life. Sean was into crazy little things like sneaking and having a quickie in the alleyway behind their favorite bar and making out above the stars in the back of his car. But Hope was more conservative, always afraid that someone might see. Slowly, she was beginning to push herself beyond her insecurities, and was trying hard to keep the fire between them burning.

Looking at him now, she could see why coming here had been a good idea.

Sean was a classically handsome man. At six feet, three inches, he was tall, and gorgeous. Everyone always complimented him on his physically stunning appearance - long dimples in his cheeks, a strong square jaw, smooth perfectly golden tan skin, freckles splashed across the bridge of his symmetrically perfect nose, rose-colored heart-shaped lips, perfect white teeth, auburn-colored eyes, long black lashes, heavy arched brows, deep voice and a head full of curly black hair.

He was lying in the bed naked curled up to a pillow with the street light from outside to shine in and illuminate the small, well-maintained bedroom. The bathroom door was closed and the smell of a fresh shower permeated the room with mist.

To put it in his mother's words, he was the perfect catch.

Hope had to agree.

She reached down at ran her hand through his hair and was surprised to find it dry. He always washed it when he took a shower.

"Mmm, come back to bed. Let's make love again," he said, reaching for her arm in the darkness. He grabbed her small forearm and pulled her closer to him.

The word *again* rather threw Hope for a moment.

Instinctively, Sean's eyes flashed open when he smelled Hope's perfume. Surprised, he sat up in bed and pushed up against the headboard, startled and visibly confounded by her presence.

Hope smiled gently. "Where you dreaming of me?" she asked, sitting by him on the bed. Touching his face, she leaned in to give him a kiss.

Sean stuttered. "I..." he looked toward the bathroom door. "Hope..." He said her name apologetically.

His demeanor was so out of place until she could not help but stop and analyze him. *What was wrong? Why did he seem so afraid?* Hope followed his gaze to the bathroom door and stood up beside the bed again. It was then that she noticed his clothes thrown on the floor, a purse and heels beside it.

He wasn't alone.

"Who's in there?" Hope asked, walking around the bed toward the bathroom door.

As she asked the question in a strained voice, the door opened quickly. "Who are you talking to in there?" a female voice asked back. A petite brunette stepped out with a towel wrapped tightly around her body. She looked over at Hope and frowned. "I thought you said that you two were having problems," the woman said, swallowing down anger at Sean.

Sean, realizing that the situation was quickly escalating, jumped up from the bed and stood in between the women.

"Is this the woman that you work with?" Hope asked, voice trembling. Her mouth flew open in shock. "You're fucking your co-worker behind my back?"

"Wait," Sean said, pulling Hope back toward him.

"Don't you dare touch me!" Hope exclaimed, pushing him away. "How could you lie to me?" Tears erupted from the corners of her eyes.

"How could you lie to me?" the woman behind him asked, hitting Sean in the back with her small fist.

"I didn't lie," Sean said, turning toward the woman. "I didn't lie to you, Ashley. Just give me a moment to explain. Everything that I said to you about Hope and I is true. This just looks all wrong, but it ain't how it looks."

It was that small decision to turn to Ashley instead of her that seemed to push the slow knife deeper for Hope. She stepped back, hand over her mouth and tried to control her sudden desire to scream. "Well then, how is it? You lying son of a bitch," she growled at him.

Sean turned to Hope. "You're right. I am a son of a bitch," he said, shaking his head. "And I'm so sorry, but things just ain't working out for us."

"You think!? When were you going to tell me?" Hope said, voice growling at him. "How long has this shit been going on behind my back?" Tears and sobs clouded her vision in the dark room and all she could do was try to keep it together.

"You've been busy. I've been busy. I thought it was obvious, Hope. My mother is damn near having a break down over our relationship."

To Hope, that was a cop-out. "You knew how your mother was before you brought me into her home! How was I supposed to know that you couldn't handle her?"

He put up his hands defensively. "Look, I take the blame for this okay. I'm not blaming anything on you, I'm trying to explain."

In the middle of the fight, Ashley grabbed her clothes and went back into the bathroom, slamming the door behind her.

Sean's shoulder sank. "I never meant for you to see this. I was going to find some time to tell you...alone."

"Why couldn't you tell me before you screwed her?" Hope asked, wiping tears. "Why couldn't you just be honest with me?"

"Harder said than done," Sean admitted. He threaded his fingers together as he pleaded with her. "I'm sorry. You're a real nice girl, but I've never been in an interracial relationship before. The pressures are coming from *literally* everywhere - my work, my home, my family and friends. They all didn't mind when they thought this was just a fling, but when it was starting to get serious, so did their contempt for it."

"So you're ashamed of *me*?" She asked, pushing him in his chest.

He stepped back and recovered his footing.

Hope's heart broke in front of him. Was he really so small of a man that he would hurt her like this to appease the people around him?

Sean realized that he was naked and grabbed his underwear. Sitting on the side of the bed, he slipped them on. "I'm just not strong enough to deal with it. This is a small town. It's where I grew up. We aren't in New York City somewhere. People look to me and my family, and no matter how educated you are, no matter how pretty you are, *and God knows that you're pretty*, it's just not going to work here...not yet."

"So what you're saying is that *in your mind*, you're too good for me?" Hope couldn't believe her ears. "Because I'm Black?" she dug deeper.

"I don't want to get into a race debate. This is hardly the time," Sean huffed.

Hope folded her arms. "But you're saying that a Black woman is...beneath the good White people of Hernando, Mississippi?"

"He's saying that, not me!" Ashley screamed out of the bathroom. "He doesn't speak for everyone in this town!"

They both looked toward the bathroom door, and then Sean continued.

"I'm saying that it won't work. I like you; hell, I think I love you. But I worked my ass off to get that job, and I want partner. I'm never going to get it with you on my arm. My parents won't hear it, and my brothers won't either, although they are nice to you when you come around. So, instead of ruining each other's lives, we have to do the mature thing and part ways."

Hope straightened her back despite the agony of his words. With tears still flowing down her cheeks, she pursed her lips together. "You have..." she sniffled, "no spine Sean Pritchard, and to be honest, you're not worth the time or effort it would take to disgrace you the way that you have just humiliated yourself with that backward ass logic and that false sense of self." She wiped the tears again from her now reddening cheeks. "Not to mention that you are a coward and a lair, and it doesn't matter what you want or don't want, because I don't want *you* anymore."

Covered in embarrassment, Sean wanted to say something, but every word would have a double-edge sword attached to it. Silence was his only option. At least, it gave him a reasonable cop out.

However, there was no denying that he felt absolutely horrible for how this had happened, only he couldn't deny the more dominant feeling inside was one of relief. He could go back to his life before race was an issue, before he was the one-half of the odd couple of their small town.

"I'm sorry, Hope," he whispered.

"Go to hell Sean and take your bigoted ideals, family, friends, and promotion with you," Hope said, turning on her heels and out of the bedroom.

Deciding against stopping her or even apologizing anymore, he allowed Hope to dash out of his home back into the rain, while he focused

on making things better between him and
Ashley – his better choice, his only choice now
that she had seen the truth.

***

Bursting through the front door, out onto
the porch, Hope finally exhaled as a strong gust
of wind and rain blew past her and cooled her
burning face. Grateful for the change in envi-
ronment, she stepped out into the storm in a
complete daze.

Almost in a trance, she moved through the
night air in slow motion. Getting into the truck,
she barely noticed the sudden downpour pre-
venting her from being able to truly see the
road or the fact that the wind had picked up and
the lightning and thunder with it.

Instead, she blankly stared ahead, thinking
about how many hours, days, weeks, and
months she had devoted to a man who didn't
even classify her as human.

"I'm not good enough?" she said aloud. "Is
he serious?" Tears ran down her cheeks, warm
and salty.

The wind began to pick up, beating harder
against her truck. The rain poured down,
blinding her sight as she drove down Main
Street.

Seeing in the darkness, the street light ahead
turn yellow, she slowed to a stop by the time

that the light finally turned red. With her hands clutching the steering wheel and the defroster on to clear the windows, she waited, trembling all over and soaking wet with rain water. Her long hair stuck to her face, down her neck and back. Shivering, she wiped her eyes.

The CD player switched songs and another B.B. King ballad played. The *Ghetto Woman* turned on, making the already dismal scene more depressing.

Hearing the words and playing of Lucille in Hope's ears made her stomach knot up into little balls, and the tears that she tried hard to stop poured out from her diaphragm.

Damn you, Sean, she thought to herself as flashes of his face haunted her. The sad thing about all of this was that she truly was happy with the man. She didn't know if that made her a bigger fool or not, but she certainly felt like it did.

His voice echoed in her mind. "Hell, I might even love you..." She could hear him say.

What did he know about love? What did he know about anything at all?

Bending over the steering wheel, she sobbed hard until she realized that the light had turned green. If she could just get home, she knew that she'd be all right. But Lord, 10 minutes had never felt so long.

Easing up off the break, she pushed down on the gas and headed through the light. As she did, out of the corner of her eye, to her right, a blaring light came toward her. Even in the high winds and heavy rains, she could hear the belting of a horn booming.

Foot down on the gas pedal, she now realized that the car was going to hit her instead of stopping. She tried to get across the intersection, but the large truck came crashing right into her.

Hope screamed out in fear at the large, metal bending clang. Her head jerked; glass broke everywhere around her and the truck rolled over and ended upside down. Suddenly she could smell smoke coming from the hood and something that smelled an awful lot like gasoline, but she couldn't see.

"No," she mumbled. "God. No!"

Fumbling with her seatbelt, Hope felt blood dripping off her face and hitting the roof of her truck. Dazed, she finally gave up. B.B. King's voice started to fade and with it her consciousness.

"Hold on ma'am," a male voice said as he crawled into the truck with her. "I'm going to get you out of here."

"I can't see," Hope cried, reaching for the voice. "I can't see!"

Chapter 3

Royal Deeside, Aberdeenshire Scotland
Balmoral Castle

It had been a lovely flight over from London to Scotland with not a cloud in the bluest of August skies, but Michael hadn't taken the time to notice. All he could concentrate on was the long list of emails on his phone that he had gotten over the last 12 hours from everyone *except God* condemning him for ending his relationship so suddenly with Thalia.

The most noted came from his brother, which he deleted immediately. He read the first two lines and knew that *pissed-off* was a dish best served cold.

Spoiled brat that she was, Thalia had made him out to be a monster to everyone who would listen, instead of telling the truth about what had caused their sudden end. Namely, the fact that she was a fraud.

Not in namesake. She was royalty. In fact, that was the only thing real about her.

The rest was just a well-orchestrated lie.

Evidently, her family in their haste to defend her honor had also already issued a statement to the public, which of course every rag in the UK happily ran. And because of his reputation before dating her, despite the fact that he had never once cheated on her during their relationship, everyone was taking her side.

Go figure.

Now his mother, the Queen of England, wanted to weigh in. And while he could not blame her for wanting to know the details, he was certain that she'd agree that it was entirely his fault, as was everything.

As soon as the door of the bulletproof truck opened and Michael's foot hit the ground, the front doors of Balmoral Castle opened and a small succession of staffers.

Since he was a young boy, he had always hated being waited on. No one believed him, but he rather envied young men who grew up without all of the pomp and circumstance.

But there were at least two people in the mansion in front of him who would definitely disagree.

Stepping out into the cool breeze, he looked up at the lavish granite estate in all of its glory and felt ill. Even among all of this decadent beauty, today's meeting was going to be ugly, and he already could feel his mother's hot as hell-like wrath emanating from the very pores of the structure.

Yet again, he had disappointed her. Only this time, it was with good cause.

"We are most honored to have you back in our presence, Your Highness," the butler said, bowing as Michael passed. He was stereotypically old and haggard in a tailored uniform with silver hair and liver spots, but he was also Michael's favorite servant.

"Hello Albert," Michael answered as he walked briskly past. "Where is *she*?" he asked. He stopped in the foyer and slipped his hands in his pockets.

"The *queen* is indisposed at the moment, however, she has asked that upon your arrival, you meet her in the sitting room for a conversation," Alfred said, closing the front doors behind him.

"Good. Then I'll just head to the parlor for a drink before," he said, rolling his eyes. There was no way that he was going to take his tongue-lashing sober in a place that distilled its own whiskey.

This glorious, historic estate that outsiders coveted with a certain amount of absolute glee carried many memories for him, *not all of them good*. He was here when his father passed away, here when Margaret Dunning first broke his heart, and here when his first bones were broken from falling from a nearby tree.

This was the place he went when nothing was right in the world.

It was exactly why he had not brought Thalia here to propose to her, but exactly where he should have brought her to break up.

Now, he was again, facing another pivotal point in his life, and it irritated him to no end that he was doing it at the Balmoral.

Taking off his winter green North Face jacket, he laid it on the back of a finely upholstered wing-backed chair in the gilded golden parlor colored by fresh bouquets and fine furniture and went over to the bar.

Without apology or restraint, he wanted whisky, and not the crap distilled a stone's throw from the estate. He wanted American whiskey. He wanted to get properly drunk. That was the simple and complete truth.

Picking up a rare and hard to find bottle of Jefferson's Presidential Select, his mouth watered. He poured a hefty helping of the Kentucky made bourbon into a crystal tumbler and raised the glass to admire the attractive copper color – flickering from amber to mahogany in the dim light.

"You've managed to make the news again," a deep English baritone echoed from behind him.

Michael looked up from his glass into the large mirror behind the bar to see his brother's regal reflection glaring at him.

Great. An ambush.

"Bloody hell. I wasn't aware that you were here," Michael said, quickly putting the glass to his mouth and taking a large gulp. It went down smooth, barely burning.

Without pause, he poured another.

"You've made a mess, so of course I'm here," Richard said, taking a seat. He crossed his long legs and looked at the fireplace. The embers danced about and warmed the drafty room. "While you're up there playing bartender, why don't you pour a glass for your brother? Mother should be finished soon. That gives us just enough time to talk."

"What is there to talk about?" Michael asked, pouring Richard a glass that equaled his. He walked across the room and handed it to him, then sat in the chair across from him.

"You asked publicly for Thalia's hand in marriage and then you broke up with her. This is not the way of a Prince of England, Earl of Wessex, on and on," Richard said, taking a sip of the drink. He had done this entire song and dance for so long until he could not bear to finish the lecture.

Michael's chest began to swell. He didn't need another speech from his more than accomplished, over achieving, perfect do-gooderbrother, especially on matters of the heart.

"This isn't about you," Michael huffed. "This is about principalities..."

"*This* is about our entire family, and your inability to commit to anything longer than it takes for paint to dry." Richard cut his eyes at him. "You've always been spoiled."

"Not this again," Michael said, preparing to get up from his chair.

"*Don't* move," Richard said voice stern. His eyes narrowed on his brother.

"Don't use your *king voice* on me," Michael growled as he sat back down. He hated when his big brother tried to play *the father role*. He was nothing like their father had been, although he looked just like him.

"Don't make me," Richard said, easing up just a bit. He wiped his face with his hands. "As I was just saying, you've always been spoiled. And I blame Mother for it. You were always the fair one with your wheat blonde curls, your blue eyes, perfect aesthetic features, and muscles like a caveman, charisma and what not. Women respond to a boyishly charming fellow, regardless of his stature, but add the title of prince and you've got utter free-fall. So we've treated your beauty like a handicap most of your life. And I'm sorry to say, but it has made you stupid."

Michael bucked his eyes. "I beg your pardon."

"It. Has. Made. You. Stupid," Richard repeated slowly and loudly, adding insult to injury. He took another sip casually as if he had not just offended his brother, and then continued with his explanation. "No teacher would fail you when you were a boy, *regardless of how horrible you were at making good marks*. No woman would deny you, *even though you had no idea how to treat her*. You were the first person anyone picked for a team because of your agility. You were the last person a woman would break up with because you were *Michael*. Everything socially obtainable, you have obtained, and it's mostly due to your handicap of being beautiful, rich, and royal."

Richard said the word *beautiful* like it was a cardinal sin. It wasn't like he was an ugly man. Broad chested, brown haired, serious and noble, Richard had always been regarded as the stately, intelligent aristocrat that was a result of impeccable breeding while many of the same people labeled Michael as the child that the queen must have drunk a few glasses of wine while carrying.

Richard was day.

Michael was night.

It had been that way since they were boys.

"So, you've just called me a hopeless, beautiful idiot, and I'm supposed to say thank you?" The frown lines in Michael's well-tanned face showed. "This is very much like pissing on a man and calling it rain."

Richard gave a half-grin and threaded his manicured hands together. "How is it any different from pissing your life away and calling it *looking for yourself*?"

"This comes from a man who has known exactly what he wanted to be since the day he was pulled from his mother's womb," Michael snarled. "All hail the king."

"Well, Michael, as much as I love you, it's a well-known fact that you were born without a compass at all. That is not my fault, but it has been my burden."

"Was I brought out here to be chastised, or is there a real purpose for this meeting?" Michael asked, rolling his eyes. He was growing tired of the conversation.

Richard cut to the chase. "Mother wants to know details. She doesn't understand why you broke up with Thalia and neither do I. She's beautiful and bright. She comes from a good family, and she understands protocol. What is there not to love about the girl?"

Michael's cool façade broke. With slumped shoulders, he shook his head. "She doesn't love me – not Michael...the man. I would think that such a thing would be a prerequisite for marriage." Michael finished the contents of his glass and stared into the bottom of the glass. He smiled as he recalled the encounter. "We were having a quiet night in and after a few drinks, we started to talk about our relationship and that's when she dropped the bomb on me. She said that she had known since she was a child that she would be a princess. When we started to date, she picked out her wedding dress. By the time that I proposed, she had already picked out our children's names." He paused. "*Dreadful ones by the way.*"

Richard raised a brow. "I don't see the problem. She's aggressive and knows what she wants. What's wrong with that?"

A chill ran down Michael's spine. "It wouldn't be an issue if she loved me, but she does not."

Richard audibly gaffed. "How can you be sure?"

"She told me!" Michael's voice rose. He hit his knee. "I asked her out right if she would have given me a second look had I not been *the Prince* and she said no. She said sure she would have slept with me, but there was no way that I was marriage material." He threw up his hands. "But the consolation prize was that she was sure that she would grow to love me, because right now she was incredibly fond of me. *Fond of me*, Richard! She's been lying the entire time. Normally, she's demure and so well-poised until you completely miss that under all of those hours of etiquette training and charm school."

"So what made her suddenly be so honest with you?" Richard asked.

"The wine. The notion that we'd gotten so far in the planning stages of this fucking wedding that it was too late to end things. Maybe she just wanted me to know that she'd gotten over on me." He felt himself hyperventilating little bit.

"Stop your dramatics. Maybe she was just drunk," Richard rationalized.

"Well, here is a question for you. If you weren't going to be the next King of England, would Madeline have married you and given you children?"

"Yes." Richard defended, as if any other situation would have been ludicrous.

"My point exactly." Michael said, point made.

"This isn't a reason to call off a wedding that millions have already been spent on," Richard said, feeling badly for his brother, but unwilling to show it. "You have no idea if she was just drunk. From what I've heard, you ended things and stormed out. There was no clarification on anything. It was a slip of the tongue and too many drinks. You can't possibly hold that against her."

"Wouldn't you clear out if a woman told you that? This is my life we are talking about, Richard. The woman whom I choose to be a permanent part of it should at least know something more about it than the fact that I'm second in line to be king." Michael rolled his eyes under his heavy lashes and clutched the glass closer in his hands. "She's just like the others, only with better breeding. And what is that anyway? Her family has money and titles and what? How does that help me be happy?"

Richard twisted up his lip in contemplation. "Why did you not know this before you asked the woman to marry you?"

"I was infatuated at first, I guess. You've seen her. She is beautiful."

Richard had to agree. She was drop dead gorgeous.

"But she's hollow," Michael added. "And eventually that body and that face will go away and all we'll have is love. And if we don't have that, then I have nothing more than I had last night with the Brixton sisters."

Richard's neck snapped. "You didn't go to Brixton."

"I had a minor relapse," Michael explained. "I went back to my less than honorable ways for a night. *Kill me.*"

"If you didn't use a condom, then you may have already killed yourself." Richard stood up. "Has anyone been sent to deal with this?"

Michael huffed. "I saw the condoms and the wrappers on the floor by my clothes when I went to get dressed. I'm fine." He put the glass on the table by the chair. "Is that all you heard? You're supposed to be my brother, and I'm telling you that this woman doesn't love me."

"Haven't you discovered that men in our position face this all the time? How are you to be really sure that anyone truly loves you? You were born a prince for goodness sake. You can't be that naive."

"*I'm not naive*, but a man can set reasonable expectations, and being loved is reasonable. Father loved mother. You love Madeline. Do I not have the same right, even if I am stupid in your eyes?"

"Like a poor woman would love you. Think of what you're saying."

"Are you really that much of a snob, Rich-ard?"

"And what are you? A common man?" Rich-ard laughed cynically. "A man of the people, perhaps? You may have served in the Queen's Royal Guard. You may have volunteered and worked among the common people, *but you,* my dear stupid boy are no commoner. You are one of only two sons of the Queen of England. It's a pity that with that, I am the only one gainfully employed. You are still trying to find yourself and now on top of that, you expect to find true love." He shook his head and laughed. "You're impossible is what you are. *Im*possible."

"Don't diminish my character just because yours has been so perfectly exalted. Since the day that you were born, you were prepped to be king."

"And you weren't?" Richard defended.

"No," Michael said, shaking his head emphat-ically. "I was just groomed not to be an embar-rassment."

"Don't be silly. If you hadn't been around, then my accomplishments would have never seemed so great." He smirked playfully.

"So, I'm not only handicapped, I'm worth-less?"

"Not worthless, just a little out of touch with reality. If a woman loves you, she loves you because you're beautiful, royalty and/or rich. Look anywhere in the world, you'll get the same answer. You can't change who you are, and if even you lied to her, you couldn't change how you look. At least Thalia was honest with you. It's the mark of a good wife."

"Do you really believe that?" Michael asked defeated.

Richard walked over to the window and pulled the curtain away to look out at the grounds. "No." He smacked his lips together. "I thought she loved you too, brother. At least, that is what she confessed to the world."

"Maybe I am incapable of being loved. You said it yourself; there are too many cosmetic barriers."

Watching the gardener tend to the flowers, Richard had a thought. "Do you plan to completely call this off, even if she's willing to prove herself to you?" He knew his brother well and he also knew that the young man was driven by pure emotion, despite their best efforts to discourage such a thing.

"Thalia would be happy with Uncle Graham if she thought he'd be the next king," Michael said, burying his head in his hands. "I won't go back to her. I don't care what you say about me."

"Then maybe getting out of the public eye would do you some good. I know that it would do this family some good. Like I said, millions have already been spent." Richard closed the drapes and turned to him. "I can appreciate your situation, but can you understand ours?"

"Yes, I can. But the last time you all thought I needed some time to myself, I ended up in Afghanistan." Michael rested his head back on the chair and looked up at the painted ceiling.

"Actually, I was thinking of something a little more livable."

Michael raised a brow. "I'm listening."

"But you'd be used as an experiment..." Richard winced.

Michael sat up. "Again with your experiments. You know my life is not one big petri dish."

"If you could go somewhere and live as a commoner, on a commoner's salary and without being recognized as an heir to the crown for 6 months, then I think that you'd be more respected in the public eye. Everyone thinks that you're spoiled rotten..."

Michael threw up a hand. "I already know what everyone thinks."

"Well, the point is, since we are waging a serious PR war against the public consensus, if you were to go off the grid for a while and do something noble, then when you returned it might be shocking enough for people to forget your breakup, and if not forget it, then forgive it." Richard crossed his arms across his chest. "It would give us the opportunity to fight fire with fire. And it would prove that you truly are trying to find yourself."

"Didn't Eddie Murphy do this already in *Coming to America*?" Michael asked playfully.

"I'm sorry, *going where*?" Richard was not familiar with the American movie classic.

"Never mind. Continue." Michael's interest peaked. "Where would I carry out this experiment?"

Richard twisted his lip up and thought hard. "You did mention America. The US would be perfect. We could still monitor you from a distance with our men and keep you safe."

"*Good*ness, man. They are royalty crazy there." He said nearly dismissing the entire notion now.

Richard could see that he was losing him. He pitched harder. "In the mainstream, metro areas, yes, they are *royalty crazy*. However, I was thinking small town, sort of roll up your sleeves, working class people," Richard added. "The kind who would be less likely to be interested in the crown." He walked over to Michael and sat down. "Somewhere Southern."

"Why Southern? Don't they even hate the Yanks down there?" Michael was not about to go to another country and be lynched.

"You're an educated man. Can you please act like it? Yes, they have a problem historically with the Northerners there, but they are also less likely to know who you are. Remember when we were boys. You used to be able to pull off an impeccable American accent. Can you still?"

"I've actually gotten better at it," Michael said with a grin.

"We could pick out one of those small southern towns for you to go and work. Somewhere where all they have is an Internet café, not even a Starbucks."

"Work how?" Michael asked, confused. "What would I do?"

Richard shook his head. "I don't know. You'll have to figure that out. You're good at collecting rare books...fine art...maybe something in western literature."

"Do they read in the south?"

Richard chuckled. "You won't last long cracking jokes like that. They are very proud people. They're still waving a flag from a war that they clearly lost over 200 years ago. It's all quite depressing, but so is your situation."

Suddenly, thinking of having to face more media about Thalia made Michael reconsider the challenge. "Well, since we're going completely rebel, we might as well go to Mississippi Rebel."

Richard shuddered at the thought. "Alright." He threw up a hand. "I did read an article about them in the *New York Times*. They're becoming more progressive. I think that they finally abolished slavery."

Michael snickered. "This sounds like something I'll actually enjoy. Living among the people. Helping. Teaching even." He rolled his shoulders and clasped his hands together. "I'll have Geoff do some recon work, and we can get to it. Marvelous idea, Richard."

"Yes, well, I do what I can," Richard said, proud of himself. He had finally found something that he and his brother could agree on. Plus, he had possibly found a way to save face for his family while giving his brother an opportunity to see the world for what it really was. When this was all done, he was certain that Michael would come back to London and beg Thalia to take him back.

Problem solved.

Chapter 4

St. Benedict Hospital
Acute In-Patient Rehabilitation Center

Guided by her best friend, Bree, who had come back home from Dallas to help her get on her feet for a few days, Hope was carefully escorted from her private restroom back to her hospital bed. She made her journey in complete silence, but with a lot less distress than the many times before, where she had fallen, banged her legs and feet or simply sat on the floor and cried.

Despite the feeling of defeat eking at her very core, she kept her head up and eyes dry, ignoring the dull nagging pain that still reminded her that she was only six weeks out of a horrific car accident.

Noting her progress, Dr. Netters observed her from the corner and wrote on his clipboard before clearing his throat, making his presence known.

"How are you today, Hope?" the impeccably groomed doctor asked, stepping closer to her.

Hope's head moved toward his voice. "Better," she lied.

"Much better from what the nurses tell me," Dr. Netters added with a sympathetic smile.

"I'm glad to know that I meet their approval. Does this mean what I think it means?" Hope asked, pushing back on the bed and letting her feet swing off the edge.

"I'm keeping my side of the bargain. You can go home today with the assistance of your best friend, but you have to do all of those things we discussed, including finding a nurse or someone who can assist you in the home until your situation changes. I'll be sending a case worker by to check on you soon."

Hope's eye twitched. "You mean until I gain my sight back," she quipped woefully.

"I want you to stay positive," the doctor urged. "We don't know when your sight will come back, but we've seen significant improvements. When you first came to us you couldn't see colors, light or shadows." He reminded her with a careful tone. "It's my belief that within months, you could be back to the full eye sight that you lost."

Hope nodded. "I'm praying for the same."

"I'm praying for a miracle," Bree added, sitting beside her on the bed. She rubbed her back. "Everything is going to be okay."

Bree's voice was calming to Hope. She clung to it in the darkness.

"Well, let me get your discharge papers ready. Do you have any questions for me that we haven't covered over the last six weeks?" the doctor asked.

Hope nodded no. "Thank you for helping me."

Dr. Netters was a professional man, but he couldn't help extending a hand and placing it over Hope's. She reminded him so much of his girls when they were younger. "Stay positive, my dear. You're stronger than you think," he said, winking at Bree.

"Thanks, doctor," Bree said, as she watched him walk out of the hospital room and close the door behind him. Bree shook her head. "I wish he wasn't married," she said under her breath. "He'd be a great catch for Momma."

Hope snickered. "Are you still trying to get your momma married?"

Bree laughed. "Girl, the Lord said that he who finds a wife finds a good thing. He did not say that the man couldn't get any help in finding her."

Hope laughed. "Yeah, you right." Without meaning to, she instantly thought of Sean. She hoped God found him a psychopath. That was all that he deserved.

"I've packed all of your things. As soon as we get your walking papers, we are out of here," Bree said, standing up. "I just don't know what to do with all these flowers. There are so many of them." She cut her eyes at Hope.

"I told you what to do with them," Hope sneered. "Get rid of any of them that came from Sean."

"That would be...almost all of them," Bree corrected. She put her hand on her hip. "Seems like an awful waste."

Hope didn't care.

Bree begged. "At least let me give them to the other patients in here who don't have someone groveling after them." She looked around the room at the many vases of roses and daffodils, Hope's favorite flowers, and the many balloons and cards and almost felt a smidgeon bad for the man.

"I don't care who you give them to," Hope said, staring blankly into the glib, twilight coming through her pupils.

Bree saw that even the mention of the man was bringing her friend down and chose to change the subject. "While you were napping, I went to the house and started dinner." She knew that would cheer her up. "And because I know that you didn't inherit any cooking skills from your grandmother, I took the liberty of preparing fried chicken, greens, candied yams, okra, fresh cornbread and pineapple cake."

Hope ducked her head and smiled again. "Damn, girl. Why you aren't married yet yourself is beyond me."

"The Lord is going to have to find someone extra special for me, darling. I don't take hand-me-downs. Now, come and let me get you ready so we can get you home."

***

Even though Hope couldn't see a thing, she still looked out of the window while Bree drove her home from the hospital. With her eyes picking up the light of the cloudless day, she could imagine all of the cypress and oak trees as they made the short drive from the neighboring town of Southaven to Hernando. Supplementing her sight, she focused on her other senses, specifically the smell of fresh air tumbling through her cracked window. She hadn't smelled clean, fresh air in six weeks. Just to have the wind blow through her hair and the sun shine directly on her face felt like a blessing.

Within minutes, Bree pulled up in the long drive of Hope's home and headed up the gravel road to the house on the hill. Hope tilted her head up and smiled.

"Mr. Jernigan cut the yard for me, didn't he?" Hope asked, smelling freshly cut grass in the breeze. It instantly brought back memories of her childhood.

"Yep. I told him that you were coming home today, so he did it this morning. He's been keeping it up weekly since you've been gone," Bree answered, putting the car into park. "Oh shit," she said under her breath.

"What?" Hope's ear perked up.

Bree looked over at her friend and shook her head. "Sean is here."

"What!" Hope growled. "What does he want?" she asked as she held on to the handle of the door.

"Well, I don't know yet," Bree said, opening the door.

"Tell him to go away," Hope said after her as Bree closed the door.

Sean was patiently waiting on his trunk, sitting in his three-piece suit, looking at his iPad. As soon as he saw Hope, he stood up, threw down his pad and walked toward the car.

"Sean," Bree said with a warning voice. She put up her hand to stop him. "What are you doing here?"

"I came to see her," Sean said, looking over Bree to the window of the car.

"She's not in the best of moods. Can't your groveling wait?"

Sean sucked in a frustrated breath. He was about to say something rude but saw the distinct glare of a woman ready to kick his ass and calmed down. "No, it can't." He side-stepped her. "I'm going to help her out of the car."

Bree turned and followed him, refusing to say anymore. Maybe he just needed to hear it for himself, and he was sure that Hope would tell him. Their relationship was not only over, their friendship was too.

Sean opened Hope's door carefully and looked down at her.

"Is he gone?" Hope asked.

"No," Sean answered, moving in closer.

As soon as the wind blew again, she smelled his cologne. Ralph Lauren Black. Ironic really. The smell used to make her bow down and beg more buttermilk, but now it only made her stomach turn.

He reached gently for her arm to help her, but she pulled away. "What do you want?"

Sean cocked a brow. "First, I want to help you get out of this car and into the house. Secondly, I'd like just five minutes of your time. I need to say some things directly to you without your bodyguard over there giving me the evil eye." He rested his large arm on the roof of the car.

Hope had to repress her smile. She could always count on Bree.

"Well, I don't want your help," Hope said, trying to help herself out of the car.

As soon as her foot hit the gravel, Sean wrapped his arms around her and picked her up off the ground. "You can hate me later," he said, ignoring her struggles. "Bree, can you please get the front door."

Already ahead of them, she had made her way to the porch and was inserting the key when he called out to her.

With her wrapped in his embrace like a mother coddles a newborn, he held her close to his chest and carried her up to the front door. He wished at that moment that there was not so much tension in her body, that she could find in her heart to forgive him and at least lay her head on his chest the way that she used to, but Hope stayed rigid.

Hiking up the stairs that led up to the porch and then over the threshold of her home, he headed for the stairwell to take her to her bedroom.

"She can't stay up there," Bree said, stopping him. "I've arranged all of her things downstairs in the guest bedroom until her...." She lowered her voice a little, "until her sight comes back."

"I'm not deaf," Hope quipped.

"No, but you are stubborn," Sean said, following Bree to the bedroom.

"Who says that I want to sit in the bedroom? I've been locked up in one room for six weeks. I want to move around my own house," Hope complained.

"Well, you can move around after we talk," Sean said, setting her down on the bed. He looked at Bree with a plea in his eyes. "Can you give us just a few minutes? I know how you feel about me, how you both do, but I need a minute alone with her anyways." He looked back at Hope and hung his head in guilt.

Bree rolled her eyes, but quickly turned and left the room, closing the door behind them. "Five minutes," she called out.

Taking off his suit jacket, he threw it over the foot rail of the gold iron bed and pulled at his red tie.

"I've been trying to reach you for six weeks," Sean said flatly. "So, you'll excuse the imposition, but when I called again for the 45th day and they told me that you had gone from the hospital, I knew that I'd have one opportunity to see you before there was someone else blocking me."

"Haven't we said all that needs to be said here?" Hope asked.

Sean ran his hands through his hair. "I'm sorry. I'm so damned sorry," he blurted out. "I never meant for this to happen. I never meant..." He wiped his face. "I didn't come over here to play with your sympathies. If anyone should be seeking it, it's you."

Her voice was much calmer than his, almost still. "I don't need your sympathy. I don't need anything from you, Sean Pritchard."

"Can you just stop saying my name like that?" he huffed. He looked up at the ceiling. "Geez, you say it like it's a damned curse word."

Hope was silent. It was a curse word to her.

"I accept your apology," Hope said with finality. "Now, go."

"That's not what I came here for?"

"Then why are you here?" she snapped.

"Bree doesn't live here. You don't have any family. Your artsy friends are in New York, Miami and LA, but none of them are here. Your agent is in New York. All you have is Mr. Jernigan, an 85-year old, half-deaf senior citizen who can't run up here every single time that you fall or you get scared or..." he couldn't bear to finish the sentence.

Hope shifted in her seat, feeling helpless at the moment, but refusing to show it.

"I called a lady I know, a real nurse. Her name is LouAnn Hartfield. She helped my grandmother when she was on her way out. She's professional. She's hard working and trustworthy. I've already contacted her and she's got plenty of time on her hands."

Hope stiffened.

"This will all be on my dime, considering it's my fault. And I want to do this for you. Just let her come here and stay with you. I mean, this is a big ass plantation house for God's sake. When you get your sight back, then she can leave."

"I don't need your handouts," Hope answered politely.

"This isn't a hand out. Let's face it. The only reason that you're fucking blind right now is because I couldn't keep my dick in my pants or look you in the eye and tell you the truth about what I could and could not handle in my life." Strangely, it felt good to finally say it. He bit his lip in desperation, but lowered his voice as he heard Bree's footsteps making their way back toward the bedroom. "Take this from me, Hope. You need it. Now, you are not poor. No. But you and I both know that not even Obamacare is going to cover all the bills associated with this accident."

Hope rolled her eyes despite not being able to see him. One thing they had never agreed upon was the fact that she was a liberal democrat and he a conservative republican. It was only fitting that he'd find a way to push his agenda down her throat even while blind.

"That's what the trucker's insurance is for," she answered.

"I've been doing research on your behalf. He's spent. He doesn't have a dime more. He went to sleep while driving his truck. He's a small business owner. Your bills and some other expenses have basically run him out of business, won't be long before he's run out of town."

Moving in front of her, he bent down and looked her in her eyes. "Damn you, Hope. You're breaking my heart into little bitty pieces. If you have any mercy at all, do this for me. I need to know that someone is over here taking care of you. If you don't like LouAnn, I'll do it myself."

"No," Hope said quickly. She huffed.

Bree leaned into the door and cleared her throat. "Take it, Hope. He owes you."

Sean shook his head. What was it with that woman?

Hope ducked her head and pulled her fists tight to her. "Send her over tomorrow. If I like her and if Bree likes her, then she can stay."

Sean broke into a bright smile. Dipping into her, he kissed her forehead. "Thank you for this."

"Don't ever put your lips on me again."

He nodded. "Yes, ma'am." Walking to the door, he looked back at her one last time. "I really am sorry, Hope."

Chapter 5

Southaven, Mississippi

In Michael's very privileged life, he had had the opportunity to visit every continent in the world, travel every ocean; he had sat with royalty from over fifty countries and dined at their personal tables; he had stood on battle fields and observed destruction and victory; he had drunk champagne 8,850 meters above sea level atop Mount Everest; he had played volley ball with a sheik on sun bleached sand with exotic beauties and charted a $4.8 billion yacht with a Malaysian general across the Baltic Sea, but never once had he had the pleasure of visiting a Super Wal-Mart.

This dynamic retailer was packed with everything from sugar cookies to radio tires to double-barrel shotguns, all in one very convenient location, all reasonable priced, all on sale 24 hours a day and all under devil-awful florescent lights. This place was so liked by Americans until it only closed on Christmas Day.

And he could see why.

He loved this place.

The only thing that he didn't love was having to wait in line like the rest of the working-class blokes.

As he passed by the many families scurrying about the large store in deep conversation or maneuvering with their cell phones stuck to their faces and hands, he found himself completely entertained by the varying wardrobes, the deep southern drawls and overall informality of the place.

To his amazement, he was knee deep in common life. He saw sagging pants, too tight skirts, shorts that were more like briefs, women wearing way too much makeup, old women with bad wigs, and kids with offensively snotty noses. So not only could one get everything that was on their shopping list, they could also get a communicable disease.

Genius.

In a leisurely stroll with a gentle smile on his face, Michael walked beside Geoff as they loaded up their shopping cart to the top with miscellaneous things they would need for their newly rented house in Hernando. There was something calming about shopping for all of his own personal items, cleaning needs and food. He got a chance, first hand, to decide each and everything that went into his home, unlike the mansion that he had grown up came pre-furnished with centuries-old wares, and maids and butlers, chefs and designers that decided on his daily life.

This had been there second run to the *adult toy store*, but he rather enjoyed it and found any reason at all to come back. Plus, it wasn't like someone else was going to do the work for them.   They were supposed to be incognito. *Commoners.* The only people who knew where they actually where was his brother, his mother and MI6, who had posted up not far from their home in case of emergency. However, they had strict orders to stay out of the way unless a situation became a concern for national security.

In their process of vetting an ideal place for him to stay, it had been a sheer turn of luck that an old man by the name of Rousey Jernigan with a broken hearing aid needed to rent out the smaller home on his 5-acre lot.

It was a nice, late-model, bricked home that had been built for Jernigan's daughter and her husband when they were first married.   But since then, they had moved out and there was no one else to manage it. Mr. Jernigan was a widower and an anti-social butterfly, so he never bothered them as he was sure that they weren't *funny* people.

Upon answering the ad in the paper and seeing the home for himself, Michael thought it was perfect for his exploits. It was a charming three-bedroom closet of a house with all the updated amenities and even Wi-Fi. He'd blend into the small sleepy town flawlessly with his set up.

Geoff, however, was completely unnerved. He thought that Michael's arrangement with his brother was reckless and potentially dangerous. He thought the house was ridiculous, and he wanted nothing more than to return to his native country. But he was just his liege's man, not his counselor. So, he settled for sharp looks and heavy sighs of discontentment, which Michael happily ignored.

A young woman, barely in her 20s, with red hair glanced over at Michael and gave a flirty smile. Unfortunately, Michael had not noticed her until now, but she seemed awfully close to be shopping. He stepped back a foot and smiled.

"Hi," she said, reaching beside him to pick up something from the shelf.

Geoff audibly huffed in the background.

"Ma'am," Michael said, using his southern accent. "Pleasant day."

"Pleasant enough," she answered, sweeping her eyes across his broad chest.

Instantly, Michael felt cheap, like a steak on a paper plate, but he rolled with it. "Am I in your way?" he asked.

"No, you're *fine*," she said with mischief in her tone.

Geoff quickly stepped in, hitting Michael's chest with his rolls of toilet paper. "Dear, he's taken," he said, baritone stern.

Michael blinked hard, but stayed quiet.

Geoff shrugged. "It's a new day. What can I say? Find someone else to flirt with on the ass-wiping aisle. This one is batting for the other side."

Michael tried hard not to laugh and dipped his head in the customary southern way and winked at her. He rather liked playing a south-ern gent in his jeans, t-shirts, John Deere base-ball cap and leather work boots. He had gotten his motivation from a country music video and mimicked it down to the last detail. And too his surprise, with his faux southern accent, his face always covered by low-brimmed hats and an absolutely 180 degree-appearance, no one anywhere had noticed who he really was.

The woman quickly turned on her heels and threw her toilet paper in her cart leaving the men alone.

"Now that wasn't nice," Michael said, return-ing to his shopping.

"We're not here for you to go on a southern panty raid," Geoff reminded.

Geoff on the other hand, chose something more to his liking and closer to his true character. Khakis, plaid button down, loafers and a smug glare that he wore better than most women wore makeup.

"You stick out," Michael said, turning from the woman as she pushed her cart away to the opposite direction.

Geoff turned from picking out his own selection and narrowed his eyes at Michael. "Begging your pardon, your majesty...your highness...sir?"

Michael knew the slip was more of a slap in the face as Geoff was supposed to just call him by his name, but he couldn't help but be entertained by the fish-out-of-water experience that his friend was having. "Michael will do just fine," he answered with a smirk. He looked Geoff up and down with disapproval. "And you stick out in that get up. You look like a Brooks Brothers ad. What happened to jeans and simple t-shirt?"

"Based upon the love for camouflage in this community, I think that anything goes," Geoff said under his breath. He picked up a 12-pack roll of Charmin and looked at it.

"Oh, I like that brand," Michael said, setting his brand down. "It's supposed to be softer for your bum."

Geoff raised a brow. "I'm only getting it because it's on sale."

"So the little bears don't do anything for you?" Michael joked.

***

As soon as Michael and Geoff arrived back to their new little house from Wal-Mart, they saw Mr. Jernigan checking the mailbox at the end of the drive. He waved them down as they approached and fiddled with his hearing aid before the conversation could commence.

Dressed in tattered denim overalls and flannel shirt, he bent in to their brand new Ford F-150 and smiled at both men.

"How are you boys doing today?" he asked, scanning both of them, still not sure if they were a couple or not, despite their denial, especially the quiet English one, Geoff.

"Doing well," Michael answered first from the passenger side. He dipped his cap in Jernigan's direction.

Geoff simply nodded, refusing to take part in any southern gentile behaviors that Michael had so quickly adopted.

Mr. Jernigan swatted a bug in front of his leathery tan face and hid his tired green eyes from the sun. "The post lady dropped off the wrong mail again. I was hoping that one of you might run this over and put it into my neighbor's box. She's not doing well. So, I don't expect her to come down here and get it herself."

"Of course," Geoff answered. He took the envelopes and set them in the middle compartment. "We'll take care of it directly, Mr. Jernigan."

"How are you getting settled back there?" he asked, ready to go back inside out of the heat.

"Just fine," Michael answered. "The house is very nice. Thank you. We've just come from Wal-Mart getting more supplies. It's a very accommodating place."

Accommodating? They behaved as though they'd never been to a Wal-Mart. One was just the same as any other. "Good," Mr. Jernigan said, tapping the door. "Well, you boys have a nice one. Since the wife passed a year ago, I go into town for Saturday dinner. Not much for cooking, myself." He spat tobacco on the ground and wiped the side of his silver beard. "So, I'm going to get ready. I might be able to get some lemon ice box pie if I hurry."

"Well, enjoy your trip," Geoff answered, sensibilities raring quietly. Spitting tobacco was yet another vile tradition that he did not care for.

"If you can call it that," Mr. Jernigan said, slowly moving away from the truck so that they could pass.

Pulling off, Geoff huffed. "I'll take the neighbor the mail after I'm done unloading the truck."

"No, I'll do it," Michael said, taking the mail. He clutched the envelopes in his hand. "I haven't been for a run or walk in weeks. It will do me well. Plus, it would be nice to see a new face. I'm sure she's just some old lady who likes to talk a lot."

Geoff didn't complain. He was ready to retire for the day. "Very well, I'll take out all of the groceries and put them away. Then I'll run over and check in with the team. They might have news from your brother."

"Oh yes, our friends at MI6. Seems hilarious really, don't you think? They're doing nothing at all over there but searching the Internet for porn." Michael looked down at his phone. He was used to a hundred text messages; it seemed now that he barely got one.

"Expecting a caller?" Geoff asked curiously.

"No." Michael opened the door as soon as Geoff parked. "I'm bored. I need something else to immerse myself in besides the riveting sights of Mississippi."

"Like?"

"A job," Michael answered. "Something that will allow me to be put to good use."

Geoff raised a brow. "Don't blow your cover? The whole point of this is to keep you out of the media."

"Yes, yes, I know." Looking across the way at the white house on the hill, Michael rotated his broad shoulders. "I'll be back in a little while."

***

Bree hated to have to leave Hope so quickly, but she had to return home to Dallas and get back to work in the next day or so. And considering that Hope was only a friend by law even though in every other way she was family, she had not been able to file for FMLA in order to stay for an extended period of time. Plus with Hope unwilling to go back with her, she had no choice to make sure that she had adequate care in her absence.

It had been a knuckle sandwich to swallow. The same man who had caused all of this was now in a position to be her friend's savior. She knew that taking Sean's help was not what Hope wanted, but it was the only plausible option that they had.

Sitting in the living room perched on her favorite window seat, Hope allowed the sun to soak through her skin while they listened to

D'Angelo on the stereo. He had a new CD out that Hope was dying to hear.

Bree, on the other hand, cooked up a storm, preparing plate after plate of ready-made dishes that Hope would be able to simply pull out of the refrigerator and put into the microwave for the next few days.

"What time is it?" Hope called out for the third time.

"She should be here in just a few minutes," Bree called out from the kitchen.

Hope huffed. "I hope that she's nice. I know that I'm getting on your nerves. Sorry, I'm just nervous."

Bree looked around at the finely decorated kitchen and all of the crystal, pottery and fine pots and smirked. "I'm sure she'll be nice, I just pray that she's not a thief."

Hope heard Bree mumbling under her breath and laughed.

"Can you hear me?" Bree asked, amused.

"I can hear everything now that I can't see," Hope answered. "It's strange. I never thought so much about the five senses until I lost one."

"Well, at least you're up in spirits. It seems that being home has made you feel better. Before you know it, you'll have your sight back."

Going rigidly straight when she heard the front steps creek, she paused. "She's here," Hope said, standing up.

Bree quickly stood up from the stove, placed the hot bread on the oven and pulled off her oven mitten. "Okay. Here I come. Just sit down." Hearing Bree breeze past her and her perfume linger, Hope followed her friend's footsteps to the front door.

"I'm coming with," Hope insisted.

As they came to the door, Bree saw a shadow behind the white linen drapes. Opening the door up slowly, she saw a boney little woman in teddy bear scrubs and a painted smile on her thin lips stood in front of her. The woman's hair was pulled back in a bun, streaked with gray. She looked at Bree and then at Hope.

"Hi, I'm LouAnn. The Prichard's sent me over," she said waiting for them to invite her in.

Bree looked her over while Hope simply looked passed her.

"Thank you for coming," Hope said first, "please come in."

Bree smiled and moved, allowing the woman to come into the open foyer of the home.

"You have a lovely place here," LouAnn said, tucking her purse under her arm. She looked up above her at the crystal chandelier.

"Thank you," Hope answered. "It's been passed down for generations."

"Please come have a seat in the living room," Bree said, grabbing Hope to guide her.

Hope liked LouAnn's voice, although she could do without the loud perfume. It smelled like a knock-off of Sunflower by Elizabeth Arden.

"How have you ladies been managing?" LouAnn asked sitting down on the brown antique Allistair sofa. She looked around as she talked, admiring everything, perfectly placed in the house.

Hope sat across from her on the wing-backed chair directly under the painting of her great grandmother. "We've been doing okay considering..."

"She's doing much better now that she's at home," Bree followed up by saying, taking a seat in the opposite chair.

"Well, Sean told me about the situation. He said that Hope might need some in-home assistance for a while...indefinitely." She reached inside her purse and pulled out a small folded piece of paper. "I have about 27 years in home health as a nurse. I recently retired, but I'm looking for work now that my grandson is in private school. I need to help my daughter out. She's a single mother."

Hope smiled. *A saint.*

Bree took the folded paper and read it out loud to ensure that Hope could hear her. When she was done, she set it on the coffee table and nodded at LouAnn, pleased with her experience.

"Well, you have all the proper training," Hope said impressed.

"When can you start?" Bree asked.

Hope frowned. *That was a bit premature.* She didn't know if she wanted this woman in the same house with her...at least not yet. "Would you like some tea or coffee so that we can talk? Get to know each other," she said, turning toward Bree's voice.

"Coffee would be fine," LouAnn said, standing up. "Why don't you tell me where it is and I can fix us all a nice cup." LouAnn was a simple woman who believed a lot stronger in actions than pretty words.

"I'll show you were it is," Bree said standing.

As they walked off, Hope sat in the living room listening to birds chirping out in the trees near the open windows and contemplated how she could find out more about LouAnn and make a serious decision before Bree left for Dallas. Normally, she would have liked the woman, but the mere fact that Sean had sent her over made her feel uncomfortable, especially since she knew how his mother felt about her in general.

Hearing the doorbell ring again, she rose up. She wasn't expecting anyone else, and if Sean had shown up to oversee this, she'd kick him out herself.

"I'm coming." Bree called out.

"No, I've got it." Hope said, eager to do something on her own. She loved her friend, but Bree had to give her an opportunity to see how much of her own life she could manage.

Standing up, she slowly made her way to the door without help. It felt good to make the journey unaided. While short, it was a step in the right direction.

As the doorbell rang a second time, she opened the door feeling mildly accomplished. A broad smile crossed her lips. "Yes."

There was an instant hesitation from the visitor.

"Hello," the deep voice answered. "Are you Hope Daniels?"

"Yes, I am," Hope answered, glad to hear that at least it wasn't Sean. "Can I help you?"

Michael stared at her for a moment. It was as if she looked right through him. The wind blew through her long black hair and perfumed the breeze with sweet fragrance. He stumbled over his words. "I'm your new neighbor. I took over Mr. Jernigan's smaller house on his property. When I arrived back from shopping today, he asked me to drop your mail by your home." Extending his arm, he offered her the mail with a shaky hand.

Hope smiled, eyes sparkling like black diamonds in the sunlight. She ran her fingers past a wild strand of her unbound hair and tucked it behind her ear. "He finally found someone to take over Kelly's house. Good. He's been looking for months now." Reaching out for the mail, she moved her hand right past the envelopes and into his wide chest. It felt like warm concrete to the touch. Her fingertips lingered there for a moment.

Getting control of herself, she recoiled, embarrassed at her misstep.

That had been his first physical interaction with a human being who did not work for him since he arrived. It wasn't normal for people to touch royalty, *unless they were incredible drunk*. The small touch felt odd, like zingers coursing through his blood stream or maybe it was just being in her presence. Whatever it was paralyzed him.

Michael looked down at her hand and then back at her with a clever smile. Two things stuck out. She was absolutely breathtaking and based upon her wedding finger, she was single. But there was something off in her gaze at him.

"Sorry, I'm newly handicapped," she explained with an embarrassed laugh.

"How so?" he asked, stepping closer. *Why did she not react?*

"Oh, I was blinded in a car accident about a month and a half ago. I haven't gotten the whole depth perception thing down yet. I hear you fine, but I can only see shades of light. Good thing that you weren't a woman. I would have felt you right up," she joked, twisting her lips into a rueful smile.

You still sort of did, Michael thought to himself.

He liked that she couldn't see him, it prevented the obvious, which was his inability to take his eyes off her.

But Hope could smell him. Sandalwood danced in her head. He smelled like heaven. Without knowing what he looked like at all, she knew that he must be beautiful. No man could ever sound so charming and not be.

Gently, Michael reached out for her hand and placed the mail inside of it. Holding on to her soft hand and feeling her fingers just a second longer, he looked into her eyes. They were soothing, despite her blindness and

kind...so kind. "I'm sorry for your recent mishap. I hope it's not permanent."

"Oh, it's not permanent," she answered
quickly. "The doctor says that it will come back
as soon as they heal themselves." A sigh followed, indicating that she wasn't really as sure
as she led on to be.

"Well, I'm Michael," he said, heartstrings
jerking inside. His body shadowed over hers,
hiding her face from the sunlight. "It's very nice
to meet you."

"I'm Hope Daniels," she said, enjoying his
voice. "But you already know that." His lyrical
accent wasn't all Southern, but she couldn't
properly place it.

Finally realizing that they were not alone,
Michael looked passed her to see two women
glaring at him from the background. "We have
a bit of an audience," he whispered to Hope.
"Are they your caretakers or bodyguards?"

Hope laughed, more than she had done in six
weeks. "The tall pretty one is the nosiest woman you'll ever meet. But she means well. Now, I
don't know much about the other one. I'm
trying to figure out if she'll be my new nurse
until I'm better."

"Well, she looks pleasant," Michael said,
nodding toward them. "Ladies."

Bree raised a brow at Michael, but did not speak.

LouAnn on the other hand, glared at him with a look of surprise on her face. *What was with this girl and pulling attractive white men? What did she have that her daughter seemed to lack?*

"Are you ready to finish our interview?" Bree asked, trying to pull Hope away from the conversation with Michael.

Hope glanced back toward her friend's voice. "Just a moment."

Michael smirked. *He knew what Bree was up to. Cock blocking was an international pastime.*

"Well, I had better get back to things, but it was nice to meet you, Michael," Hope said, wishing that she could see his face. She turned back toward him.

"It was nice to meet you as well," he said, drinking her in one last time.

She clutched the side of the door for balance. "Don't be a stranger. If Mr. Jernigan liked you, you must be alright." Her nervousness finally betrayed her and showed.

Michael chuckled. "He's a nice old man, but I think that he thinks that I'm gay."

"Why would he think that?" Hope asked, now even more curious about the strange man.

"I live with my best friend, Geoff. He's a bit English and a proper asshole."

Hope chuckled. "Well, are you gay? I mean, it's alright if you are, but I'd be incredibly disappointed."

"No," he said, voice fading. He couldn't take his eyes off of her even though he tried with everything in him to do so. The warmness of her brown perfect skin, the curve of her heart-shaped lips, the sinfully thick, wing-like flaps of her eyelashes and long natural arch of her brows made her look like an angel or the most beautiful devil he'd ever seen.

"Good," she said, flirting just a little. "Then I'll see you around for more than just mail service, *maybe*."

"It would be my pleasure," Michael said, ending his stay. "Have a lovely evening, Hope."

Hope giggled. "You too." Closing the door behind her, she left him there to contemplate her on the porch.

Chapter 6

The nights in Hernando were like something out of Mid Summer's Night Dream. Perched on towering oak trees, owls hooted, crickets chirped, the moon blazed with nocturnal fury and a fresh, inviting breeze crept through the slightly open window.

It was a perfect setting for a peaceful evening. In fact, Michael could hear in his head quotes from Shakespeare even as he tossed and turned in bed. He was tormented but for once, not with the agony of his life but the idea of what it truly was. This peculiar woman and her millisecond of an introduction into his existence had birthed intrigue back into his consciousness.

I know a bank where the wild thyme blows,
Where oxlips and the nodding violet grows,
Quite over-canopied with luscious woodbine,
With sweet musk-roses and with eglantine.

Despite the peace around him, Michael simply couldn't sleep. Every time that he closed his eyes, he thought of Hope and his eyes flashed back open to remind him that he was only a house away from her. Over the course of the night, he had committed her every feature to memory and played out every possible scenario that would cause for him to see her again. *He had to see her again.* Only, he didn't know why...yet. But he intended to find out why she had become the flame and he the moth.

Maybe it was the fact that he had gone the longest he had ever gone without sex since his decision to come to the U.S.

Maybe it was because no one knew who he was and he lacked the very attention that he had fled, along with the incessant demands of his title.

But maybe there was something else that niggled at him.

He heard his brother's voice suddenly and remembered the conversation with Richard back at the castle. "If a woman loves you, she loves you because you're beautiful, royalty and/or rich. Look anywhere in the world, you'll get the same answer. You can't change who you are, and even if you lied to her, you couldn't change how you look."

Funny. She didn't know that he was rich, royal or beautiful. And yet, she seemed to like him.

Sitting up in the small queen sized bed, he finally pushed the covers off his naked body and stood up. The moonlight from outside illuminated his room and all six-feet of his muscular frame. Another thought crossed his mind, but this time it was sexual in nature. He imagined what she might feel like in bed with him, naked and sweating under the moon, wrapped in his embrace while he kissed each and every inch of her beautiful body.

That thought sent him over the edge and forced him to fight a growing erection. The last thing that he needed was that, less he find himself in the bathroom with a bottle of lube and his phone properly placed on Pornhub.com.

Slipping on a pair of pajama bottoms, he walked down the hall in the darkness, past the cameras installed by MI6 to watch their every move, to Geoff's bedroom and found him up looking at his tablet.

"You can't sleep either?" Michael asked, glad that he was not alone.

"It's morning at home. I'm watching the news from London," Geoff answered, not bothering to look up. "Why are you up? Please don't tell me that you'd like to go to Wal-Mart again. I can only stomach that place once a day."

Michael scratched the back of his neck. "I'm thinking about a girl."

Geoff paused. Putting down his tablet, he huffed. "Who is she?"

"The neighbor," Michael answered, leaning against the door. A brow rose. "She's funny."

"The senior citizen?" Geoff was extremely disappointed. He was hoping to get some rest on this remarkably boring adventure, but he knew that look in Michael, when he saw it.

"No, she's not a senior citizen. From the looks of her, we're very near in age," Michael answered. He shrugged reluctantly. "But she is blind."

Geoff huffed in relief. "Thank God."

Shock overwhelmed Michael. "What? That's a horrible thing to say."

A yawn escaped the large, brooding man. "If she's blind, it means that she can't see you, and if she can't see you then she can't blow your cover." Geoff picked his tablet back up and continued watching the live stream. *And she can't ruin our plans*, he said to himself inwardly.

"Hope." Michael said her name with complete reverence.

"Excuse me," Geoff said.

Michael wiggled his nose. "Her name...it's Hope." Her face flashed in his memory again. "She's Black," he said as an afterthought. "She's a beautiful, exotic woman."

Geoff was not surprised. Michael had always been attracted to women who hailed from exotic locales or had exotic looks. Still he corrected his friend. "African-American. They don't like to be called black anymore in this country. You should probably get that right before you say something to offend her and ruin the moment."

"I'll remember that," Michael said, walking over to the chair in the corner. He plopped down most ungracious like. "It was the way that she looked at me that keeps playing in my mind."

Geoff's voice was flat and matter-of-fact. "How could she look at you? She's blind."

And there it was. Geoff's off-color comments. "I know that she's blind, Geoff. Damn. I just told you that. What I am saying is...," he paused and looked over at his friend. "I'm saying it's the way she looked through me. It's been a while since I have met someone who seemed so calming. She was real."

A real live girl, Geoff mocked inwardly. "Jernigan is quite calming once you get pass his constant and abhorrent tobacco spitting and his situational deafness. Maybe you should try to make a match, since you're not in the market."

There was a long silence as Michael stared out of the window.

"Do you believe in destiny?" Michael asked.

"I believe in directing your attention toward what you want," Geoff answered, a little more responsive than before. But he quickly shut off his emotions. "But I also believe that you can see what you want to see, or in her case…"

Michael huffed and stood up. "I give up. Good night, Geoff. Do get some sleep. You are absolutely crabby without your rest." He picked up a pillow from the bed and threw it at Geoff's head. "Don't quit your day job. You're a dreadfully unfunny bloke."

Geoff smirked. "I'll remember that. Good-night, sir. Do try to get some rest."

"Good night," Michael said, leaving Geoff alone with his news broadcast.

Michael knew that going to sleep was not really an option, but talking to Geoff had given him an idea. This was a social media age. Sure-ly, there had to be something about her on the Internet. Closing the door behind him as he entered his room, he turned on the light and grabbed his computer. Since it was far too late to stop by her home, he'd Google her.

***

Just a few hundred feet away from where Michael sat surfing the internet for Intel on his new muse, Hope sat up in bed under a mass of colorful patchwork quilts, while Bree oiled her scalp. With the windows open listening to the same chirping crickets that serenaded Michael and the same moon bathed the night, the two women drank tea and ate chocolate chip cookies while Ed Sheeran played on the stereo.

Like school girls, they laughed and played, forgetting all the troubles that came with the day. Unable to sleep on their last night before Bree's departure, they decided to spend some much-needed quality time just talking like they used to do before things had gotten so complicated.

For Hope however, there was another motive for the late night chat. Today, unlike the ones before it had brought intrigue back into her life. For hours after the stranger had come to her door, she had recounted their conversation. How funny he was and quick witted. He had made her laugh and for a moment, forget that she was blind. While LouAnn was trying to convince her that she was qualified to work for her, Hope had been lost in her thoughts, trying desperately to figure out the brand of cologne that Michael had worn. When she moved from his cologne, she was only left with his funny accent and the brief touch of her skin and his when he held her hand. Was it possible that he liked her too?

She curled her legs under her and finally asked the question that she'd wanted to ask since earlier in the day.

"Tell me how he looked, Bree" she said, trying to repress her smile.

Bree parted Hope's hair. "Who?"

Hope huffed. "You know *who*. Michael."

"Oh, him," Bree said, smiling. She chuckled. "He was handsome."

"Like school boy handsome or Facebook post hot?" Hope asked, biting her lip. "Don't leave out any detail."

Bree couldn't lie. Although she had only seen the man briefly and from a few feet away she could see that he was Facebook hot. "Well, he had wheat blonde hair, natural though, not the bleached kind. He had crystal blue eyes, great bone structure, wide lips for kissing and thick eyebrows." She could feel Hope shift in the bed.

"What else?" Hope pried.

"He had a long thick neck, muscles and a wide chest and wide shoulders with a lot of definition and a flat stomach. And I liked that he had incredibly long legs and big hands."

"Damn, you noticed all that?" Hope joked.

"Well, it's not often that you see someone that attractive in Hernando." Bree snickered. "He had big ass feet."

Hope laughed. "He seemed really nice."

"Yeah, you said that earlier," she frowned. "You aren't thinking of..."

Hope cut her off. "I'm not interested in going on the rebound. I just like the idea that a cute guy showed up while LouAnn was here. So, she can go back and report it to Sean. I hope he chokes on it." Hope lied.

Bree didn't believe her. She had known her friend for too long to be deceived. "You were flirting with him."

"I was not," Hope said, turning toward Bree.

"You were," Bree taunted, straightening Hope's head to continue her hair. "You were *blind* flirting," she said, adding insult to injury.

"Well, maybe just a little. What harm could a little flirting do?"

"Don't get hurt again," Bree said seriously. "I don't think I can bare it."

"Neither can I," Hope said, more solemnly. "I really liked Sean. I mean, I *really* liked him. Don't get me wrong. I knew it was possible that we'd break up. That's a possibility in any relationship. I just never thought that we'd break up over my race or what his family thought. And I never thought he'd cheat on me. And I wasn't physically blind then. I just didn't see it coming."

"Men are pigs," Bree said with finality.

"Yep, some of them are," Hope agreed. But inwardly, she was hoping that Michael wasn't. Something about him was different, though after only one interaction, she didn't know what.

"Just promise me that you'll get your sight back before you decide to get your groove back."

Hope laughed. "I will." She fiddled with her fingers. "I hope my sight comes back soon. Not for Michael, but because I don't want LouAnn to be here long. I'm used to being my own woman. I don't like the idea of having to depend on someone. Plus, every day that I spend like this, I can't finish my work."

Bree finished Hope's hair and brushed the long tendrils back. Hugging her friend from behind, she prayed over her. "God is going to give you more than your sight back, little girl. He's going to give you peace. You have to believe that. But you have to let Him do it in his own time."

The soothing words brought tears to Hope's eyes. "I really don't know what I'd do without you," she said, hugging her back. "I love you."

"Love you too girl," Bree said, kissing her shoulder.

Chapter 7

In the high-rise offices of the popular gossip magazine Perk, there sat a very unhappy employee. Hannibal Ross was absolutely in knots over the sudden disappearance of Prince Michael from the celebrity gossip headlines. *Not that he cared on a personal level*, but it was his job to report on the constant terrible choices of the beautiful mess, and for over six weeks, Hannibal had been tearing his hair out calling all of his sources trying to get a lead on the whereabouts of the missing prince.

So far, no reports had been credible. Rumors were circulating around the globe, but none could produce pictures or proof. And the royals were about as helpful as tits on a bull, with their simple statement saying that the Prince needed time to reorganize his life.

Reorganize?

Really?

And what was the rest of the world supposed to do while the Prince figured what his next steps would be? Whole industries depended on knowing every single move, including RQL.

Hannibal was only a step away from producing his very first fully fabricated story just to keep the powers that be off his tail, but he knew that even that would only sate the wolves for only a short period of time. The world needed photos; they needed a story!

He had been up nearly 24 hours on Red Bull, 5 hour energy drinks, coffee and cupcakes, a combination that did not bode well for his wide and very unsettling gut tucked into black jogging pants and covered by large Lakers jersey. Cookie wrappers, old canned cokes and pizza boxes lined his office as he had refused to leave the confines of his work space as he relentlessly toiled over the phone.

His boss had told him that at 10 o'clock this morning; he'd receive a personal visit to find out what new developments had transpired. Normally, such a visit would not have created such havoc for him. He had been dubbed the golden child of RQL because of his gritty stories on the prince and his ability when no one else could to get the dirt on a man who had been historically the easiest royal to be tracked and ridiculed. However, now the visit would surely be ball busting.

As he glanced at the clock for the hundredth time, sweat beads began to form on his balding red head. It was exactly 10 o'clock on the dot. Immediately, the tension in his back rose up his spine and exploded into a headache.

"Hannibal," his editor said, blowing into his office and slamming the latest newspapers from around the globe on the glass table. "What have you got for me?" The words were like sharp knives inside of his head.

Hannibal turned from his computer monitor reluctantly, feeling emasculated. "Nothing yet, boss." He looked up at Chief Editor Anna McGregor with hesitation, afraid to make eye contact.

While she was a beautiful woman by the societal definition, she was also a fire-breathing dragon from hell that lived and died by the number of online and physical subscriptions, and point of sale magazines RQL sold.

Glaring red daggers back at him; she placed her long red manicured claws on the desk and bent closer. "Do you know why I hired you?" she asked, blonde hair spilling over her shoulders.

"Because of my good looks," Hannibal said with a crooked yellow smile.

Clicking her nails against the glass, she sucked in a deep breath. "You wish. I hired you because you can get the dirt on anyone, not just anyone, royalty. In fact, I've damn near given you an entire page in a time when in the world of publishing, that is pretty much an impossible notion." Her hunches rose. "But what am I paying you for lately? No comment from the soon-to-be-king and photos of the boring brother going to dinners doesn't sell copies of RQL."

"I've looked everywhere. Michael is missing," Hannibal explained.

Anna stood and rolled her neck. "Well, find him...if you want to stay employed," she said, raising a brow. Turning on her red back high heels, she stomped out of the office just as she had come, full of fury. "Or I can always hire someone who can. You've got one week to come up with something that will sell magazines."

"I hate that woman," Hannibal said out loud, when he was certain that she was out of earshot. "How am I supposed to find missing royalty?"

Then the idea hit him.

She didn't say find him per se. She said to sell magazines.

Looking down at his notes, he came up with the perfect story. "WHERE IS MICHAEL?" If the bad boy of royalty wanted to hide, he'd make

him work for it. A nationwide manhunt purporting that he was right here in the states and
giving a reward would create a whole new story
and give him all the leads that he'd need to
actually find the man.

***

LouAnn arrived at dawn to begin her day
with Hope. Letting herself in with the key that
Bree had given her, she made her way quietly in
the house and slowly tiptoed down the corridor
to the kitchen. As soon as she flicked on the
light to the kitchen, she nearly jumped out of
her skin. Surprisingly, Hope was there sitting
quietly with a cup of tea.

"Oh my goodness," LouAnn said, grabbing
her heart. "You gave me a start."

"Sorry," Hope said with a smile. "I sort of
don't need the light right now."

"Logically," LouAnn said, setting down her
lunch bag on the counter. "Why are you up so
early?"

"Bree just left not too long ago. I didn't want
to miss saying goodbye." She picked up the
coffee mug and sniffed the lavender tea. "I'm
hoping this will put me back to bed, but it's not
likely. When I get up, I tend to be up for the rest
of the day."

"Me too," LouAnn said, looking around the
kitchen. "Want some breakfast?"

"Not really hungry," Hope answered. "But I woke up with a bit of good news. I'm seeing more than just a little light. I saw shadows."

"Progress." LouAnn came to sit down by her. "I was talking to Bree yesterday about some things that need to be taken care of around the house. I'm thinking that you might need a handyman."

"Lay the list on me," Hope said, ready to hear the bad news.

"Well, the barn door needs to be replaced from a storm that passed through while you were at the hospital, the yard needs to be edged really bad, the gutters need to be cleaned, and evidently your roof has a few shingles that came off."

Hope huffed. "Those are things that I don't think we can handle on our own."

LouAnn chuckled. "I'm no good with a hammer."

"Me either. Okay, we'll get someone in here as soon as we can. I'll make that my priority."

"Are you sure you don't want me to handle it?" LouAnn offered.

"You're sweet, but no. You're doing enough."

"Well, what's on the menu today?" LouAnn asked.

"Laundry." Hope hated laundry more than she hated paying taxes, but it was a necessary evil. She cast a hopeful smile. "And then, I was hoping that you might help me take a walk. I normally run a few miles a day and being in the house has really been taking its toll on me. I think more endorphins might help my mood and help stunt my growing ass."

LouAnn laughed. "The story of my life, girl. Sounds good to me. Since I'll only be here every day until five, I'll get started separating clothes and linen ASAP and then we can take a walk before it gets too hot outside."

"Thanks, LouAnn," Hope said appreciatively.

***

At eight o'clock in the morning, Michael woke from his peaceful slumber. Somewhere in between reading the many articles on Hope's up and coming career and viewing her website, he had finally fallen asleep in the middle of the night. Only when he did, he dreamed of her. She was standing under an oak tree in a yellow sundress smiling at him with the sun at her back and the wind in her hair. That was all that he remembered, but that was more than enough.

With the laptop stuck under his left side digging into his ribs, he cracked his eyes open and looked out of the window.

Shit, it was finally morning.

Jumping up, he knocked the Apple MacBook Air onto the floor and nearly stepped on it as he ran into the bathroom to shower.

A normally sluggish demeanor had all but dissipated in him at the prospect of seeing Hope again. He had a new mission in mind, and it wasn't to find a job as much as it was to get closer to the woman in his dreams. She was more amazing than he had first thought. She loved art, so did he. She didn't mind being different, neither did he. And she could not judge him on his looks, status, thus his short comings. It was a great feeling. For once, he had a clean slate.

Now, the question was what to do with it.

After a quick shower and a change into running clothes, he zipped into the kitchen to grab a shake. Geoff was waiting at the table, fully dressed in his normal khakis and plaid button down. Pushing a pot of coffee across the table, he sent a text and looked up at Michael.

"You seem to be in a very chipper mood," Geoff said, checking out his running clothes. "Getting back into the swing of things?"

"I'm going for a run," Michael said, turning on the blender. He leaned against the counter and crossed his long legs over each other. "What time does the mail run?"

"The mail?" Geoff frowned. "Are you expecting something?"

"No," Michael said, looking at his watch. "I'm going to pick up some."

Without explanation, Geoff knew what Michael's intentions were. Moving the conversation right along, he pulled his coffee mug up to his mouth. "Look behind you, I took the liberty of looking up some possible job openings for you. I figured that the American saying could prove to be true for you, so I wanted to get in front of it."

"American saying?" Michael asked.

"An idle mind is the devil's workshop." Geoff smirked.

"Oh, but my mind is not idle," Michael said, looking behind him and grabbing the paper. "I assume this came from our friends down the street."

"You assumed right," Geoff answered. "Also, someone will be following you on your run. Please try to understand that you are still the Prince of England."

"Really?" Michael said, pouring the protein shake into a container as he read the list of jobs. "There's nothing sexy on here at all."

"There is nothing sexy in Hernando that won't get you caught."

"It's sort of exciting really. I feel like one of our specialists on a mission."

Geoff couldn't agree. "I feel like I'm in the twilight zone." There was no lie in his voice, no inflection.

Michael huffed. His friend simply didn't know how to have fun.

***

Michael had to admit there was something absolutely breathtaking about running the roads of Hernando. So many trees, bushes, land, horses and cows. He'd never been so immersed in the country land before. With his headphones on, he maneuvered over the hills and down the rambling roads for several miles, all with his men trailing closely behind him in a Yukon Denali, passed every once in a while by someone who refused to go below the limit. He rather missed his team of MI6 and their more personal attention. If he had not been under-cover, he would have insisted that they take a run with him, but obviously considering what he was trying to do; one would have noticed men running nearly in cadence together.

After a brisk five-miler, he headed back down his road covered in sweat, but deter-mined to do one final thing before the day went on. As he passed Hope's house, he stopped abruptly and went over to the mailbox.

His men slowed behind him. "What's he do-ing?" Benjamin, one of the men in his MI6 detail asked.

"Looks like he's checking the neighbor's mail," Bradley, the passenger in the Yukon said astounded.

"Well, why would he be doing that?" he asked in his British accent.

"Shall I step out and ask his highness?" Brad-ley said snidely.

"It's illegal to touch anyone else's mailbox," Benjamin reminded.

Bradley simply shook his head. There was no reason to respond, it would only fall on deaf ears.

Luckily for Michael, the postman had al-ready run, thus enabling his plan to move forward. Taking Hope's mail in his hand, he turned and saluted his men, then ran up the gravel driveway to the door.

"I think he fancies the neighbor," Benjamin said, pulling off before they were noticed.

"Well, we need to get some ears and eyes on that house if he plans on being there," Bradley huffed, calling up to Geoff. "Be advised. ETA 5 minutes. We need to debrief on Brown Bear's run and the *neighbor*."

"Copy," Geoff responded over the radio.

***

Michael could feel his heart beating out of his chest as he moved up the steps of Hope's home to her door. Taking a deep breath, he pushed the doorbell buzzer and stepped back. He hoped that she was up, prayed that she wasn't busy. After a few moments, he saw a silhouette behind the sheer covered door.

LouAnn opened the front door cautiously in a pair of Care bear smocks and Ugg shoes. Smiling curiously at Michael, she pushed open the screen door for him. He was a sight for sore eyes. Twice in two days.

"Hello," she said, putting her hand on her hip.

Michael smiled. "Good morning. Is Hope available?" He passed her into the house.

LouAnn looked back behind her to find Hope walking toward the sound of Michael's voice from the hallway.

"Are you available, Hope?" LouAnn asked playfully.

Hope tried not to smile as brightly as she wanted. "I think so," she answered.

"Hi," Hope said, twisting her fingers together.

"Good morning," he said, thinking that she looked like Christmas morning in her black yoga pants and her pink form-fitting t-shirt. He couldn't help but notice that she only had socks on.

Just then LouAnn's phone went off in the front pocket of her smock. "Hold on one second," she said, pulling the phone out and looking at it. "This is my grandson's school."

Stepping away from Michael and Hope, she left them to talk for a moment. As soon as she did, all the air in the room seem to be sucked out and both of them found themselves fumbling.

"What brings you to my doorstep *this* morning?" Hope asked.

Michael stepped closer to her and took her hand. Pulling the envelopes into her hand, he bent and whispered into her ear. "You've got mail."

"Thank you," Hope giggled. She liked him being close, but she tried hard not to put her hand on his chest again, this time, although something about him drew her near.

LouAnn walked back into the room and huffed. "I'm so sorry. Hunter is sick, and his mother works in Germantown. I need to go and get him."

"I'll be fine," Hope answered. "Go get your grandson."

"Are you sure?" LouAnn asked even though she was relieved. "What about your walk?"

Michael immediately seized the opportunity. "I'd love to take you," he said, quickly. He hated himself for sounding too eager. "I haven't gone on my run yet," he explained a little less spastic.

LouAnn looked at the man drenched in sweat, obviously from a seriously exhausting workout, and raised a brow. "Are you sure it won't be putting you out?" she asked, turning up her lips at him. If only Hope could see how big of a lie he was telling at the moment, she might find him more adorable than he already was.

"It would be my pleasure," Michael answered with a smug smile. "I was just going to work out myself. So, it will be no imposition at all." He looked down at Hope with a determined gaze.

LouAnn shook her head. It didn't take a genius to see where this was going. "Well, aren't we fortunate?" she said, putting her hands on her hips. With a huff, she digressed. "Alright, I'll leave you kids to it. I'll be back as soon as I can."

"Take your time," Hope answered, reaching for Michael's hand. She caressed the smooth ridges of his fingers. "Follow me to the den," she ordered.

"Yes, ma'am," Michael said, winking devilishly back at LouAnn.

"Be good, young man," LouAnn warned as she headed out the front door.

"Alone at last," Hope joked.

Michael didn't laugh. It was exactly what he had in mind the entire time. "So where'd you like to walk today?" he asked as he looked around.

"The park would be nice." Hope smirked. "Are you sure that you won't be too put out?"

"No, why would you ask?"

Hope stopped walking and turned to him. Reaching out, she touched his chest. Her fingers trailed in the heat of his body and the dampness of his shirt. "I can smell your sweat," she answered with a grin. "Didn't know if you had one more workout in you."

He looked down into her beautiful face again and fought his urge to kiss her full mouth. "Damn, I'm caught," he said ruefully hiding the lust boiling under his surface. "Guess I should have freshened up first. I hope my *fragrance* isn't too offensive."

"Not at all. I like sweat on a man," Hope said, shaking her head. "I thought it was cute." She removed her hand, but not before patting his chest.

"Do you?" Michael ran a hand through his hair. "Well, aren't you clever?" *Or am I just an idiot*, he asked himself inwardly.

"Not clever just more in tune with my other senses."

"All of them?" Michael asked suggestively.

"Yes, all of them." Hope started to walk with him again.

"How do you walk around without bumping into anything?"

"I'm a clean freak. I keep most of the house in perfect condition, all except my work room."

"Where is that? What do you work on?"

"Nothing at the moment." She avoided the questions.

Michael had never been so far into Hope's home before. Even when he came to the front door this morning with her mail, he only half-way expected to get into the foyer. But now, he was here – an opportunity that he could only attribute to a mix of preparation and luck.

Something about being here with her was like being a teenager again. Excitement coursed through his veins like a boy about to experience his first kiss. Bliss. Pure unadulterated bliss.

"Your home is beautiful," he said, loving how cozy and warm it was. And it wasn't just small talk. He could smell candles burning all around him. The air was crisp and clean like fresh linen. Wilted flowers bent over crystal vases. The smell of cleaning products danced in the air with bleach and fabric softener. It was homey and perfectly decorated, like the American romantic comedies that he was forced to watch when he was with Thalia.

"Thank you," Hope said, praying the house was as clean as when she had sight. With other people helping her, she had to depend on their version of clean, instead of her own, which was more OCD than anything.

"It's very pre-Civil war," Michael noted.

"It's been in the family a long time. There is a whole story behind it. When you feel the need to be bored out of your gourd, then come by and I'll tell it to you."

He laughed. She was funny. "I'll do that."

Her home was definitely authentic antebellum architecture. There were shiny hardwood floors, tall ceilings, wide boxed archways and tons of antique furniture. It was a pure southern home meant for a southern belle. Perfect for her.

Looking around as he walked her toward the den, he noticed how everything was in place. Many of the pieces were from different eras, which suggested that the home had been in her family for quite some time. But everything blended together.

She smiled as they arrived into the large, airy den. There were some noticeable modern touches to the tall, crown molded ceilings. An oak entertainment center sat mid-way off the back wall with a 70 inch television, media center and stereo.

Now this is more like it, Michael thought to himself. His new little home was much smaller; needless to say the smallest and most modest place that he'd ever lived in his entire life. However, it did have character, or at least character building characteristics.

Michael's mind began to turn. "So what are we doing in here?"

Without seeing his face, Hope knew that his mind was if not in, sitting near, the gutter. She couldn't lie, there were parts of her that had been untended to and regardless of how she tried to repress them had started to come alive at just the thought of them being alone. She chuckled and rubbed the back of her neck as a naughty thought crossed her mind. "You are going to help me...find my shoes," she giggled. "They are somewhere in here, but the room is pretty big. And then, we're going to the park."

Michael eyed her pink Nike's in the corner. Leaving her side, he walked across the room and picked them up, while she sat down on the sofa. Coming to her side, he knelt down in front of her and grabbed her foot gently.

"I can do it," she said quickly.

But Michael didn't let go.

"Please, allow me," he insisted, voice deep and full of strain.

She sat back and crossed her hands. "Alright." Hope could feel his large hands around her calf and foot. She could also smell his cologne and sweat competing for equal aroma.

Swallowing hard, she felt herself getting lightheaded.

With care, he ran his hand up her leg and wrapped his fingers gently around her muscular calf. Trying hard to focus on the rest of her supple thighs and the perfect V-shape between them, he slipped the little gym shoe onto her socked-foot, applying just enough pressure to make sure that it was completely on.

"How does that feel?" he asked, gazing up into her eyes.

"Perfect," she said, barely above a whisper. Never had anything so small been so intimate.

A smile crept across his mouth. Pleased with himself when he saw the attraction looming on her warm face, he did the same for the other foot.

Taking a deep breath, she bit her lip. "Thank you."

Michael wanted to stay there on his knees in front of her, but he pushed himself to stand. "So where to?"

"The park," she answered. "It's only about five miles away."

"Well, then, we'll need transportation. I'll just go and get my truck." He looked around and clasped his hands together in front of him. "Right. You stay here and I'll be right back with the truck."

She grinned, wishing she could see his face. "I'll be right here," she said playfully.

Nearly sprinting out of the den, he headed out of the house as fast as his feet would take him.

Chapter 8

What the hell was that? That was the only question that continued to ring in Hope's head when she was finally left alone.

Sitting on the sofa in complete darkness, she suddenly didn't feel so alone. This man who had just swept in her life over night was proving to be quite an adventure.

Truthfully, she was grateful for just a few minutes of alone time while Michael went to get his truck from next door. If nothing else, she needed to wipe the sweat forming on her upper lip – a nervous tick that she could not help. And if time permitted, she needed to pull herself together after such an intense interaction. *Certain parts of her felt suddenly moist and alive.*

Just a shoe, it was supposed to be just a shoe. But it wasn't.

Something about his touch drove her insane. But it was more than his touch. It was his presence. Just him being around, made her a completely different person. It was as if her molecules reconfigured around him.

It was as if he knew that she had spent the entire night thinking about him, praying that he would show up for no particular reason at all.

And he had done just that. Under the guise of delivering mail, he had delivered something else.

Courage.

Courage to put Sean behind her.

And faith that all men were not dogs.

Now, back to freshening up. Patting her hair, she cringed at how truly frizzy it was. "Good grief," she said, imagining how she must look with someone else doing her hair. Running her fingers through it, she pulled at the small tangles and cuffed it around her shoulders, then raised her arms and checked one more time before he returned to make sure that she was pleasant, especially since she had not been running today.

"Stay calm," she barked at herself, hearing the house phone ring at the same time.

With a few movements, she was up. But the sound of the phone echoed around the room. *Where was it? Argh!*

Trying to move toward the sound of the phone, she finally gave up right before it went to voicemail. Whoever it was would just have to call back later.

Making her way through the house guided by the dim lights and shadows, she vaguely picked up; she finally came to her make-shift bedroom, and felt around on her vanity for her perfume and brush. She'd have to make do with trying to be as cute as she could by memory. Spraying perfume on her chest, she heard him come through the door.

That was fast.

"Hope," Michael called out.

She liked the way that he said her name. "In here," she answered, setting down her brush and at the same time knocking some of the other contents on the vanity onto the floor. Butterflies erupted again. Feeling for her lip balm, she smeared it on quickly.

She could hear his large steps come towards her room. With each single echo, her heart lurched more.

Stop being nervous, she said to herself. *He's just a man.*

Michael looked around her bedroom and smiled. Again, another place in this magnificent home that felt like a warm blanket. There was so much love in it, so much history.

"It's nice in here," he said, walking up to her. He found a certain amount of privilege in being in her bed chambers. It gave him more clues about her life. He liked the many colorful silk scarves, the checkered flower comforter, the warm green walls, the muted carpet and rugs, the antique lamps and the smell of sweet, intoxicating perfume. It was like a garden.

"Thank you. It's not my real bedroom. That's upstairs, but Bree brought my things down here until I get my sight back," she said, seeing a shadow as he approached her. "Oh my," she gasped, hands over her mouth.

He paused. "What?" *Did he not freshen up enough?*

"I can see something," she said with a bright smile. Excitement rang in her voice like bells. "I can see...something!"

"You can see me?" he asked, walking closer to her.

"Shadows. That's progress, right?"

Her smile was intoxicating. "It is," he said, taking her hand in his own and fighting the urge to kiss her. "Are you ready to go?" he asked, moving a piece of her hair from her face.

"Yes," she said, letting him guide her.

***

Michael was thankful for Hope's blindness yet again as he looked in the rearview mirror. How else would she be able to ignore his entourage unless she was blind? Pulling into the park, he eyed the black Yukon behind him. *They could ruin a wet dream.* But Hope was in her own world. She rather enjoyed the ride. All the way to the park, she kept her window down and her face toward the wind while he played 107.5 The Q. He liked the station. Its pop music kept the mood light with the exception of Hozier's *Take Me to Church*. Strangely, the tune reminded him of her.

Putting the truck in park, he looked over at her and felt accomplished. Whether she knew it or not, this was their first date. It was a first for him in many ways. He'd never gone on a literal *blind* date before, never put on a woman's shoe, never assisted a woman on such an intimate level and quite frankly never felt this way.

Ready to get out and explore the park, Hope found the handle and opened the passenger door.

"Wait. I've got that," he said, quickly jumping out. He waved off the men as he rounded the truck and mouthed, *go away*. But he knew that as long as he was there, they would be there also.

Michael looked up at the sky and the low dark clouds that were starting to form. Earlier it was a sunny morning with blue skies, but now rain was in forecast for the afternoon for sure. Only, he didn't want to tell her that. What if she decided that she wanted to go back?

Hope inhaled the strong, fragrant breeze that met her, picking her hair up and carrying it over her shoulders. "Mmm. That feels so good," she said, extending her arms. "I can smell the freshly cut grass and everything.   It's like a dream."

"First time out?" He shut the door behind her and locked the truck.

"Yep, you just sprang me from jail." Her face was covered in glee. "I bet its beautiful today, isn't it?"

He couldn't take his eyes off her.   "Very beautiful." Michael meant it. She was absolutely breathtaking and as much a breath of fresh air as the breeze she enjoyed.

"I love the walking trail. You can just lose yourself in it, you know. No worries. No drama. Just you and the trail. When I'd come here alone, I'd pop in my ear buds and blast my iPod for hours. Straight powerwalking."

"Sounds like a Nike commercial," Michael quipped.

"Don't laugh. It would be a great one. Now, let's *just do it*." She giggled.

Guiding her to the paved walking trail, they began their stroll. Michael pulled down his baseball cap and slipped on his shades to ensure he was as discreet as possible, especially as they passed a few other runners. One young woman was especially nosy, however, making sure to make eye contact with him from nearly 20 feet away and until she passed him completely.

Talk about forward. These southern women always pretended to be genteel, but since he had been here, he had found that they were some of the most forward and direct women on the planet.

At a comfortable pace, they made their way down the narrow path lined with magnolia trees, yellow honeysuckle flowers and green wooden benches. Birds chirped from the tree limbs above, and dogs barked in the distance. The entire park was peaceful and beautiful. And it felt as though they were there completely alone.

She clutched his hand tightly, like they were an old married couple, and relished in the blissful sounds of the afternoon. The plus for her was that more than ever, since she had been blinded, she really could *see* shadows in the daylight. There was a quiet calm flourishing in her because of that fact, making the day even more of a dream.

Michael shared her feelings, unbeknownst to him. "It really is a perfect day," he finally said before realizing that he was even speaking aloud.

"It is," Hope answered in a soft whisper. She turned towards him awash with pure gratitude. "Thank you for doing this." The only thing that would have made this more perfect for her

would have been if she were able to see him,
but she could feel him through his soothing
voice and his graceful touch.

Without her knowing, Hope was eliciting
some indescribable joy in him. It was amazing
that such a small gesture pleased her so. Such
humility.   In his history with women, they
normally wanted incredibly expensive gifts or
exotic trips to *seem* so pleased, yet all he had to
do for her was put on her shoes, which had
been perversely erotic for him, and take her for
a walk. No money involved. No trips. No name
dropping. No airs. Just time and those priceless
resources that people in his position often took
for granted. *Quality time. Precious words.
Simple and non-assuming acts.*

A chuckle escaped him. "I can't pretend that
my intentions were completely honorable.   I
just wanted to get you alone," he confessed. "I
wanted to know more about the girl behind the
door. Something about you has me besotted."

Hope found his word choice odd, but she
appreciated the compliment all the same. "I'm
glad your intentions were less than honorable
then."

"Really?" He wanted so at that moment for
her to expound upon her surprising statement.
True, she had been open to his advances, but he

wasn't sure that she was as enamored with him as he was with her...until now.

The walk began brisk but it was slowing with each enlightening lap, not because either was tiring out, but neither wanted it to end.

Finally getting the nerve, she turned her head toward him.

"Tell me about you, Michael. Where are you from? What do you do?" she asked like she was begging for the secrets to eternal life.

Shit. Michael wanted to avoid those questions though he knew it would be impossible. If he wanted to get closer to her, he would have to allow her to get closer to him. Only he didn't want to lie. Not to her.

Hope Daniels was special, more special than any of the other women before her. If anything, he needed to find a way to be more honest than he'd ever been. His brother's words echoed in his head again, taunting him. And for the first time, he felt like he could prove Richard wrong. He was not just a beautiful mess. And a woman could love him for more than being just a prince. But right now, he was putting the cart before the horse.

He scratched his stubbly beard. "I'm...not from around here."

Hope giggled, like she was letting him in on a little secret. "Oh, I know."

"You know?" he asked, brow raised.

"Your imitation of a southern accent sucks. Maybe not for someone who isn't from around here, but for us natives who were born with it, it's pretty awful to hear you pretend."

Michael deflated until she laughed.

"I was going to let you go with it until you felt comfortable enough to tell me the truth. Plus, I thought it was cute."

Michael laughed. She was full of surprises. *Smart. Beautiful. Witty.* "I thought I pulled off the southern charm quite well," he said, speaking in his English accent.

Wow! That felt good. He was no actor, but after six weeks of pretending to be something that he was not, he had a new found appreciation for their craft.

Hope picked up on the extreme deviation from his poorly crafted southern drawl and the natural flow of his normal tongue. "So where are you from really?"

"I'm from England," he answered coyly. "London."

"All hail the king." She didn't know that she had hit the nail directly on the head.

Michael froze. *Did she know his other secret as well?*

"So, where in London?" she continued, completely missing his quiet hysteria.

The tension immediately eased in his broad shoulders when he knew that his secret was still safe. But it did raise another interesting question, one that had to be quickly answered. *How did one explain a residence at Buckingham Palace?* "I'd like to think that I'm from the heart of it," he said with a smug grin. Every man had to have a few secrets, right?

She frowned now, trying to put the pieces together. His story still didn't make sense. "Why the accent though? Why not just be a guy from London?"

"Oh, that's a long story. Let's just say that I'm hiding out."

"From the police?" Now she was intrigued. Has she met a real international criminal?

"No, from my family, from my friends and my life," he answered truthfully. "I needed a break from it all. So, I came here."

Her voice hardened. Was it all lies? "Is your real name Michael?"

His voice softened. "Yes."

The domino effect created so many questions for her; she didn't know where to begin. "What do you do?"

A Richard question. "I'm finding myself." He slipped his free hand in his pocket. "But I am looking for a job." And a wife, he thought inwardly.

"Okay. What do you like to do then?" A reasonable second question.

"I like to read. I love art. I love traveling. I
love teaching. I've been all over. And the most
calm that I ever was would have to have been
when I was in Zimbabwe. I taught a small group
of young men there for a few weeks. It was
exhilarating. Their thirst for knowledge was
addictive. I stayed up every night with them
talking and teaching until my eyes were so
heavy, I could barely keep them open." Talking
about it brought back nostalgia.

Hope liked the way that traveling abroad
sounded. So, he was an adventurer. "I've
always wanted to travel, but I could never get
away from my work." Hope didn't say, but her
work included taking care of two elderly
grandparents. One died and then the other. It
took a lot out of her both emotionally and
physically.

That gave Michael the much-needed segue
into Hope's life. "What is that you do anyway?"
He already knew exactly what she did, but he
asked to protect his cover. No man wanted to
seem like a stalker, even if he was guilty of the
act. Plus, it was better that she talked about
herself instead of him.

She knew that he was trying to redirect. "I'll
tell you what I do when you tell me what would

drive a man across the world to a small town in North Mississippi and force him to change his accent."

He laughed. "You are something."

"I am listening," she corrected.

"Bullocks. You are listening. Okay, in truth, it was a woman." He made sure to explain that one. He didn't want her to think he was still wrapped up in that nasty business. "She broke my heart, and I...ran. It seemed like the most logical thing to do."

"What did she do to you?"

"It might sound silly to you, but I found out that she didn't love me, and I used that to justify me being stupid and behaving like a juvenile. But in my defense, I was mortified. I realized - while having a quiet evening over wine and dinner and music and all the things that couples do when they are in love - that the woman that I had told the entire world that I was going to marry, was with me for all the wrong reasons." He immediately regretted the whole world part of his purge but telling the truth was like turning on a faucet. His cup was running over.

Hope smacked her lips like she was the authority on the matter. In truth, she was if nothing but by experience alone. "Now *that* I can understand," she said with a wave of her finger. Her heart lurched, but this time because of the pain she felt inside. Her smile was a rouse for the anguish Sean had caused.

Michael was expecting her follow-up question to be something along the lines of what the world meant, but he was pleasantly surprised to find that she had all but ignored his slip. "Can you? How so?" Something in him eased as he watched her face. Nothing but pure acceptance of him. *That was a first.* He wasn't used to not being scrutinized. Every word was normally twisted and turned and analyzed like he was sitting on a therapist's couch. But not her. She simply listened and identified. It was such a surreal experience.

There was a varying reaction on Hope's face – a mix of salty sweet resolve. She fought tears as she said the painful words, causing a twitch of her full lips. Uncovering her emotions like a woman pulling off a veil in a cathedral, she confessed. "I thought that I was in love too." She nodded her head. "Okay, *in truth*, I was on the way to being in love. But the night that I came to the realization that it was all in my head was when I caught my successful little boyfriend cheating on me with a woman from his work. The bastard brought her to the same bed we had made love in a hundred times before. The same bed that he had told me that he loved me in a week before. When I caught him, it was a rainy night. That I do remember. He stood up in that dark bedroom and broke up with me literally while she got dressed in his bathroom. Pissed off and hurt and defeated, I jumped in my truck in a mild hysteria and drove off in a storm. Well, a man on a two-day run with little sleep crashed into me and wrecked out. Among other smaller injuries, I was blinded and left like this."

"All in one night?" Michael asked mortified.

"No man. All in one *hour*," Hope answered with a nod.

"Bullocks. That's pretty...," he looked for the best words, "fucked up."

Hope laughed, despite her dismal situation. It felt good to find some humor in what had been a complete tragedy. "Yes, it is," she said, holding her side.

Michael threw up his hands. "My dear, you've won," he said, nearly speechless. "My story is not nearly as catastrophic as yours. I think I need a Valium after hearing it."

"Thought I would win," she said, feeling him hold her hand tighter.

"Yes, you won." He laughed and at the same time hid his quiet disdain for the mysterious coward of a man who had hurt her.

Hope found a way to make the mood lighter. "Sooooo…you're not a killer." Mock disappointment covered her face.

"No," he said with a smug grin. "Sorry."

"Bummer. That is a real let down. I was hoping to be gutted by my next dream guy, since the last one blinded me."

He chuckled, but stopped abruptly. "Wait. I'm your dream guy?"

"I'm being facetious," she said, rolling her eyes. "I just met you. You can't be my dream guy". *That would be crazy*. She hated herself for letting that slip from her vault of ridiculous emotions. It was just a fairytale, something to fantasize about when no one was around.

Michael didn't think it was crazy at all. "Well, I'm being hopeful. Maybe I can change your mind eventually."

"Maybe you can," Hope answered. Only this time, there was no humor in her sweet voice, only the sound of promise.

The walk became even slower as the talk became more intimate. They were no longer just at the surface of getting to know each other, and they did so with impeccable ease.

Every once in a while, Michael would look back and see in the distance a few very conspicuous group of men walking behind him, but he was able to ignore them for the most part now. *If they knew what was good for them, they would back completely off now that he was finally making head way.*

Suddenly, Hope stopped. Raising her head toward the sky, she took a deep breath. "Rain is coming," she said, clenching her jaw tight. Fear laced her words.

Michael could hear the angst in her voice, only he didn't know how to soothe her. Something in him felt possessive at the moment.

A bolt of white lightning cracked across the dark gray horizon like a leather whip across the back of a tortured soul and a few seconds later thunder rumbled in the distance.

Hope gripped Michael's hand now, all softness gone. Her voice was urgent. "The last time that I was out in the rain, something horrible happened to me."

"Then let's get you out of the rain," he said as the bottom broke out of the sky. Rain fell down in heavy drops on top of them, drenching their bodies. Moving her under a large oak tree a few feet away, he fished out his keys from his pocket. "I'm sorry, Hope. Really, if I had only known of your tragedy's origins before I brought you here, I would have told you about the clouds." *The fucking clouds!* Grabbing her hand, he prepared to escort her back to the truck as quickly as possible. He had to tell her the truth.

"It looked like it was going to rain when we arrived." He felt horrible about his decision not to tell her. "But I wanted so badly to have some time alone with you…"

"Wait," Hope said, pulling him back toward her. She could feel his rapid heartbeat through his wide wrist.

"Yes," he said with a frown. "What is it?"

Hope ran her hand over his chest. "I don't want every time that it rains for me to think about Sean or that night or even my handicap." She pushed up closer to him. "I want a *better* memory."

Michael's heart began to pound in his chest. "What kind of memory do you want," he asked, lightly touching the small of her back. At that moment, he would have given her anything.

Pushing up on her tiptoes, she smiled innocently. Water splashed against her rosy cheeks and her heart shaped mouth, making her even more of a temptation. "Kiss me," she whispered. "Make me forget."

He could feel the words as they left her mouth and hissed against his ear like the promise of sweet ecstasy. While he had imagined what kissing her would be like, he would have not dared make the first move – only because of her situation. To take advantage of her would have been lower than low. But this was a request.

Closing his eyes as she spoke, he stilled his beating heart, reminding himself to do this right, make it perfect. *It's not about you*, he reminded himself quietly.

As his blue eyes flashed open, he slipped his large trembling hands around her petite face, resting his fingers around the nape of her neck and pulled her close. Her skin was on fire, begging for him to quench the thirst of need boiling inside of her.

Tilting his head, his mouth lingered just above hers for a moment before he dipped his head and tasted the sweet nectar of her soft lips. As soon as their mouths met, fireworks erupted inside of him.

Push off!!!

Immediately, Hope let out a sensual moan and snaked her long body around him. He tasted like she thought he would. Decadent. Warm. Lush. Wrapping her arms around his neck, she pushed her torso against him as closely as she could. Her rigid nipples grew hard against the fabric of her shirt and pushed into him. *However, it did not go without notice.* Tangling her nails in his curly hair, she twisted her tongue around his.

Michael fought his overwhelming desire to devour her whole and the growing, aching, painful agitation in his loins. After all, an unwelcomed hard on would ruin the moment. But in his defense, it had been so long since he had been intimate with a real woman and at this moment, he wanted nothing more than to tear her clothes off in the rain and make love to her under this tree.

Deeper and deeper they fell into the kiss, breathing hard, ignoring the raindrops and holding on to each other for dear life.

Wrapping his arms around her waist, he picked her up off the ground. As he did, he felt himself losing control. His eyes opened and looked directly into hers.

He stepped back. "Did you forget?" he asked, wiping the raindrops from her face. He knew the kiss had not lasted as long as she would have liked, but any longer and he would not have been able to be the gentleman that she needed.

A smile laced her curled lips. "Forget what?" she said with a wink.

Chapter 9

Even after an intentionally slow drive back from the park, the summer rain didn't let up much, except far out on the horizon where the sun tinged the sky pink in the distance. Listening to jazz on Sirius radio, they both basked in the moment.

However, their peaceful moment was quickly interrupted. As Michael and Hope pulled up into the driveway of her home, he noticed a BMW parked out front and a man standing on the porch, arguing with LouAnn.

"Were you expecting someone?" Michael asked, putting the truck in park a few feet back from the car.

Hope rose up in her leather seat, jolted from her previously relaxed state. "No." Her hands gripped the black vinyl dashboard. "Who is it? A man or a woman?" *She had an idea, but didn't want to say.*

Michael touched her hand, trying to relax her. "Do me a favor and stay in the car," he asked, stepping out in the rain before she could reply.

The black Yukon of MI6 men pulled over on the road right across from the driveway and lowered their windows to get a better look. But Michael quickly signaled them to stand down for the moment. He didn't want to complicate things if he didn't need to. For all he knew, this was someone that LouAnn knew.

In a heated discussion, Sean slapped his right hand into the palm of his left hand in frustration. "I've been calling for over two hours," he said, nostrils flared. "Two hours!"

His strained tone irritated the older woman. *What happened to respecting his elders?* "She went for a walk," LouAnn explained. "That's all." Eyeing Michael as he walked up the steps, she paused. "Here is the neighbor who took her now. See, you got all riled up for nothing. They're back and no ambulance or sheriff was needed."

"Who in the hell is this?" Sean asked, sizing Michael up. Despite his attempt to hide his true reaction, his eyes betrayed him. Evidently, Sean was not expecting such a well-put together man to be Hope's escort. When LouAnn referred *the neighbor*, he thought of some scraggly nobody pulling up in a broke down Honda, not some *wanna-be runway model* with good bone structure pulling up in a $60,000 shiny new truck.

"Is everything alright?" Michael asked LouAnn while at the same time completely ignoring Sean's presence – an intentional snub.

He made sure to use his Southern accent, just in case the man might recognize him. *One could never be too careful.*

"Yeah," LouAnn sighed, rolling her eyes. "This is my employer, Sean Pritchard."

Michael knew of only one Sean and figured this was him. *The asshole from the rain.*

"Who. Are. You?" Sean asked, jumping into the conversation.

Michael glared daggers at the man. Standing at least three inches shorter than Sean, he stepped up on the porch curling his lip.

This ex-boyfriend wasn't at all what Michael expected. Maybe it was just that he knew what a slime ball Sean had been to Hope that made him smaller, but whatever the case, he was extremely unimpressed.

"I'm Michael," he answered dismissively, body tense. He turned his attention back to LouAnn and lightened his voice. "Do you have an umbrella? I'd like for Hope not to get soaking wet while I escort her up here. She's had an exhausting afternoon."

Another jab just for Sean, this one even more of a gut check than the one before it.

"I'll run in and get you one," LouAnn said, shaking her head at Sean one last time. *What a disappointment.*

Now alone with his new adversary, Michael turned tersely and tilted his head. "Why are you here, anyway?" he asked with a frown. "Hope wasn't expecting you. I know, because she told me," he added just to cut Sean off at the knees.

After the conversation and the kiss with Hope, Michael felt like he was more than within his rights to probe the man for information. Plus, it sort of felt like he was on his territory now.

Sean's mouth nearly dropped open. *What the fuck?* He pointed at himself. "I'm paying for Hope's care. And as such, I have the right to be here whenever I feel that she needs me." He poked at his own chest like he was going to put a hole through it. "Now, I called for two hours, and I got no response. And I'm paying someone to be available, so I left work and came over here to see what the hell is going on."

Michael shrugged his shoulders. "LouAnn has done a good job here, and Hope is not a prisoner in her own home," he said, chest rising in anger. However, he kept his voice low because of the women. "Just because you are paying for Hope's care, doesn't mean that you are allowed to spy on her or keep tabs on her. Surely, that is in breach of some kind of law."

"Spy on her?" Sean growled. "Where the fuck do you get off waltzing up here and barking orders. Hell, you're just the neighbor."

"Am I?" Michael taunted. *He was a lot more than that.*

LouAnn stepped out quickly. Nearly shoving the umbrella into Michael's hands, she walked toward the edge of the porch and folded her arms across her. "Is she alright in there alone?" she asked, staring at Hope sitting impatiently in the truck.

"She's fine." Michael turned his attention from Sean for the moment. "I'll be right back," he said, headed back out in the rain to get Hope. As he did, the rain water continued to soak through his soft cotton shirt, giving greater form to his well-sculpted back that was tense with anger and cut to perfection with detailed muscle.

LouAnn couldn't resist the urge to look over at Sean and gauge his reaction to the attractive young man. Just as she thought-pure jealousy.

As soon as the door to the truck opened, Hope reached out for Michael. "What's going on?" she asked as he wrapped his arms around her petite waist and picked her up. His embrace was suddenly intimate and possessive – a thing that Hope immediately noticed, and he made sure to let Sean see the motion, and prayed that he'd choke on it.

Yes, my hands are all over her, you smug insect of a bastard, Michael thought to himself with a smirk.

Setting her down on the ground carefully, he covered her body from the rain with the umbrella. Moving her hair from her face, he broke the news. "Don't get too upset, but that Sean character is here. Would you like for him to leave?"

"What?" she huffed. How could she not get upset? "Yes, I want him to leave."

Michael was relieved. "I'll be happy to relay that message directly...just as soon as I get you inside."

She grabbed his hand tightly again. "Michael," she said under her breath.

"Yes, dear." He looked down at her.

"I don't want to be embarrassed by him anymore," she confessed. "Every time he comes around, it feels like it's just to demean me some more."

"What did you have in mind?" Michael asked, guiding her slowly through the rain.

There was a sharp bite of desperation in her voice. "Be my make-believe boyfriend, for at least long enough to run him off," she stumbled over her words. "I know it's juvenile, but..."

He cut her off. "It would be my pleasure," he said, eyeing Sean. "And it's not juvenile at all. The prick deserves a lot worse."

As soon as they arrived at the porch, Sean came to help, but Michael quickly stopped him. Raising his palm, he snapped, "I've got it."

"Hope, just who is this man to you?" Sean insisted, stepping back.

Hope drew back her shoulders with as must strength as she could muster. "He's my boyfriend," she said proudly. *Damn, that felt good*. Even though she couldn't see Sean's expression, she was sure that it was priceless.

"Your what?" Sean's eyes bucked.

Michael made sure she didn't have to repeat herself. After all, he was playing the new boyfriend. "You seem like a smart man." He helped Hope up the last step and into the arms of LouAnn. "Surely, you know what a relationship is. Or maybe it doesn't quite compute for you if the woman isn't the right *shade*."

Sean sucked in a begrudging breath as he processed the Hiroshima-like bombshell that had just been dropped on him. She had a boyfriend? What was this, The Twilight Zone?

"This wasn't part of the deal," Sean reminded Hope. "I'm paying a pretty handsome fee for LouAnn to be here, all because I felt bad about her being blind. And I'll give you that I should have been more honest about my own *preferences* but it shouldn't cost me to the tune of several thousand dollars as penance."

Michael understood right then what Hope had been afraid of. Every opportunity that Sean got, he was going to throw this favor in her face.

Sean continued. "However, I agreed to it, because I know your situation and the fact that you don't have any friends." He cut his eyes at Michael. "But I won't be paying LouAnn when she isn't needed while you're off gallivanting around Hernando with some Prince Michael look-alike and making a mockery of me."

Michael's eyes narrowed. *Was this guy serious?*

"You get that a lot, huh?" Sean said, looking him up and down like he had him all figured out. "Oh, I've got your number. Moving in on a helpless blind woman trying to pass yourself off as a royalty look-alike. Well, let me tell you something. On a scale of 1 to 10, you rank a low-rent six."

Giving away to the reality of the situation, Michael smirked but did not blink.

"Enough!" LouAnn exploded at Sean. "You're being a child, Sean."

Hope pulled away from LouAnn apologetically. "I'm sorry," she said under her breath before she turned toward the general direction of Sean. She could see enough shadows to know that she was looking at him. "I don't want your handouts anymore. LouAnn has been a great help, but the expense of having you around it's not worth it. Plus, you suddenly made me very glad that we broke up, regardless of who ended what. You can't hide crazy forever, and you just proved that you're a certifiable jackass and psycho."

"So glad to hear that you're not taking handouts, because I'm not offering," Sean snapped back. "LouAnn, I'll be happy to refer you to some people who actually need your care, but I refuse to spend one more dime on *this woman.* Consider this your last day." He waved a hand in the air and corrected himself. "Scratch that. Consider this to be your last hour."

Michael had heard enough. "Take her inside," he said, snapping his head toward LouAnn. "I'll be in directly." The authoritative tone of a true noble reared its head in his anger.

LouAnn didn't say another word. She was still in shock. Sean had always been a pleasant and respectable young man in her dealings with him before. But now, he was just being a jerk. Shaking her head at him, she opened the door and guided Hope inside.

As soon as Hope was out of sight, Michael turned back toward Sean.

"You can have her," Sean said, turning to walk off the porch. "Good luck footing the bill."

"One last thing before you go," Michael said, reaching back.

"What?" Sean said turning around.

As soon as he did, he saw Michael's fist coming straight toward his face. The impact was loud and jarring. Bone met bone and broke the perfectly linear nose that Sean had been so proud of before.

The next thing Sean knew he was on the ground below, wallowing in large muddy puddle.

Michael stomped down the rickety wooden steps and stood over Sean's body. An overwhelming disgust took over as he stared down at the pathetic excuse for a man. *Who did this bastard think he was?* He bent down over him, rain drenching his face and curling his blonde locks. Pulling Sean up by his Oxford until his knuckles went white, he growled. "Don't act so fucking surprised. You know that you've had that coming." He snatched his collar tighter to the point of ripping it. "You're a piece of shit. I know you know it. And they know it. Don't show up here again or the next time, I'm not going to behave like a gentleman. I'll tie you to the back of that shitty little BMW, drive you off into the woods and leave you for the fucking dogs."

Sean looked up into his adversary and knew that he had more than met his match, a feeling that evoked a sudden feeling of fear.

Michael knew that he had bested him, and that was all that he wanted... for now. "Now, get off her property and don't come back." Pushing Sean back down in the murky water, Michael turned on his heels and headed back up the stairs to the women who now stood in plain view of the altercation.

He wasn't expecting them to witness it, but what was done was done.

Benjamin watched from the Yukon completely entertained. Getting on the radio, he wiped the sides of his eyes wet from tears of laughter. "Get a complete background on the wanker who just landed arse first in the mud and put a tail on him until further notice," he said, releasing the button on the radio.

"Copy," a voice answered.

Taking the money from the men in the back seat, Benjamin reached for his pocket to put away his earnings. "I told you that he was going to knock his lights out. You could see it in how his shoulders got all tense."

Chapter 10

After Sean left, beaten and bloody, a triumphant golden sun came out and stayed affixed
in the sky with a rainbow arching across the
horizon brightening further the playful conversation between Michael, Hope and LouAnn that
had gone on for hours.

Passing cups of flavored coffee and finger
foods between them, they all enjoyed each
other's company without the airs of position. It
was a perfect culmination to a completely
chaotic afternoon. But for Hope, it was more. It
was the end of something that had drug on for
nearly two months – the lingering stench of a
foul relationship. She was quite happy to be on
her own, even if it did mean feeling around the
house and knocking things over even more. It
didn't matter to her if when she got her sight
back, everything in her house had been broken,
tipped over or ruined; it would still be better
than owing Sean Pritchard any favors.

Knowing that today was her last day;
LouAnn went to the kitchen and prepared her
famous chicken casserole as a going-away gift
while Hope and Michael sat across from her at
the kitchen table talking about everything from

blood sausage to contemporary artist Andreas Gursky. Everything was relative, everything exciting.

Feeling his emotion through his words and his warm, soft hands, Hope held on to his every story, and he held on to hers. They were, in a word – enraptured.

Michael found the conversation strangely enlightening. He had never sat at a kitchen table with women like these discussing such simplistic but wonderful things. To his surprise, LouAnn had quite the personality and was a wealth of knowledge on all things maternal. She reminded him of a living, breathing dummies guide to being a good mother. However, nothing could top the conversation with Hope. While witty and clever, she was also serious and insightful with a big-picture look on life that he didn't normally encounter except with Oxford scholars and heads of state.

For LouAnn, any fear that she had about leaving Hope on her own, quickly dissipated. She learned through her conversations that the young woman was quite strong and capable of taking care of herself, and on top of that, Michael seemed very eager to help in any areas that she might need assistance. She giggled under her breath at their growing love connection.

Serves you right, she said to herself while thinking of Sean, *you didn't deserve her anyway.* When she had first been approached by Sean, the story of his relationship with Hope had already been blown out of proportion.

Sean had painted Hope as a weak and chaotic woman who had ended up in the car accident as a result of a very dramatic and volatile exit from his home of her own making. He forgot to mention that a woman had been there naked or that he had broken up with her only after Hope found them together right after sex. He had forgotten to mention that he had been the one to approach Hope with the idea of him helping and not that she had asked him for help, as he was telling everyone. He had also failed to mention that somewhere in between being a great kid and a dependable young man he had grown up to be such an ass.

But as these things do, the truth had found a way to come to the light.

At dusk after a delicious home-cooked dinner, as the sun receded back into the shadows of night, LouAnn said her goodbyes, gave hugs and kisses to them both and departed for the last time.

Michael stood with Hope in the doorway while LouAnn pulled out of the drive, and then closed the large door to be left alone, finally.

Hope could feel his strong hands on her shoulders as he guided her back inside. There was a loving touch to his guidance, a sort of caress through his fingertips. She only prayed that he couldn't feel the reaction that he was having to her. After so many hours with him, all the tension of unfamiliarity had vanished, but the sexual tension between them had grown exponentially.

Michael could feel the dramatic change in the atmosphere. The house took on a different feel at night. The tiffany lamps and translucent lights made the house glow with warmness and the smell of freshly cooked foods and sweet candles made him want to cuddle with her.

Grabbing her hand, he led her back to the sitting room and placed her in a comfortable armchair across from the sofa.

"Well, this has been quite a day," he said resting beside her. His body ached a little, but he couldn't take his eyes off of her. She seemed even more beautiful now than when he first met her – now that he knew so much about her, that he had begun to understand her.

"Tell me about it," she said with a smirk. Nervously, she fiddled with her fingers.

Michael felt nervous again. They were finally alone and he was lost for words. "Is there anything that I can do for you? Now that you have to try to do this all alone..." He stumbled over his words and crashed into another confession. "I feel responsible for it, I have to admit. At the time, it felt right to knock that prick off the steps, but now I feel as though I've put you in a more difficult predicament."

She smiled. "I'm glad that you did." Licking her lips, she raised a brow. "Did he look shocked when you decked him?"

Michael laughed. "Very much."

"I'm so glad. I wish that I could have done it myself."

"I'd be happy to assist you until you get your sight back. I was looking for something to do – something worthy." He cringed. This was not coming out right. What if it sounded like a complete come-on instead of a true offering? "What I'm saying is that I could come by and sit with you, like LouAnn did...at no cost, of course." God, he was bombing this entire proposal. If he didn't get it together, she might just see him right out of the house.

Hope cut him off. "I'd like that...all of it. It is very kind of you to offer, but I wouldn't want to put you out. This isn't your problem."

He quickly responded. "It would be no imposition at all. It would be an honor." His chest swelled with excitement. "I'm not a good cook, but I can manage. And I'm not very good with most household duties, but I could surely tend to whatever you needed." He laughed nervously. "I want to, Hope." His voice was eager.

Unable to turn him down, she sat back in the chair. "What would be great is if you could run me a bath." The request felt odd but it was needed. She quickly clarified. "I don't need you to bathe me or anything..."

"I'll be happy to," he said, jumping up. He rolled his eyes. Another flub. "What I mean is that I'd be happy to run your bath." He didn't say it aloud, but he'd be even happier to do the other as well, but he was sure that such a statement wouldn't go over well.

"Okay. We can start there," she said, unable to hide her blush. "But you must allow me to pay you something. I'm not broke. I have plenty of savings..."

"Neither am I," he said, walking over to her. Taking her hand, he knelt before her again. Sure that she could feel the sweat forming in his palm, he kissed her hand gently. "I've never wanted to help a woman more than I've wanted to help you. I think it's because you are so willing to help yourself, and because after all of our conversation today, I understand. And..." He paused and slowed his words. "I want to do this."

She leaned toward him and slowly raised her fingers to feel his cheek. "I wish that I could see your face," she said, fighting tears. "You seem so kind." Shaking her head, she stilled her rapidly beating heart. "I'd be happy to have your help as long as you'll be happy to accept some form of payment for your services."

"A small fee then," he said, determined to find a way without her knowing to return it back to her. "Good, then we're in agreement." He stood up. "Well, I'll just go and run a bath for you. Upstairs or downstairs?"

"Downstairs," she said, standing up as well.

"Where are you going?" he asked, ready to start his job.

"I'm going to get my personal things." She giggled again. "You know where the bathroom is, right?"

That he did know. He nodded. "I've been a few times today. Yes," he said, moving out of her way. "Should I take you to your room?"

"No. I better learn this on my own," she said, walking right into the coffee table and knocking down a picture of her grandmother. "Shit!" She bent over but Michael was right there to help her. Picking up the frame, he sighed in relief.

"Did I break it?" she asked hesitantly.

"No, it's perfect." Putting the frame back on the table, he rubbed her back as he helped her stand. "This will take some getting used to, but you'll do fine. I believe in you." Just then, his phone went off. Pulling it from his pocket, he saw that it was his brother, Richard. He quickly hit ignore.

"Do you need to take that?" she asked.

"No, it's just my brother. I can call him back. I'm sure he doesn't want anything." *Except to get on my nerves*, he thought to himself.

"You have a brother?" she asked intrigued. They never really got around to talking about siblings. After all, it had only been a day. There was so much discussed, but so much still left to talk about. She was overwhelmed with questions for him, but decided against a true Spanish Inquisition, at least until tomorrow.

"Yes," he guided her to the room. "I have an older brother."

"What is his name?"

"Dick," Michael said with a smug grin.

"Is he like you?" she asked.

"No. He is very much like his name. Come now. Let me help you to your room."

While Hope grabbed the hygiene basket that Bree had made for her and used the simple drawer system that she and her friend had devised to find her underwear and night clothes, Michael went into the bathroom and prepared her bath in the refurbished pearl claw tub.

Lighting candles, he placed them up on the mantle away from any possible fire hazard; he also opened up the many bottles of salts and soaps to make a perfect relaxing mix of tranquil scents to relax her. When he was done, he set out a large towel and hand towel where she could easily access them and then placed a brand new bar of soap in the gold rack.

"Voila," he said proudly. He had never done that before, but it had turned out pretty nicely.

"Are you done?" she asked, standing at the door with a handful of her things.

He turned to her. "I am," he said, proud of himself. "It's all yours." *So am I*, he thought inwardly.

She walked into the bathroom and found her way over to the tub. Dipping her finger in, she smiled. "It's perfect. Nice and warm. I couldn't have done better myself."

"Wonderful. Well, I'll leave you to soak. If you need anything, I'll be…around."

"Am I holding you up?" she asked, feeling as though she had used up his entire day. She didn't want him to leave, but she also didn't want to hold him up from the rest of his life.

"No." He felt his phone buzz again but he ignored it. "I don't mind one bit. You relax here, and I'll go and grab a glass of that wine that I saw in the kitchen...if you don't mind. When you are dressed, we can talk a little more before I take my leave."

"Please, help yourself," she said, sitting in the chair Bree had placed in the bathroom for her to get undressed. "When I come out, I think I'd like one as well."

"I'll have it ready." Michael closed the door behind him and took a deep breath. She was about to be naked in the tub that he had pre-pared for her and like a teenager, it made him giddy. He rather needed that glass of wine to take the edge off.

Moving toward the kitchen, a little more re-laxed, he stopped curiously in the living room and opened up her tall wooden stereo cabinet. It was full of music from nearly every genre that he could think of – all in alphabetical order - making it nearly impossible to just pick out one thing. She had all the classics: Prince, Michael Jackson, The Isley Brothers, and Al Green. She had B.B. King and Stevie Ray Vaughn. She had Rage Against the Machine and U2. She even had New Edition. It had to be over 500 CDs, hun-dreds of bands. So many options. So very much like her other eclectic tastes for life.

Picking out a CD by John Coltrane, he slipped it in the player, turned up the music and meandered into the kitchen where he pulled down the small rack of wines from on top of the stainless steel refrigerator beside a bowl of breads. It was then that he noticed all the pictures attached to magnets. There were several pictures of her grandparents and several of a woman who had to have been her mother. Hope had mentioned that they were all dead now, but she didn't really explain how. It must still be too painful to talk about. But he also couldn't help but marvel at the pictures of her as a baby, a toddler, a teen and as an adult. In each, she looked just as beautiful, strong and majestic.

Picking out the perfect bottle of red wine, he surveyed the rest of the tranquil room. He loved the aloe Vera plants, ivy vines and multi-colored teapot roses that she had lined the top of the vintage cabinets in colorful porcelain pots. It showed how much time she spent nurturing her surroundings down to the very last detail. There were nearly 50 cookbooks stacked up in decorative little piles around the large kitchen with neon post-it notes peeking out of the pages, indicating that they were not just for show. Playful little mats with red roosters covered the gray ash ceramic tile floors and rows of spice racks lined the back of the yellow countertop. Cumin. Mustard. Peppers and celery. Salts and sugars. Cinnamon and Ginger. Evidently, she loved to cook, loved music, loved to read. Loved the simple but most enjoyable parts of life. Just being in this room caused a stir of genuine motivation to create something.

Going through her well organized cabinets, he finally ran upon the glasses and pulled out two crystal wine goblets. Then he dug through her many drawers of well-organized utensils to find a corkscrew. It was funny. Although she didn't have a maid or a butler, she took special care with each and every part of her home like she had a team of servants – a very commendable accomplishment he thought.

After pouring both of them a glass of wine, he placed hers on the table and made his way out into the rest of the house. He felt like a child exploring. Each room told a story of warmth and peacefulness that he knew wasn't staged. Many of the women in his past had pretended to be something that they were not by simply paying someone to come in and create an illusion of uniqueness. However, she had actually created a safe haven from the world that he was easily drawn into and honestly found it hard to leave.

He didn't want to go back to the coldness of his little house with stuffy Geoff. He wanted to stay here, but that would surely have been an imposition on them both. For no other reason that he was finding it harder and harder not to keep his hands off of Hope.

As he came to a room he had not yet seen, he noticed the French doors were painted with brilliant colors on the windows, making it impossible to peak in. Opening it quietly, he turned and found the light switch on the wall and found himself in awe. Her working room was a place of pure beauty and the large canvases of beautiful Nubian faces pulled him into their beauty.

He stood sipping his wine and staring, gawking, soaking in the powerful images in front of him, and at that moment, he realized that Hope was in the truest sense a remarkable artist.

***

The hot water cascaded over her skin and soaked into her aching bones. Letting out an exhale, she pushed her body deeper down into the tub and shivered at its hold on her. She needed this. Running the sponge over her arm, she soaked in total ecstasy.

"Thank you, Michael," she whispered, listening to the music coming from the hall. Coltrane was a good choice, perfect for the night that they were having.

She was betting a lot on this stranger. For all she knew, he could have been a murderer or a rapist, but something about him told her that she could trust him. It was risky, and something that she normally would have never considered. However, in the last six weeks, she had learned to trust some people a little more and not trust others at all.

Sean crept into her thoughts and at the same time her muscles tensed. That rat bastard! The moment she had let her guard down, he had found an opportunity to betray her once more. It was because of him that she was allowing Michael into her life – literally, but what choice did she have? If she went at this alone, it could honestly be more painful than it had to be. But she also could wake up tomorrow to an empty house, robbed by another snake in the grass.

The thought made her laugh.

Damned if I do, she thought to herself. This was one time that she was just going to have to gamble on her gut and trust that it would not lead her in the wrong direction again. Besides, her grandma had accused her of being a good judge of character most of the time.

Only life had never been quite so complicated for her, and she had faced some pretty serious situations. However, not having her sight was teaching her a lot about herself. For one thing, she realized that she needed to listen to people more. Tone went a long way when there was little else to build upon. It was also making her appreciate God's true gifts. When she got her sight back again, she promised that she'd never complain again about having painter's block. Just being able to see shapes and colors and people again would be motivation enough.

She prayed quietly. Lord in heaven knew how badly she wanted her sight back. Maybe she had been blind to Sean, blind to her decisions to trust him, blind to the way that he had treated her, but if He would just give her back her sight again, she promised to pay more attention to the person behind the face. She promised to be a better person. Just PLEASE. All she wanted was her sight back.

The prayer brought tears to her eyes.

"You can heal anyone at any time. Heal me," she pleaded. "Please, Father. I beg you." Her words were barely above a whisper, but powerful enough to make her cry. Even as she pleaded, her body trembled with emotion. "Father, I need you," she called out to God. "Help me. Please. Give me my sight back."

She sat in the tub for a while alone in her thoughts, in the silence of the room, in the darkness of her despair, before she finally decided to break away and pull herself from her pain. There was no room in her life for self-pity. She had enough to deal with.

After washing up thoroughly, she pulled the plug out of her tub and stood up. The steam moved off her body in waves. Naked and still trembling, she reached out for the big towel Michael had left her and dried off her upper body. Slowly negotiating her way out of the tub, she reached for the sink to stabilize herself but missed it by a few inches.

Before she could get her bearings and plant her feet solidly, she felt herself falling. Fear ripped through her. Grabbing for the shower curtain frantically, she tumbled, hitting her head on the hard, cold floor and bringing the world down around her.

Michael heard the clang from the other side of the house. Turning, he bolted in a sprint toward the bathroom, sloshing wine out onto the floor. "Hope!" he screamed out, twisting the knob. Setting down the empty glass beside the door, he tried again.

The door was locked, but he could hear her moan in pain behind it.

Stepping back without thought, he quickly kicked the door in and found her twisted in the white linen curtain on the floor, blood mingling in the water around her from a busted head.

Swooping her up quickly in his arms, he grabbed the towel and nearly slipped himself in the mess.

Dazed, Hope mumbled something before her head flitted back. Dangling in his arms, her long hair spilled over and her naked body curled into his embrace.

She could feel herself being carried swiftly to her bedroom and then Michael laid her on the bed and covered her body. Pulling off his shirt, he used it to cover the wound just above her eye to stop the bleeding.

"Hope," he called to her.

Reaching for him, she touched his bare muscular chest and then fell back into the pillows.

"Darling," she heard him say. "Stay with me."

"I'll be okay," she finally said, getting her bearings as best as she could. She lied despite the agonizing pain.

"Where is your medic kit?" he asked, running back to her bathroom.

"Under the cabinet," she mumbled.

He came back with a towel of ice, bandages and ointment. Sliding up beside her on the bed, he put her head in his lap and tended to her gash. She winced in pain, but tried not to complain. Blinking as the blood ran in her eyes, she suddenly saw more than shadows.

First fuzzy, now the room had color.

"Michael," she stuttered in disbelief. Words wouldn't form fast enough.

"I'm right here," he assured her.

She blinked again. This time the color had more shape. "Michael," she said again.

"It will be alright. I promise," he answered her in a soft, soothing tone.

She grabbed his arm as he gently wiped her face and then stared up at him. His beautiful face slowly and more precisely came into view, though not as clear as a picture. Swallowing hard as tears erupted, she made herself speak.

"Michael," she said again.

"Yes, what is it, dear? Do you need to go to the hospital?" he asked, face warped in fear.

Her breath nearly left her. "I can...see you," she said, gazing into his bright blue eyes.

He looked down at her and frowned. Moving her long locks of wet, bloody hair out of her face, he shook his head. "What?"

She smiled. "I can see you."

Chapter 11

Michael couldn't breathe despite his best efforts. As his eyes blazed down into Hope's angelic face, his heart literally stopped. *So beautiful.* The intoxicating fragrance of bath soaps and perfume mixed with the glistening of her soft brown skin was pure unadulterated torture. To be so close in proximity to her - this magnificent woman who was now a part of his deepest fantasies – but not being able to really have her had him paralyzed.

He had never had a muse before, but he knew that she was without a doubt that to him. It was the way she blinked with her wing-like black lashes, the way the sweet sweat rolled down her swan-like neck and pooled at her throat, the way the heat emanated from her curvy body and soaked into his own skin that pushed him to the near brink of giving in to his domineering hunger for her.

His body whispered, *I want you.*

Forcing himself to exhale, he swallowed down the fear of what she must be thinking as she looked up at him. The innocence in her eyes confounded him. *How much of me can she see*, he thought to himself? *How much has she already put together?*   There were so many questions in such a short space of time until he almost did not process the fact that she was lying here with him naked. That was, until she abruptly moved.

"Ouch," she muttered suddenly.

The pain of her busted head caused an involuntary spasm followed by her arm rising to touch the bandage he had placed on her wound. As soon as she did so, her towel slipped below her bust line, exposing her beautiful ripe brown nipples.

Damn. That was over kill.   His mouth watered incessantly.

Although he quickly looked away, his arousal was immediately apparent. His primitive reaction was almost painful, it happened so fast. Growing without his approval or control, he tried to adjust her off his erection, but it only made it worse and more obvious.

"Apologies," he said, hating himself for his mishap.

Hope smiled. "Is that for me?" she asked, voice teasing.

His baritone was low and husky. "You shouldn't make fun." Placing a careful hand on her back, he raised her up. "It's been a while for me. I'm afraid your breasts are quite a break from the normal excitement of Hernando,

Mississippi." His facetious tone did nothing for the sexual tension in the room, though he tried hard to mask it.

Breasts? Hope hadn't realized until that moment that she was even exposed. Looking down, she pulled the towel up as fast as she could. "Holy shit! Sorry." Her nervous laugh told on her.

"Not so funny when it's you is it?" he asked with a devilish smile. Refreshingly, he felt better when he saw her cheeks burn with embarrassment. Plus, it was also a thrill to know that those perfect little Hershey-kiss nipples happened to have been erect as his own discomfort. She wasn't as innocent as she appeared.

"Stop laughing at me," she said, hitting his arm as she held tight to the towel with the other hand.

He caught her hand playfully and paused, looking at her long beautiful fingers. "How much can you see anyway?" he asked.

Taking her hand away slowly, she sighed and blinked hard. "You're fuzzy," she said, looking around the room. She lied about the clarity only because she could see his erection just fine, and it was much larger than it felt on her back. Gazing up toward the ceiling, she held back a smile, "Everything has a glaze on it. But it's the most I've seen in so long, so I'm very grateful." Her words carried dual meaning. Truthfully, she was quite glad to have her sight come back and have something so sexy to behold.

Michael quickly put one of her decorative pillows over his lap and diverted the conversation to a safer place. "Do we need to get you to a hospital for your injury? You might need stitches." He tried to guide his mind back to the thing that was most important for now.

"No, but I should get dressed," she said unable to take her eyes off of him. "Your bandaging should be enough. The last thing I want to do is see the inside of a hospital." She gawked at him again.

"What?" he asked. Her stare made him nervous. *Did she find him unattractive now that she could see him?*

She reached out again and touched his face. "From what I can see, you're beautiful, Michael," she answered sincerely. "What a difference a day makes." Her eyes sparkled with approval.

Michael could barely look at her. "Don't do that," he warned as he ducked his head.

"Do what?" she asked, knowing the type of reaction she was having on him, because she could feel the force inside of her. Still, she pushed him to admit it.

"Provoke me," he said, eyes rising to lock on hers. He did not blink. "It's so hard to be here with you right now like this." And in just a minute, the pillow would not be enough to disguise it.

"Why?" she whispered. "What's so hard about being around me?"

Michael could almost feel the pheromones in the room. "Because of the effect that you have on me. I've only known you two days," he said with a chuckle. Wiping his chin, he sighed. "This is crazy." However, so was every other part of his life.

"I know," she said, pulling at her towel. "What is even crazier is that I'm still talking to you naked even after flashing you." Standing up, she tried to smirk as she cleared her throat. "I should change into something more presentable."

That was his cue to leave the room.

But Michael didn't move. Of course, he knew that he was supposed to do so, but stubbornly he sat on the end of her bed, legs apart and shirtless. Even as he slumped, his tanned muscles bulged with definition.

"Should you...get dressed?" he asked, as a fair brow shot up at her.

Hope stuttered. *The elephant was officially in the room.* "I...don't know." She had to look away from him. He was too beautiful even as a mosaic to continue to gawk at any longer. "Michael, I'm not one of those types of women."

"What type?" he asked, even though he damn well knew.

"The one-night-stand type." Even as she said it, she tried to convince herself that she could just say no. But it was so hard. Everything she was feeling now, she had never felt for a man before. And she knew that because of that, she wasn't sure what she was capable of doing with or for him.

Michael clarified. "I would never assume that you are *that type of woman*," he said with the truest of conviction. "Now, have I been that type of man before?" He shrugged his wide shoulders. "Unfortunately the answer is yes. And I can't lie; it wasn't two months ago that I made some horrible choices." Normally, he would have never told a woman that but with Hope he felt the need to be completely transparent.

Hope licked her lips. *That was more information than she wanted to know.*

"But in the short time that I've gotten to know you, I am absolutely certain that you are nothing less than a lady. And what we decide to do, *if anything*, will be regarded with the utmost respect."

She blushed despite her desperate desire to remain serious. "You and your words."

Michael took a deep breath, putting his fear behind him, and stood up. As soon as he did, a zinger shot through Hope. She didn't realize how tall he was. He towered over her by nearly a foot.

Reaching out, he offered his hand. At the same time that she took it, he pulled her close and ran his nose and lips down the side of her neck.

The sensuality of it sent chills up her spine and caused an unmistakable wetness between her aching thighs.

"If you tell me we shouldn't, we won't," he whispered. Aching to have her, he kissed a trail down her neck, cooling her hot skin. His eyes flashed at her, full of promise. "But if you tell me you want to, we will."

Hope felt suddenly overwhelmed. "That's not fair." Her voice barely carried above a whisper.

"Life isn't," he said, moving her hair out of her face. His mouth curved into a smile. "All I keep thinking about is why I couldn't have met you first."

She turned into his words. Looking up at him, she licked her lips. "I want to," she said, kissing his bottom lip. "But I'm so afraid."

"For once, so am I." He put her hand on his chest to allow her to feel his racing heart. "But we'll do it together...all night until we get it just right."

There was something about his words that soothed and excited her at the same time.

An exasperated moan escaped her. "Michael," she said with confirmation, wrapping her arms around his neck. "I don't want this to just be a thing."

"Hope," he responded, eyes flickering with understanding. "It's not."

"But I barely know you," she tried to reason.

"People spend their whole lives together, barely knowing one another for what's on the surface. But I don't want that. I've had that. I want you." He smiled at her. "I want you so much; I'm willing to ruin everything by telling you who I really am."

She loved his accent. Smiling back at him, she shook her head. "Who are you...really?"

Michael raised a brow. It was very rare that he had to explain who he was, for most people, it was just obvious. "I'm Prince Michael. Duke of Cambridge, Earl of Strathearn, and Baron Carrickfergus," he sighed like the titles were heavy and troublesome. "And so on, and so on, and so on. I was born a prince; I may very well die a king, but I am at all times at your disposal, madam."

There was a long pause as he waited for Hope's response, to which was a hearty laugh. "You always know how to make me laugh," she said, thinking he was joking.

"I'm glad that my life is amusing to you," he said nonchalantly. "I'll be here all night. Don't forget to tip your waitress."

"Oh, I'll tip you alright." Planting a kiss on his lips, she shut him up. "I hope that you don't plan on making me laugh all night."

He ran a finger down her side. "I had some other things in mind."

Her long, muscular back arched toward him as he pulled down the towel and allowed it to pool around her feet. Heart racing, she prayed that he was happy with the way that she looked completely naked. God knows that she had put on a few extra pounds since she had been blinded.

But Michael was more than satisfied. For a moment, he was stunned.

Melting into him, she allowed all of her inhibitions to give away to the want exploding out of her. *This felt right, it felt good, it felt so damn exciting.* And for once, she would not deny it or him or herself.

Her rigid nipples pushed into his rock-like chest, prodding him to take her, to recognize the desire blooming. Emotions knotted in her stomach as his fingers trailed her soft skin, wanting so badly to explore every inch of her exotic temple. He could feel her heart beat against his own – an indication of her vulnerability. He could smell her glorious scent wafting up to his nose. Inhaling it gladly, he clenched his square jaw – reminding himself to be gentle, to take his time with her, not to lose control.

"God, you're beautiful," he confessed with a cool gleam in his lusty eyes.

Dipping his head down into her atmosphere, he kissed her beautiful, full mouth slowly. It was just as sweet as the first time. Only this time, she was naked, closer and most importantly attainable. She tasted like cool mint and sweet honey, and he couldn't get enough of her nectar, no matter how he tried. The deeper the kiss became, the more the room began to spin. The laws of gravity began to give way and they began to float in each other's arms.

The blood in Michael's veins began to boil. Every time, that she flicked her nimble tongue up against his, he grew harder. Every time that he inhaled her, he became hungrier.

Picking her up off the floor, he lifted her up into his embrace. Like a muscle memory, she locked her long legs around him.

Carrying her to the bed as quickly as he could, he laid her back on the bed of colorful pillows as he trailed kisses down her neck to her shoulders. Undulating beneath him, she ran her hands down the length of his back to his jeans. Pulling and yanking at them, she managed to get one down over his left buttocks out before he reached his hand between them and undid the clasp of his belt, then his pants.

Rushing to get closer to her, he pulled them down completely.

Naked between her thighs now, aching to be inside of her, he paused and moved down her shoulders to her breasts. He grabbed her orb gently, wrapping his fingers around it, and then lapped a heavy tongue atop her nipple over and over again until she cried out all while keeping the other hand firmly pushed against her clitoris.

The milk of her aching sex began to flow freely between her thighs dripping into his hand. He stroked and petted her gently before he finally slipped a curious digit inside of her. The tightness of her made his mouth open with pleasure. It wouldn't be long before he was there instead of his damned fingers. Making her watch, he pulled the finger from inside of her and slipped it into his mouth. "You taste like I thought you would," he whispered. "Delicious."

Taunting her with the eroticism of the act, he allowed his shaft to run between the lips of her vagina and over her clit. The pressure began to build as she felt the thickness of him against her. Eyeing her as he moved slowly on top of her, he smiled.

"I want more," she begged, lifting her head to bite his bottom lip.

Ecstasy nearly overwhelmed her and a familiar quake rushed over her body. Before she could cry out, he covered her mouth with another kiss.

"Love, stay with me," he ordered her. "Don't come just yet."

"Then don't make me," she whispered.

He couldn't help but laugh.

As she opened her thighs further to rest the head of his steely manhood at her apex, he could feel her heat drawing him in. She let her hands wander up the thick column of his neck and pulled him down to kiss her again.

His mind shot from her womb to his jeans. Pulling away from her for just a second, he reached into the back pocket of his pants and grabbed his wallet.

"Condom," he said, pulling out a Gold Magnum Trojan.

Quickly, she nodded in approval and reached over toward the nightstand. "I have plenty."

"I love a woman who always comes prepared," he said, tearing the sheath of the package with his teeth. When he was satisfied with his placement, he grabbed both of her legs by the back of her knees and pulled her toward him. The smile on her face quickly disappeared into the seriousness of the moment.

Bending down to steal one more kiss, he tasted her slowly. With a deep kiss full of fervor and demand, his hands found hers and pressed them into the mattress. At the same time, the tip of his manhood pressed into her flower.

She wanted to scream as his muscles tensed, but she didn't want to miss a moment. Instead, she watched what she could see of him, his blurred image move toward her – inside of her.

She gasped as the muscles of her flower clenched tight around his erection. Wet with anticipated pleasure, she guided him in by arching her back and legs as he held her down to the bed. His eyes closed in rapture. Biting his own lip, he fought the temptation to empty himself inside of her.

She moved against him wantonly, enjoying the smell of his cologne as his skin melted into her own. His kisses trailed down her face, neck, mouth and ears. Finally letting her hands go; he wrapped his arms around her and held her tight – not wanting to ever let her go.

Their bodies both trembled under the weight of their action. Intense physical pleasure mixed with equally intense emotional bonding wrapped them together in an embrace that ignited all of their fantasies.

Even as she shuddered under him, she could feel her body responding to each and every stroke. The sound of sex filled the room with a melody of sweet love. Dancing synchronically together, they rolled around in the bed, kissing, rubbing, touching and moaning, taking care to memorize each and every single curve, fold, and dip of each other's bodies.

The force of his thrusts drove out all reasoning for Hope. She held on to him as he drove into her mercilessly. With ever gentle touch he provided, he also gave an equally powerful thrust. But she gave as good as she took.

When she found herself on top of him, looking down into his glazed image, she placed her hands atop his mountain of muscles. Moving her hips wildly, she took him inside of her and raised her body nearly off of his tip before she plummeted back down. Grabbing her by her soft hips, he pulled her into him, made her take every inch that he had to give.

"Yes," she moaned, feeling her vision blur.

"That's it," he said, lifting her up and pulling her back down into the gravity of sex. "That's it, love. Take me." He growled again; sweat pouring down his chest and face. "Take all of me."

Rolling her over, he grabbed one of her shapely thighs and raised it over his arm. Pulling her by her hips into him, he moaned as he felt the walls of her sex start to spasm.

Her hands found his back in their passion and sharp nails dug into his sweaty skin. The pain released endorphins and that made him moan aloud.

"Oh God," she said, feeling her climax approach.

He moved her mass of hair from her face and kissed her lips, moving faster and harder.

"Oh…" she moaned again, mouth open.

"Come for me," he demanded.

"Michael," she panted.

The rush was unlike any that she had ever experienced before. As he splashed into the pool of her sex, thick and heavy inside of her, a powerful orgasm erupted. Nearly paralyzed with pleasure, she wrapped around him as a tide of pleasure washed over her.

It was too much for Michael despite his every effort to control himself. Knowing that she had reached her peak, he lifted up and pressed his body as far as he could inside of her. Releasing, he roared like a wild beast – the vibration bouncing against both of their diaphragms – as he flooded into her body only protected by the sheer condom between them.

As Hope finally let go, she felt her body completely explode, her vision went from blurred to crystal clear. Looking up at him, sweating and weak, she pulled his face to hers to kiss him. When she did, she finally saw his face for the first time.

"Oh my god," she said, blinking hard.

"What's wrong?" he asked, startled and out of breath.

Hope was nearly lost for words. "It really is you."

Chapter 12

It had been four full days since Hope and Michael had emerged from her house for any reason at all. Basking in what seemed to be the most pleasant weather of the season, they opened all the windows in the two-story home to enjoy the bright blue, cloudless skies and fresh breezes during the day and star-filled, full-mooned view of the night.

They tore through the media cabinet and played every jazz CD that they could find and lit all the scented candles they could burn.

There in their self-imposed solitary confinement, they spoke of every love lost and every dream imagined. They spoke of childhood losses of both her parents and grandparents and his father. They spoke of crushes and heartbreak, of best friends and worst enemies all while catering to each other's bodies with sweet kisses and passionate embraces.

It had been the best four days of their lives, and they relished in the privacy of it.

While cooking his best eggs benedict and humming to Nora Jones, Michael watched Hope in her St. Louis Cardinal's T-shirt and red lace panties while she combed through the refrigerator for jams and honey to go on top of their bagels.

He fancied her nearly-naked look more than any other. While effortless, her mismatched attire always seemed to evoke the lion lurking inside of him. Her long sculpted legs were a pure work of art with all the soft curves and hard muscles from years of running. She had defined calves and strong hamstrings, a heart-shaped backside that made him want to reach out and grab her and a curvy waist that had an adorable little pooch. She had the longest back he had ever ran his fingers down and peaks and valleys of tender muscle that made her shoulders strong yet feminine.

He enjoyed the way that her body felt in his hands when he held her and the way that it felt when she pushed it up against him. He loved the smell of her hair and the way she looked with no makeup.

The conclusion was hard to admit, but in less than a week, he honestly felt like he was falling in love with her.

It was such a strange feeling; he dare not say it aloud. What did he know about love anyway? What if this was simply the euphoria of not being alone? Plus, regardless of his feelings, what if she didn't feel the same? Then it would be just another Thalia situation and he couldn't

bear one more confession of admiration without love. No, he'd keep his secret close to his
chest for now as to not ruin the best few days of
his adulthood. And if something came from it,
then...

"Michael," Hope said, invading his deep
thought.

He turned to her in only his black boxer-
briefs and smiled. "Yes, love."

A flush rose up her neck. She loved when he
called her that. "Are you allergic to anything?"
she asked, lining up containers of jam on the
counter.

"Peaches," he said, placing one of the eggs on
the plate that she had set out for him.

Picking up one of the jars, she walked back
to the refrigerator and placed it inside. "Well,
that narrows it down a little."

He licked his lips. "Some peaches," he said,
looking in between her thighs.

Hope blushed, cheeks visibly turning red.
"You're insatiable." Walking over to him, she
slipped her arms around his back and locked
them around his chest. Kissing his shoulder,
she closed her eyes. "This is great, isn't it? No
one to bother us. No one to interrupt us."

Placing the other egg on his plate, he put
down the spatula and turned around to look
down at her. Lifting her chin, he gazed into her

eyes. "It's perfect," he said, kissing her mouth. He savored the taste. "Mmm," he moaned. "I can never get enough of kissing you."

She giggled in between puckering. "Who says that you have to?" Another kiss followed.

Was that a possible sign that she wanted to keep him around?

"Good point." Picking her up, he took her over to the table and placed her atop of it. The cool surface sent a chill up her spine. His firm hand ran down her side and pulled at her panties. "I'm hungry for something else right now," he said, wickedly seductive with his small touches.

She giggled incessantly. Resting back on her elbows as she watched him rip and remove her panties. She spread her legs wide. The hiss of his hot breath on her sex made her moan, but it wasn't until she felt the sharp tip his long tongue slide inside of her that she whimpered.

Grabbing her by her hips and sinking his fingers into her soft skin, he buried his kiss deep, sucking at the folds of her as she grabbed the end of the table.

"You, my dear, have such a sweet peach," he said, sucking in her taste and raising up to look at her. A smile formed on his lips. "And it's the only kind in the entire world that I'm not allergic to."

Hope grabbed the top of his mop of curls and pushed him further down. "Don't stop," she begged as he kissed her again, flicking his meaty tongue against her clit until she fell back flat on the table.

He stayed there in between her glistening thighs, enjoying her until she begins to quake.

Trembling under him, she barely noticed in her own pleasure that he had pulled his under-wear off. Grabbing her quickly, he pulled her to the end of the table, his erection standing hard and ready. Before she could look up, he was inside of her. They both released a moan as she grabbed his backside and lifted up, taking all of him into her body.

He kissed her lips now, lifting her up with one of his hands to make her ride him as he stood. Feet planted firmly on the floor, he held her in his embrace, thrusting inside of her as she moaned and screamed. His strong muscles flexed, carrying her like she was as light as a feather. Harder and harder he grew in her as she wrapped her arms around his neck.

"Yes," she said, feeling her womb tense.

"Are you coming baby?" he asked, wanting to see her face as she climaxed.

Mouth open, mewing and eyes rolling to the back of her head, she swallowed down a scream. "Yes!"

"That's it," he said, fighting to hold back his own release at the sight of her.

"Right there," she said, kissing his neck. She ran her tongue down his collar bone.

"Shit." He closed his eyes, feeling her wetness slide over him. She was going to make him...

The doorbell rang three times back to back – quickly and impatiently.

"Who the fuck?" he growled, still moving inside of her. He looked toward the doorway as if his frustration might send whoever it was away.

Her nails dug into his skin, dragging his attention back to her. "They'll have to wait," she insisted. "Finish."

The effect was immediate and intense. Her words set him ablaze to the point that he ignored the loud banging of someone's fist against the door. Carrying her to the wall, he propped her up by the phone dock and the wooden KITCHEN MENU sign and kissed her mouth. Moving in and out of her, he felt his skin turn scarlet red before he slammed a hand against the wall behind her and did what she commanded.

A loud echo of his pleasure carried throughout the house and surely to the front door.

Smiling as Michael slid her down onto the floor, she kissed his chin. "*Now*, go see who it is."

He paused, still breathing heavily. "Me? Like this?" he sputtered, looking down at his naked body covered in her essence. Sweat fell from his brow. "You must be kidding." His blue eyes peered at her.

Covered equally in him, she strode over to the table and bent to pick up his underwear.

"Damn," he said, feeling himself rise again. Her naked backside was absolutely remarkable. *Would he ever get enough of her?*

Throwing his briefs over to him, she giggled. "You can't expect me to go. You tore mine." Picking her torn lace panties, she balled them in her hand.

For a moment, Michael wanted to take the balled up panties from her and save them for later, but he pushed that thought to the back of his mind.

Michael growled. "Why does either one of us have to go? Callers should be announced before they just show up on your doorstep."

Hope smiled. Everyone once in a while, when he wasn't meaning to, his royal side came out – all haughty and demanding.

Boom, boom, boom!

Now out of the haze of a sex spell that she had cast on him, he heard the knock again and recognized it for what it was. His heart constricted, but he kept a straight face as to not alarm her.

Completely unaware of Michael's sudden mood change, she shrugged and yawned. "Fine, neither one of us will go," Hope said, taking a seat and yawning. She wasn't expecting anyone and she really didn't care to find out who it was.

Michael looked back toward the door. His voice was lower now. "No, I'll go," he said, running a frustrated hand through his hair. "But I'll be right back. So, don't go getting dressed. I think I still have one good shagging in me."

"Okay," she chuckled, picking up her coffee. "Meet me upstairs in *my office* after you send whoever it is away."

The naughty invitation made him smile. "Well, you had better rush up, then. I won't be made to wait."

Walking away from Hope, his smile disappeared. He knew that he had ignored all of his calls until finally his phone went dead the day before. He was also certain that ignoring his brother and Geoff would eventually lead to a knock on the door, but this was a bit untimely.

Entering into the foyer, he was met by Geoff, who had no shame in pushing his entire face up against the glass and peering into the window like a pervert. Michael huffed audibly. *The man could be a real drag when he wanted to.*

He opened the wooden door and smiled sheepishly at Geoff and two of his men standing behind him in full suits, ties, shades and weapons. Leaning against the door frame and folding his arms across his bare chest, he shook his head.

"Is this necessary?" he asked, spying one of the men's sidearm poking out of his suit jacket.

The man, catching Michael's gaze, quickly adjusted his weapon and stood up straighter.

Michael rolled his eyes over to Geoff again and twisted up his lips.

Geoff quickly looked Michael up and down. It was obvious that his liege had just recovered from a woman's embrace – ignoring the fact that they had all heard his release - but this was the first time that he had shown up at the door so relaxed after.

Evidently, there was no need to escort him out quickly with sincere apologies. Dipping his head a bit to acknowledge his prince, Geoff began his task. "Apologies for our abrupt interruption. However, we've been waiting for four days Your Highness. I was left with no choice but to make our presence known." His left eye twitched. "Prince Richard is insistent on speaking with you *at once*."

Michael rolled his eyes. "Tell him that I'll speak with him later today. I'm busy, as you can see." He prepared to close the door.

Geoff wouldn't state the obvious, but he did step forward in protest. "I'm afraid that it can't wait until later. We have been ordered to get you on the phone now," he said, handing Michael his cell phone. He nodded toward the screen, indicating a call was active, and raised his brow. It was a small gesture, but something to keep Michael from going on a tirade about Richard's overbearing ways.

Michael took the phone and threw back his head. How he tired of the never-ending theatrics. Letting out a sigh, he shrugged his shoulders. "You can't come inside. We're not decent. Sit out here on the porch for a minute. I'll be back."

"As you wish, sir," Geoff said formally.

Normally, Michael and Geoff's conversation would have included a barrage of swearing and clever banter, but in front of other men, the two friends always maintained a certain amount of professional decorum.

Closing the door behind him as he stepped inside, Michael pressed the phone to his ear.

"Brother," he said, awaiting a full tongue-lashing.

"Are you so busy that you can't accept my calls?" Richard asked, irritation evident in his arrogant tone.

"As a matter of fact," Michael began.

Richard cut him off – not wanting to hear his brother's sarcasm. "I know what you are doing there. You are making a mess of things, completely negating your reason for the entire trip. Can't you stay on task?"

Michael raised a brow. He could not deny that he had deviated. "Sometimes life just happens."

"Does she know who you are?" Richard probed.

"Yes," Michael answered in relief. "And she's not at all concerned by it. And before you start, she's not some gold digger looking to get fame and fortune by being associated with me."

"While I don't doubt your ability to read her intentions *or her mind* after only four days, may I just say that I do doubt your judgment."

"May I just say that I'm not surprised."

"You're putting yourself and this entire family into even more of a situation than breaking up with Thalia publicly, which cost us a fortune in PR and money for her troubles."

"You paid her?" Michael snarled, appalled at the thought of her reaping one more monetary benefit from their relationship. It wasn't like he had married the woman. *Thank God!*

"Of course, we paid her. It was the least that we could do after you broke up with one of the most sought after young royals in the western hemisphere. These are people of conse-quence...that we have to see on a continual basis – a *real* family that you have shamed." Richard said the words as though they were a part of his very being.

"I'm assuming other families aren't real." Michael smirked facetiously. It was amazing to him that one man could be so pompous.

Richard ignored Michael's continued at-tempt to be normal. "On top of that, you changed your mobile number. So there was no closure for Thalia. You wouldn't even honor her with a call after you went home with the Brixton sisters, who let me remind you, made the news. They were paid to talk about the size of your private parts for goodness sake."

"What did they say?" Michael asked, in-trigued.

"They were kind - generous even," Richard seethed, flabbergasted that Michael would even care about rumors at this point. "But you should be more worried about what Thalia and friends close to her said about your character in the news. They were not as forgiving or generous."

"Why should I care?" Michael's anger flared. "And the Brixton sisters had a lot more respect for themselves than you think."

"I doubt that," Richard snorted.

"They never pretended to be anything but who they were, and they never lied to me. Thalia, on the other hand, manipulated me for years into believing that she loved me so that I'd marry her. And why? So, she could have her chance at the crown and to elevate her family's position. Now, who is really more treacherous? The Brixton sisters or your precious Thalia?"

"Michael is a self-centered monster."

"What?" Michael flinched.

"That is what Thalia's family told the press." Richard blew out a frustrated breath.

"How very royal of them." His eyes narrowed. He had a few other choice words to call her and family, but he would keep them all to himself.

"And just what do you think that Hope will say to the press when you break her heart? She'll reiterate Thalia's story further damning your already-tarnished image and this family."

"Hope isn't like that. And this isn't about you or the family. It's about me."

"And what about you?" Richard asked, twisting in his leather seat. He looked out of the window at the clouds floating beneath him and cringed. "You're so incredibly short-sighted until I don't know why I'm blaming you for this, but how is it about you?"

Michael didn't want to fight, not here, not where *she* could hear him. It would ruin everything if she heard him justifying his actions with other women, whether right or wrong. And considering how open she had been with him about her life and her desire not to be hurt anymore, he could not risk her losing faith in him.

He pursed his lips together and held the phone tighter to his ear. "I won't have another conversation about how incredibly stupid I am or how my physical appearance serves as such a handicap. I'm quite aware of what I'm doing, and I'm quite aware of the implications. I happen to lo... like her." He glanced down the hall to make sure that his voice was not carrying, especially with that last part.

Despite Michael's attempt to cut off his statement, Richard knew what Michael meant to say, which elevated his already-heightened concern. Michael had never mentioned love so early. Normally, he was reserved with his feelings, almost to the point of cutting them off.

"Is Hope aware of what happens after being linked as a love interest of yours? Does she know that her life will become fodder for critics, everything from her dress size to her personal hygiene and diet?" Richard pulled off his glasses and rubbed the bridge of his nose. A headache was on the horizon – one of gigantic proportion.

"I'll protect her," Michael promised. "I won't let them hurt her."

"Like you've protected yourself or this family? No, I'm sorry. That's been my job. I protect you. I'm protecting you now. And while you were busy rolling around in the bed with a blind artist, RQL was busy releasing a large digital and print campaign offering $100,000 to the person who could pinpoint your location on the planet, but more specifically the United States."

"How do they know I'm in the states?"

Richard laughed, though he wasn't amused. "It's not about the truth, Michael. *You know that*. It's about what sells. And right now, after your breakup with Thalia and sudden disappearance, you're a commodity for those bloodsuckers. There will be a media frenzy behind this. Sightings everywhere from the Grand Canyon to South Beach. The whole world is going to be looking for you and no doubt before long find you."

"Maybe not," Michael whispered.

"Don't be naive. The nurse who watched Hope will call and get that money, as will the neighbor who rented out his home to you and the lawyer you punched. That's at least three people who all have seen you in the same place."

It irritated Michael to no end that his brother knew his every move, but he didn't speak on it. "Then, we'll go on holiday for a while."

Richard inserted more doubt. "Will her doctor clear her? Will she want to go? The dossier I read on her says that she's been commissioned to the tune of $200,000 to finish her current collection of work. Does she plan to put her career down to run around the world, dodging cameras with you with no guarantee that you won't just leave her at the next stop?"

"I would never just leave her," Michael scowled.

"Just like you'd never leave Thalia?" Richard felt he had gone far enough, but the point had been made. He was a man known for leaving when things got tough.

Richard let go of a breath. "The piece goes live tonight at midnight. After that, you, my dear brother will be on house arrest."

Michael looked around Hope's house. "First, she's not blind anymore. Second, I can handle RQL. Third, I like the house that I'm confined to and the person that I'm confined to it with."

Richard hissed again. "Have you ever been able to end one sentence in anything other than a prepositional phrase?"

Michael had to laugh. "You're being facetious, brother. It doesn't suit you."

"I want you to pack up and get back here quick smart." Richard knew that he would deny his request, but he insisted anyway.

"No," Michael said, voice stern. "I will not."

"You will," Richard said, hating to give the ultimatums but forced. "By decree of your Queen and more importantly your mother. You will end your fling and return back to London, where we will regroup."

"I'm a grown man," Michael snapped. "I have regrouped. I've found someone that actually makes me happy. And what decree? Are you kidding? She can't make me come home and neither can you. And if my mother wants to talk to me, she has my number," he said, exasperated.

"What good is it to call, if your phone is dead?" Richard snapped back.

"Don't push this, Richard," Michael warned, as he scrubbed a hand across his face. "I'm not just fooling around, and she's not just a girl. I care about her, and I won't have you ruining that for me with your bloody tantrums. Now, I appreciate the heads up about RQL and your never-ending vote of confidence in me as a man, but I have to go." Ringing off, he swung open the front door and shoved the phone back into Geoff's chest in anger.

Catching himself, Michael apologized. "I'm sorry. That wasn't meant for you."

Geoff's face was stoic but not his words. "What have you done, Michael?" he asked, afraid for his friend. Pissing Richard off in the past had not turned out well for Michael. He doubted very seriously that it would yield different results now.

Michael clenched his jaw tight. "I've made a decision. If she won't go, then neither will I. But I'm not leaving her and running back to London with my tail tucked conveniently between my legs."

Nodding, Geoff slipped his phone back into his pocket. Turning toward the entourage of bodyguards who stood stone-faced, he dismissed them with a waved hand. "Wait at the car," he ordered the men.

As soon as they headed toward the car, he let down his guard and turned back toward Michael. "Dick is pissing bricks right now. God only knows what he'll do once he arrives. *And he is on the way.* Between you and me, he should be in U.S. airspace now. We've gotten orders. We're to stay on this house, around the perimeter from now on – no matter what kind of attention it causes. And the state department has sent men as well. We're not to let you out of our sight. We are not to let anyone on the property and we are no longer allowed to pretend that we are not here. Your cover is blown."

Michael slumped his shoulders and shook his head. The utopia he was building was suddenly crumbling around him. "Let me know when he arrives. I'll deal with him then. I just don't want him to come into contact with Hope before I have time to talk to her. He'll ruin everything with his arrogant ass. At least give me one more night without your full presence. I'll take her out tonight and break the news to her about RQL and what she can expect, but it should come from me, not him."

Geoff smirked. In only four days, he sounded much stronger.

"And if you can, bring my charger. I should call my mother." Michael hated the idea. He knew that Richard was a cakewalk in comparison to that woman.

"Fine. One more night. When you take her out, we'll follow behind as quietly as possible. But with all of this, you know I have to ask."

"Ask what?"

"Is she really this important? You know what's coming. Thalia was prepared for this type of media circus – hell, she loved it, but I doubt a woman as quiet and reserved as your friend is will be. Think of her before you throw her to the wolves." Geoff had done the background on Hope. She was a great woman, but no social butterfly. The media could be brutal – something that took training and unfortunately a lot of bumps and bruises.

"I am thinking of her," Michael answered, eyes pleading for understanding. "I'm thinking of both of us."

"Are you sure it's not just a rebound from Thalia?" Geoff asked. He knew how much Michael had cared for her until her confession. He also knew that Michael had never taken rejection well. The combination could have been the reason for his sudden emotion for this new woman and understandably so.

Michael twisted up his lips. This would be a question that he would be asked for a while, so he might as well get used to answering it. He smiled at the thought of her. "Hope Daniels is no rebound," he said, placing his hand on his friend's shoulder. "I need you, Geoff. Be my ears and my eyes. Let me know what's coming so that I can protect her. But trust me when I say that I'm not blinded by lust or confused by my breakup. This is different, and she is different."

Geoff touched his friend's hand. Honestly, he believed him, but he knew that Richard wouldn't. "I'll do everything in my power," he promised.

***

In the four days since she had had her sight back, Hope had moved from the temporary bedroom downstairs back into the comforts of her second-floor master bedroom with all of its perfect amenities. And while it was a simple thing to do – to simply move from one room to another - it was a large step for her to be moving back into her own life.

Every day, she felt her independence coming back to her, and she was bursting at the seams to get back to painting and moving her life in the direction that she wanted.

From the moment she got her sight back, all she could think of was putting the brush back in her hands, being able to see colors and shapes, to be able to take in the world with her own eyes.

Only now, she would have an appreciation for it that she'd never had before. Now, she was more empowered than ever. There would be no one *carpe*'ing their *diem* the way that she planned to do.

And she had started immediately when she reached out at first sight and kissed Michael.

However, life seemed completely different after that kiss. Sure the first one in the park had been mind blowing! And honestly, she was on a high after that. If there had not been another one that day, she would have still be floating on cloud nine. But then Michael put Sean in his place, all of sudden, she got her sight back and the elation that she felt inside caused all sorts of raw emotions.

The next thing she knew, she was in bed with him. And even after four days, there were no regrets.

Looking into his eyes and holding him close, feeling him grow inside of her to silken steel, smelling his cologne all over her body – on her tongue and on her lips-, hearing him say her name and whisper sweet nothings in her ear; it changed everything.

She knew fools rushed in. Everyone knew that, but why couldn't she help herself?

In just the few days of being with Michael, she had experienced happiness at a level she had never had before him. And it wasn't that he was a prince. While that had been a complete shock, it had in no way affected how they were with each other.

In fact, she was surprised at how many simi-lar life experiences they shared. In her mind, she always thought royalty lived such dramati-cally different lives, full of pomp and circum-stance, and while that might apply to most – it most certainly did not apply to her Michael. He was a simple man who loved jam on his bagels, eggs benedict with Tabasco sauce, reading the USA Today and listening to Coltrane while lying in bed naked and playing in her hair when she laid across his massive chest.

So many vivid pictures of the last four days popped into her head, until she absolutely brimmed with joy.

She loved the way that they teased each oth-er, how he could take a joke, how he made fun of himself and never took life too seriously. She loved that he admitted that he didn't have everything figured out yet and might never get some things. But most importantly, she loved just being around him.

The idea nearly scared her. *Oh my God. Was this love*?

Was this what all those scores of beautiful music they listened to were actually about?

In truth, she'd never known this kind of love – the kind not given by family and friends. This was an intimate, bonding, electrifying thing made life itself change colors – from dim to bright.

Walking into her bedroom full of light and arguably...dust from being closed up for six weeks, she caught herself dipping her head and smiling when she saw Michael's T-shirt laid across the large bed – mixed in with silk sheets and her goose down comforter. He had picked out his most favorite coffee mug from her extensive collection and set to using it every morning and also leaving it every afternoon for her to pick up off the nightstand. *Eventually, she'd get him trained.*

He seemed to love her bedroom almost as much as her. He seemed to like her life as much too.

What did that mean? Was it possible that he might stay here with her and continue finding himself and finding what made him happy?

Was that too much? He was after all a prince with responsibilities of his own – though he never mentioned them.

She sat down on the bed and looked around her room. Funny how she had taken its beauty for granted before, but never again.

It was a spacious, beautiful old room with high ceilings accented by dark wooden beams, matching dark hardwood floors, expensive heavy drapes, plush rugs, and a colorful comforter atop an antique king-sized oak bed that was lined at every bedpost with books nearly as tall as the ceiling. Some of them had been her books, some of them her grandparent's, some of them her mother's.

Besides her studio, this was her safe place. It housed her large Mac computer on a large credenza covered in books and flowers in the corner. It housed her small Bose system that played her jazz on the mantle right below a perfect little fireplace for cold winter nights, especially lonely ones.

Only in the last few days, she wasn't quite sure that she'd be lonely again. As she waited for her water to finish running in the bathroom down the hall, she lay in the middle of the bed looking out of the open windows at the perfect blue sky. Birds chirped outside as they perched on the limbs of the elm trees below. A fresh breeze blew in shaking the drapes and airing out the room.

Suddenly, her computer began to hum a tune, indicating a call on FaceTime.

Jumping up, Hope ran over and sat in the chair in front of her desk and hit accept. Bree was on the opposite camera with a perplexed look of anger on her face. "Just where in the hell have you been?" she asked, eyebrows spiked. "I've been trying to call you for four straight days. Not one answer. I've called the hospitals, the house phone, and your cell phone!"

Hope shook her head and gasped. "Oh my goodness. I'm so sorry, Bree. Don't be mad at me. I totally forgot." Her heart lurched. Bree had been such a good friend. The least that she deserved was a call, but so much had happened, Hope had not been able to think straight.

"Girl, what could possibly make you forget your entire life for four damn days?" she asked, looking harder into the monitor. "Wait, are you looking at me?" She blinked hard at the monitor, pulling up toward her face.

Hope was about to explain her answer to the first question but stopped abruptly. "Yes, I'm looking at you," Hope smiled. *Another thing she had forgotten to share.*

"Okay, you're going to freak and tell me how selfish I've been for not calling you, especially after you came all the way here for me, but..."

"You got your sight back?" Bree asked, tears forming in the sides of her eyes.

Hope exhaled. "I got it back." She almost felt the need to cry also. Waving her hands over her eyes to fight the tears, she nodded. "I've just been really preoccupied with things. You have no idea how crazy my life has been."

"Painting? Cleaning? What?" Bree asked.

"No..." How did she explain all of this to her best friend?

As she was about to explain that the next door neighbor had recently become her temporary housemate, she saw Bree's hand go over her mouth. "My word!"

"What's wrong?" Hope asked, confused.

Bree pointed as Hope turned to see that Michael had walked into the bedroom fully naked. His muscled rippled down his chest and formed a sexy cut V-shape to his erection that he had tied a purple bow on. A boyish grin covered his face. "What are you doing on the computer? I told you that I wanted you naked," Michael said playfully. "I have a gift for you too."

Hope immediately turned and tried to cover the computer with her arms. As she did so, her bottomless vagina appeared on the screen in front of Bree. "Baby, I'm on the..."

Michael stopped in his tracks. "What?"

"She's on the computer!" Bree yelled. "Hope, I can see your entire cookie. It's like right in my face. I mean...right there."

Pulling the sheet off the bed, Michael covered his erect penis and turned scarlet red. "Is that your friend from before?"

"Why does he have an accent now?" Bree asked.

"Why is she on the computer?" Michael asked.

"Why is he talking like that?" Bree asked again.

"Both of you stop talking!" Hope exclaimed. "I can't think." Sitting back down, she put her elbow on the table and sank her head into the palm of her hand. Looking up at the monitor, she nodded at Bree. "Can I call you back?"

"You better," Bree warned, signing off.

Hope twisted around in her swivel chair and looked at Michael. She couldn't help but blush as she stood across the room covering his manhood with the sheet. "Wow," she said, shaking her head. "You are just full of surprises, aren't you?"

Michael removed the sheet and looked down at his penis. "How do you like that?"

"What?" Hope asked.

He looked up with a clever grin. "It's still hard, and it's still wrapped in a perfect little bow." Walking over to Hope, he bit his lip. "You know, your friend is right."

"About what?" Hope asked, tilting her head.

"Your cookie is showing," he said, standing in front of her. He used his foot to spread her legs further apart. "And a perfect little cookie, it is." His mouth began to water again at just the thought of taking her.

"We should bathe first."   Extending her hand, she allowed him to help her up out of the chair.

Pulling her close, he nudged himself into her stomach. "I know. I already turned off the water in the bathroom." He kissed her lips and moved her hair out of her face. "I want to take you out tonight. I don't know where. You pick. Some place low key, of course, but I'd like to get you out of the house."

Hope liked the sound of that. She kissed him again. "Awesome. We can go dancing."

"Anything you want."

"Then dinner and a movie too," she added.

"Anything. You. Want."

"Great. It will be our first date," she said, as they walked out of the bedroom toward the bathroom.

Michael corrected her quickly. "It will be our second date. Our first date was at the park."

Hope blushed. While she had not said any-thing at the time, she had thought the same exact thing.

Chapter 13

A real date.

Hope was going on a real date. She was so excited until she could barely go through her closet to figure out what to wear. Michael had left a few hours earlier to give her some time to get ready, and she was left to her very vivid imagination. She could be whatever she wanted tonight. Whimsical and fair or dark and sexy. Every woman had at least two sides to her coin. The question was which side would end up on top tonight? There were so many choices. Looking at her clock, however, she decided, there wasn't nearly enough time.

He promised to be back by six, ready to enjoy a night on the town with her. And the only thought that kept going through her mind was that she had to look pretty for him.

With the sun peering through her windows and Michael Buble blasting on the stereo, she finally ran up on a little black dress that would do her justice. It was a fitted dress that stopped right above the knee with a V-neck cut to show off her well-plated cleavage thanks to a Victoria Secret push-up bra.

Grabbing a pair of black stilettos that Bree had made her buy the summer before, she paired them with thigh highs and black lingerie that he would surely see later and pulled of her robe to begin her ascent from the girl next door to the woman of his dreams.

Another thought hit her. With the women that he had dated before her, she was certain that they had been dawned in the best clothes by the best designers, but what they didn't have on her was new sight. Being blind for nearly two months had given her a new appreciation for her own curves, and she loved them more than ever.

After two hours of detailed prepping, she looked at herself in the mirror and felt pleased. She had pulled her hair up in a wispy ponytail with tendrils that fell to her shoulders, put on make-up, painted her nails, plucked her brows, waxed her bikini area and most importantly checked her Nuevo Ring.

There was no way that this wouldn't knock his socks off tonight. He was used to seeing her in panties and T-shirts, yoga pants and jeans. But tonight, he'd see the other side of her – the side that rarely got an opportunity to come out.

Spraying on a little of her most expensive cologne behind her ears, elbows and between her thighs, she giggled when she heard the doorbell ring.

Grabbing her small purse, she headed downstairs as quickly as her feet would take her.

When Hope opened the door, Michael had to pause. Swallowing heavily and clutching a large bouquet of red roses, he nearly dropped them when she emerged. He was expecting a sundress – maybe even jeans and a blouse. But he wasn't expecting for her to look so amazing.

"I'm speechless," he said, pulling off his Ray Ban Aviator shades. His eyes glinted with approval. "You look absolutely beautiful."

Hope grinned. "Thank you," she said, taking the flowers and sniffing them. "I love roses."

"I noticed," he said, trying not to gawk at her. Looking down at his own clothes, he felt very underdressed. *It was the first time in his life.* In a pair of dark jeans, a nice tailored blue linen top and black loafers, he almost wanted to cancel to go back and re-dress. But to keep her waiting any longer would surely be a sin.

Seeing him twist his lips up as he looked down at his clothes, she quickly complimented him. "You look great," she said, grabbing his hand to pull him inside. He was standing out there like he hadn't spent nearly a week holed up in this place alone with her.

"Are we ready to go?" he asked.

"Yes, I just want to run and put these in water." Darting toward the kitchen in front of him, she heard him following behind in a leisurely stroll. What she didn't know was that he was truly enjoying the view. "You do really look amazing. I sort of want to skip dinner and go straight for dessert." That wasn't a lie or even an exaggeration. Seeing her like this was driving him insane.

Pulling an empty vase from below the sink, she set it on the counter and turned on the faucet. "You can have dessert later." As she turned to look at him, the sun setting on the horizon caught in her brown hair and highlighted all of the auburn streaks in it. Funny, he had never noticed them until now.

"I will," he joked as an afterthought. "And seconds to boot."

When she had cut the flowers and arranged them in the vase, she stood back and marveled at them. "Thank you, Michael. You're so sweet." Her brown eyes flashed with joy – again another sincere display of appreciation that he still hadn't gotten used to yet.

"You deserve an entire garden of roses," he said, pulling her close. She smelled even better than she looked. "Are you ready to start our night? Being here with you alone isn't helping my intentions." He looked down into her face and felt himself begin to stir again.

"I'm very ready."

"Good. Have you ever been to town in a big pickup truck? Because I've never been on a date in one. This will be a first."

Hope raised her brow. "That's right. You're all royal and stuff. Yes, I have been to *town* in a pickup. I used to drive my grandfather's truck all the time. It was a real classic beauty. Bucket seats and all."

"Really, what happened to it?"   Michael loved hearing about her life, but she rarely went into detail.

Hope frowned and caught herself.   Bad memory – no place in the moment. "It was totaled. But let's not talk about that. Right now, I just want to be with you."

***

Michael had never been to Memphis, Tennessee. He had seen the documentaries and truly loved the music, especially from B.B. King and the artists from Stax Records like Otis Redding and Isaac Hayes, but he'd never experienced it for himself.

However, Hope took him on quite a tour. After a scary movie at the Paradiso Theatre, where they ate tons of buttered popcorn and chocolate and no one noticed him, because

Hope stole everyone's attention with her beauty, they went downtown and had barbeque near the Mississippi River at Central BBQ. She taught him the difference between dry rub and wet ribs right before feeding him both. To his delight, he loved the saucy stuff better.

Then, completely full, they walked off some of the food with a tour around the National Civil Rights Museum, where she showed him the exact spot that Dr. King had been assassinated. He stood there transfixed by the history before him and even though the Museum was closed, he felt incredibly moved.

"He sacrificed everything," Hope explained, looking up at the white reef above from below in the courtyard of the hotel. "And look where it got us." Holding his hand, she smiled. "White and black children able to walk the streets of Memphis alone at night without being beaten and hung."

The thought sent a chill up his spine. "He was a remarkable man. I've read all his books."

Hope was impressed. "Really. All of them?"

"All of them," he said proudly. "My most favorite quote," he paused with a deep breath, "I refuse to accept the view that mankind is so tragically bound to the starless midnight of racism and war that the bright daybreak of peace and brotherhood can never become a reality... I believe that unarmed truth and unconditional love will have the final word." He looked down at Hope and felt a swell in his chest. "If I'm ever King of England, I won't allow for ruthless tyranny, hungry poor children, socioeconomic gaps that allow the least to receive adequate education or social services. I will build a legacy on the shoulders of giants like him."

Hope put her head on his chest. "You don't have to be king to do that, Michael. You can do it now. Your voice is so powerful. All you have to do is speak."

"If I were smarter," he said, chiding himself quietly for allowing his brother's judgment to take form.

Hope looked up and grabbed his face. "In the short time that I've known you, I've seen a man who knows only strength and goodness. You are smart; you are more than smart, you are blessed with the ability to connect with people. And whether they crown you king in your lifetime or not, you will always be the people's choice as long as you speak for them."

Michael shook his head. "You have such faith in me, and you don't even know me – not all of me. The side that everyone says is most prevalent."

"And what side is that?" she asked.

"The selfish man."

She bit her lip and tilted her head toward him innocently. "Are you selfish?"

"I don't want to be," he said aloud. But I am when it comes to you, he thought to himself.

"What I've found is that every day that you're alive, you can become better than you were the day before. So you might have been selfish yesterday, but today you can be a new man."

He kissed her hand gratefully. "I will remember that."

They walked along the river at Tom Lee Park and looked out at the cloudless night sky and the golden arched bridge leading from Arkansas to Tennessee, and she told him of her first Memphis in May concert where she wore rain boots and sloshed in the dirt as she listened to the Red Hot Chili Peppers.

He kissed her on Beale Street while the Memphis Flippers did acrobatic tricks and entertained the large crowd, and marveled at how no one noticed him. He was just a lucky guy out with a beautiful woman. And for the first night in his life, he was allowed to just be Michael.

He sang karaoke at a local bar with her and drank Memphis beer from a local distillery.

She danced with him on the third floor of 152 where the lights and smoke hid not only his true identity but also the erection she gave him as she grinded against him to some song by Nicki Minaj. He loved the sweet sweat that rolled down her neck and how she arched her back into him as her hips swayed. He pulled her close to him and felt her form, aching to be inside of her.

Eventually, after drinking and dancing, he decided that he wanted a cigar. So, she walked with him a few blocks over to Havana Mix, a small shop playing jazz and serving up the best cigars that the city had to offer.

Taking a seat off in the corner, they cuddled together and cut their Cohibas, ready to dig in for the rest of the evening.

"What a night," Michael exclaimed, rubbing her back and looking at the band. "This is really great."

"I'm glad you had fun. I know I did," Hope said, gulping down a cup of water. All the dancing before had her dehydrated. "I haven't had this much fun in years."

"Me either," he said, lighting his cigar. Taking a big puff, he sat back in his chair and released. "Mmm. This is heaven."

Hope laughed. "It doesn't take a lot to make you happy, does it?"

"Funny, I have been thinking the same about you since I met you." Michael scooted his chair closer to her. Putting his elbows on the table, he narrowed his blue eyes on her. "You're indescribably strong, like Teflon. How did you get that way? I know that you said that your mother died early and your grandparents raised you, but there is something bittersweet about your smile and the way that you simply let the bad things in life roll off your back. Like with Sean and the blindness. You never let it get you down. How did you come by that?"

The music played in the background and the breeze drifted in from the open doors a few feet away. Closing her eyes, Hope shook her head and smiled.

"By God," she said, honestly.

Michael frowned. "Come again?"

Hope had been trying to avoid the conversation, but eventually, they would have to get to it. Knitting her fingers together, she leaned into him as to not draw those nearby into it. "My mother was a brilliant artist. People who knew her said she was bound to do great things." Her eyelashes flitted as if to push away tears. "I only remember her through pictures now and sometimes through the jazz." She gave a painful, tight smile. "She loved Coltrane, probably more than me."

"What happened to her?" Michael asked, knowing the answer would be something tragic.

"She could never overcome her depression. The doctors tried. My grandparents tried. Eventually, she had to be admitted to a mental hospital because of her failed attempts to commit suicide. The last one was nearly successful, but evidently I had learned how to call 911. She slit her veins open in the bathtub and I called for the police. But you know, I don't remember it. The doctors say that the shock of it forced my mind to shut it out." She raised a brow. "I don't remember a thing, and I hate that because I don't remember her." She exhaled a deep breath. "We stayed with my grandparents for a while after that until she got better, but then finally my grandparents admitted her after a sleeping pill incident and I never saw her again."

"What happened?" Michael whispered.

"She found a way to do it – to umm..." Looking down at the floor, she wiped a tear from her eye. "She found a way to kill herself about a month into her treatment." Smacking her lips, she tried to smile. "My grandparents were wonderful people. They raised me with about as much love as you can give to one child. But a few years after she was buried, I picked up the same paintbrush that she had put down and started to create beauty on a canvas the way that she did. It scared the hell out of my grandfather. He didn't want me to... to be her. But I wasn't. My grandmother encouraged me to paint. They paid for classes. It slowly became my thing, my favorite thing. And even when I do it now, I feel closer to her."

Michael sat back and wiped his face. "I'm truly sorry. I had no idea." He was shocked that his brother hadn't already found out about Hope's tragic secret but was certain that he eventually would.

"I made a promise to myself as a young girl that I would never let this life consume me to the point where I couldn't survive it. I was determined to stay here until God called me. I wasn't going to check out on my own and leave everyone who loved me in so much pain. So, when things get too out of control, I find my center and I stay there until the storm calms."

"Ingenious philosophy," Michael said sincerely. "And your father? What of him?"

"Just a guy. Never met him. Never signed the birth certificate." Hope shrugged. "It happens."

Suddenly, Michael could hear his brother's voice in his head again and he knew Richard was right. The media would tear this story apart. Clenching his square jaw, he put down his cigar completely. "Can we get out of here?

We need to talk," he said, making eye contact with a tourist who narrowed her gaze on him.

"Sure," Hope said, confused. "What's wrong?"

"We should go," Michael said as the woman stood up and approached.

"Oy, is that really you?" the red-headed older woman asked with an English accent, pulling out her cell phone. "Prince Michael?"

"Wrong guy," Michael said with his faux-Southern accent. *Piss off you old cow,* he thought to himself. Giving a fake smile, he tried to explain his appearance away. "I get it all the time. Sorry, I'm not the prince. I was born here in Hernando."

Hope grabbed her purse and stood up. That was their cue. If one noticed him, more would, and his accent was horrible.

"You just look so much like him, it's unreal," the tourist said, suddenly uncertain. "Do you mind if I take a picture with you. My boys won't believe that I came all the way to Memphis and met his majesty's twin."

Michael looked at Hope and smiled. "Sure, just one won't hurt," he said, pulling the woman in for a selfie. "But make it quick. My little lady gets antsy when people stop us like this."

"Oh, I'm so sorry," the woman apologized as she quickly took the photo.

Leaving the cigars, Michael and Hope quickly exited the little bar before they had time to finish what they had come there for.

"It's only a matter of time before someone figures it out, isn't it?" Hope asked, as they walked down the street to the parking garage where they had parked the truck.

"Yes," Michael said, apologetically. "It's part of why I wanted to take you out tonight. A little shit of a reporter released a story purporting that I'm in the states, and he's offering $100,000 reward for anyone who can tell him my exact location."

"When did he release the story?" Hope asked, alarmed.

"About an hour ago," Michael said, looking at his watch.

"What?" Hope stopped in her tracks. "Why didn't you tell me?"

"Because I wanted this," he said, stopping as well. He turned to her and slumped his shoulders. "I wanted to experience what life could be like with you alone." He grabbed her hands and held them in his own. "My whole life, since the day that I was born, has been under a fucking microscope. I've never just been treated as a human being. I've never been allowed to roam the streets or go to the movies or eat at a restaurant without a camera in my face. And I wanted to know what that was like, and I wanted to know what it was like with you."

Hope nodded in understanding. "You could have still told me."

"Once they find out, everything will be different, including you."

"Not me," she snapped. "I'm not that way."

Michael hurt to say it. Running a hand through his hair, he growled. "They will...crucify you. And I didn't realize how much until now." He breathed in heavily, nearly snorting. "All I want to do is protect you. I want to keep you in this bubble of normalcy because you are the only one who makes me feel alive."

Hope grabbed his face. "Michael, nothing can change us, but us."

"They will try their hardest to take you away from me." He kissed the top of her head. "The one thing in this life that I truly want."

"Not if we don't let them," she said, hugging him tight. "Promise me that you won't let them." She looked up at him as though he held all the cards. "You happen to have some power in this world. Use it."

You can't protect her. Hell, you can't protect yourself, he heard his brother's voice say.

But Michael ignored the voice. "I will," he promised.

Chapter 14

It was the last day of a very long week for Sean Pritchard. After being smashed in the face by Hope's Neanderthal of a boyfriend, he had to work through the pain all week to be present at several court hearings, all of which his black and blue features were the point of very colorful discussions before and after the session.

Normally, he would have lied about the interaction with Michael, but considering just how small Hernando was and considering just how big LouAnn's mouth was, he settled at just saying that he had gotten into a disagreement with his ex-girlfriend's new lover by trying to be the Good Samaritan.

People took what they wanted from his explanation, but normally it was assumed that he was the savior in the story, which he could handle a lot better than the idea of a pretty boy getting the best of him on Hope's porch.

While he had gotten over the punch and the swelling had gone down a little, what he had noticed since was a black Yukon that seemed to be following him a lot lately. He knew that it could have just been the popularity of the vehicle and his own paranoia, but the unease that he got whenever he spotted the truck in his rearview mirror or passing by the window of a restaurant he just happened to be frequenting made him believe that there was no coincidence in this.

As he pulled into his normal gas station only a couple of blocks from his house to get gas, a newspaper and coffee to start his Friday morning, he noticed the same Yukon that he thought was following him. *That fucker.* He bet that it was Michael. He bet that the little shit had another vehicle and was trying to intimidate him.

Well, Sean Pritchard is not the man you intimidate! He thought to himself almost screaming it in his mind.

He jumped out of his BMW pissed, and immediately gave the passing truck the finger.

The driver of the truck nearly screeched in the street, then put the truck in reverse and pulled into the gas station, right beside Sean's car.

Fuming mad, he waited for the tinted window to lower and find Michael on the other side. No matter what, he'd give him hell this morning, maybe even break his nose!

Unfortunately, as the window lowered, he saw a gray haired man in a light sweater and polo. He furrowed his brow at Sean in confusion.

"Morning Reverend Baxter," Sean said, deflated.

"Morning Sean," the reverend said, turning down his gospel music. "Boy, are you alright?"

Sean dropped his head. "No."

"What happened to your nose?"

"I got in a fight. I thought you were him," he explained, almost like a juvenile.

Reverend Baxter nodded in understanding. "Well, whoever you got into a quarrel with, you need to let that go. Forgive as God has taught you, and in the meantime, you might want to find other ways to express your anger other than flipping off the town's folk."

"I'll do that," Sean said, completely embarrassed. "I do apologize, sir. I'm afraid that I'm not myself today."

"Well, you have a blessed day, Sean. Say hello to your folks for me. Tell them that I'll see them in church on Sunday. I hope to see you there too with your pretty little girlfriend."

"We'll be there," Sean said, noticing that the man at the gas pump behind him was shaking his head in disapproval.

As the reverend pulled off, Sean turned and slammed his door shut, nearly breaking the glass. *Great! What else could possibly go wrong today?*

Ignoring the man, who at this point had stop pumping his gas all together and stood with his arms folded, watching in protest of Sean's tantrum, he strode into the gas station and quickly went to the coffee maker. He nodded at some of the locals that he knew, poured his coffee, then went to the front to pay and pick up a newspaper.

As he perused the display cabinet waiting for the short line to move, something very interesting caught his eye.

There on the front of a national celebrity gossip magazine was a picture of Michael.

"Son of a bitch!" he said aloud, grabbing the paper.

He read the words so fast until he nearly skipped over whole sentences, he felt like he has suddenly struck gold. Evidently, the Prince of England was *missing* and reported to be hiding out in the states after the break up with his fiancée. Plus, there was a $100,000 reward for anyone who could tell the magazine where his exact location was.

Suddenly, his nose ached, but not with pain as much as anticipation. One hundred grand could go a long way with him, maybe even help him become partner quicker or even start his own firm.

Adjusting the cotton balls that he had pushed up into his nostrils, he flipped through the story until he found the contact information.

"Sir, are you going to buy that or just read it?" the cashier asked, hand on her hip.

Not looking up from the magazine, Sean pulled a twenty from his pocket and slammed it on the counter. "Where's Sue?" he asked of the normal clerk.

"Sick," the woman answered, taking the money.

"Keep the change and buy yourself a new attitude," Sean said, headed out of the store.

***

RQL had logged over 2,000 alleged siting's of Prince Michael since the article had hit the wire. A team of exhausted interns poured over each dead-end lead - some saying that he was in Manhattan, others at Disneyworld, a few swore that they had seen him at the Chicago Bears home game at Soldier Field and one woman was adamant that she had seen him in Memphis at Elvis' house.

Hannibal had been at his desk since the story went live at midnight. Now, as the sun rose on the horizon, he pours another hefty heaping of whiskey in with his coffee and stuffed a bear claw down his throat. With crumbs covering his T-shirt, he opened email after email, hoping to get something that he could present to his boss when she arrived at ten this morning.

She had warned him before she left the day before. "Your little trick might sell a few more magazines, but if you don't come up with something soon, then you end up making me look like an ass. And if I look bad, you look for a new job."

Her threats were getting old, but in comparison to looking for a new job, he'd deal with her.

While she was off giving an interview to E! Television about her extraordinary reward for information on Michael, he was actually the one working his ass off to find the man. Funny how she didn't mind him doing grunt work, but never let him go in front of a camera.

Just as he was about to give up, he saw an email come to his inbox with the subject line: Prince Richard Came to Memphis.

He opened it quickly. Nothing that he had seen had reported that the Prince had even left London.

I work at the Memphis International Airport. On my off time, I work on the private airstrip we call millionaire's row. Yesterday Prince Richard of England came to Memphis. I'm guessing that

Prince Michael must be here. If you confirm this, does that mean I get $100,000? If so, please let me know. Ralph Cooper.

Hannibal snorted at the email. If the prince was in Memphis, Ralph would still not get the money, because he hadn't provided proof. What he had provided was a crumb trail that might just lead to Michael.

He was about to pick up the phone and call his contact in London when another email popped in his inbox. The subject line could hardly be ignored. *Prince Michael is in Hernando, Mississippi and the son of a bitch broke my nose!*

Hannibal nearly spit out his food. The guy should write bylines for a living. Opening the email immediately, he read the contents with his mouth wide open. "Abby, get in here," he screamed to the intern out in the common area.

She came running in, eyes nearly as red as her hair. "Yes, sir," she said, eyeing the crumbs on his shirt. The disgust showed on her face, despite her attempts to hide it. All the interns felt the same way. Hannibal was a slob.

"Look up Sean Pritchard in Hernando, Mississippi. Find out if he is real or not," he said, making sure to watch her turn and leave his office. She had a nice ass for a sophomore.

Turning back to his work, he smiled and whispered Eureka. There were very few coincidences in this world, and they were reserved for non-famous people.

"Is he a lawyer?" Abby screamed from her laptop.

"That's him," Hannibal answered, rubbing his sausage-like fingers together. "Pay dirt."

"He's got a Facebook page, a LinkedIn page, a twitter account and he is listed on several lawyer rating sites. He's real," she said, hoping that they could go home soon.

Picking up the phone, Hannibal called the number that Sean had left.

**

Sean's office was not nearly as large as the junior and senior partners of his law firm, but he had it decked out with all of the earmarks of a partner in preparation for the big day. All of his degrees were hung in custom frames, a photo of Ole Miss's Vaught-Hemmingway Stadium hung beside a photo of he and his dad on a hunting trip, on the desk was a photo of he and former president George Bush from a fundraiser his older brother had taken him to in Dallas and to top it all off, he had placed a photo of Ashley – all blonde and beautiful - in a charming little frame right below his lamp so everyone in the office would know that he had moved on to greener pastures in his love life.

Because Hernando was so small, everyone knew about Hope's accident and some had speculated why. However, he had quickly squashed any debate by stepping out publicly with Ashley shortly after the accident. It was his way of getting in front of the situation.

Normally, if he wasn't working, he'd be online in one of the football chat rooms or surfing the internet, but today, he waited patiently by his email, constantly hitting refresh.

He knew that Michael was in fact Prince Michael, and he planned on outing him and getting that money as soon as possible.

His phone buzzed. "Sean, you've got a call," the receptionist, Arlene said groggily.

Huffing, Sean pulled his attention away from his monitor. His eyes slowly moved from the computer to the phone. "Take a message. I'm busy," he said to the speaker.

"Sounds like a telemarketer but he says his name is Hannibal. He's calling from RQL out in Los Angeles. I don't believe him though. It's only 10:00 a.m. here, which mean its 8:00 a.m. there. Nobody's open at 8:00 in the morning in Hippieville."

Sean picked up his receiver quickly. "Send the call," he said, cutting Arlene off. He could do without her West Coast antics today.

"Are you sure?" she asked hesitantly. Normally, he heeded her advice.

When she didn't get an answer from Sean, she quickly transferred the call to him.

"Hannibal, this is Sean," he said in a matter-of-fact tone.

"Sean Pritchard," Hannibal said, pushing back in his chair. Wiping off the food from his chest, he sucked his teeth. "Saw your very interesting email. You say that he broke your nose over your ex-girlfriend? The Prince of England?"

"Yes," Sean said, choosing his words carefully. "And I know exactly where he is." His eyes narrowed. "But I won't tell you unless you send me a guarantee in writing that you will send me a payment via wire transfer as soon as you confirm my information. Otherwise, I can always call another gossip magazine and give them your scoop."

Hannibal pushed up in his chair. "Whoa now, counselor. There is no need for threats. I've got your money. You have my proof?"

"I can get it in the hour."

Hannibal could tell that this man was not kidding. He had a serious bone to pick and based upon the nasally sound of his voice, so had Michael. He would have given his left leg to be there when the normally cool and collected prince punched this man in the face. The photo would have been worth a million dollars easy.

"You get me proof in an hour, I can be on a plane in two. I'll hand deliver your check as soon as you hand deliver me the prince along with an interview on your royal assault."

"Stay by your phone. I'll be calling you in an hour." Sean said, hanging up.

***

While Michael lay naked and asleep in the mass of pillows in their bed upstairs, Hope had wandered downstairs to the studio and picked up her paintbrush for the first time since she had gotten her sight back. It had been so long since she held the utensil in her hand until it almost felt foreign. That was until she turned her music down low, pulled her hair up in a ponytail and looked at her unfinished master-piece.

It had been so long, but again, her work was calling out to her.

It felt like heaven to grasp the wooden han-dle between her fingers, dip it into the paint and stroke the brush across the canvas.

Standing in her underwear and t-shirt, she begin to feel herself come alive more and more as she added color and depth to the eyes of the man's face. With each stroke her heart began thump in her chest, excitement overwhelming her. Moving quicker and quicker, she found herself nearly dancing around as she painted until finally, she burst out in pure unadulterated laughter.

Alas, she was happy again.

Pulling her hands over her head, she felt tears weld at the corner of her eyes.

"Did I miss the party?" Michael asked, leaning against the doorway watching her.

His voice made her scream, this time in surprise. She turned, a blotch of rose colored paint now at the top of her head, and smiled at him.

"You scared the crap out of me."

"I'm sorry," he said, strolling into the room in his underwear. "I just couldn't help but admire your work."

She looked back at the canvass proudly. "Yeah, it feels good to be back."

Michael pulled her close to him and kissed the back of her neck. "I missed you this morning when I woke up. You weren't there."

His kiss made goose bumps form all over her body. Shivering as he kissed her neck slow and sweet, she closed her eyes in ecstasy. "I didn't want to wake you," she explained, nearly dropping the brush as she wrapped her arms around his neck.

"Excuses, excuses," he said, moving his lips to kiss her.

This was going to be dangerous. She knew it. She could feel it. As long as he was around, how could she focus on anything but him and his amazing body, and more important than that, his amazing mind? But she also, didn't want him to go anywhere. She wanted him there forever in his underwear or in her bed. It was hardly realistic, but she didn't care.

Michael couldn't help himself. Reaching behind her, he grabbed her soft bottom and pulled it into his growing erection. "Do you know that we've made love in nearly every room in this house, except this one," he said, growling a hiss into her mouth.

She bit her lip at the prospect. "Then you should do something about that, Tiger."

He grinned, showing a deep dimple in his square jaw. He loved when she called him tiger. No woman ever had, but she made it sound nobler than being called the Prince of England.

Picking her up off the ground, he carried her over to the table and sat her down beside her paints. He massaged her thighs and pushed her legs apart.

"When will this stop feeling like heaven?" she asked.

He looked up at her and frowned. "You want it to stop?"

"No," she said sincerely. "That's the thing. I don't. Do you?"

"Since I met you, I haven't been happier, Hope. Your name describes my entire being now." Before he could think about his words, he let them slip out of his mouth. "I can't think of a life without you."

Looking up into his blue eyes, she quietly held her breath.

He pulled at her chin and blushed. "Bloody hell. You look as though you don't know already."

"Don't know what?" she asked as the doorbell rang.

They both looked toward the doorway and stood up.

"I'll get it," he said, looking down at her in her underwear. "When I come back, I want those off."

"If it's your security men, can you ask them to stop interrupting us in the middle of sex?"

Michael laughed. "I think it's their form of royal birth control."

When Michael arrived at the door, Geoff was there patiently waiting on him. Dressed in his normal black suit today and not bothering to hide his two weapons under his jacket, he nodded at Michael and took off his shades. "May I come inside, sir?"

"That doesn't sound good," Michael said, standing to the side as Geoff stepped inside the house.   He had never been in, but was impressed at the set up. "I'm sorry to bother you, but Prince Richard is here in Memphis and requests your presence at the Peabody Hotel within the hour."

Michael rolled his eyes.   "What does he want?"

"He does not share these types of things with me, sir," Geoff answered flatly.

Michael raised a brow. "I know you know. Your big brother is his number one advisor," Michael said, looking at the grandfather clock across the room. Hope would be pissed at him having to leave so suddenly. "You can't call him back in London and probe him for Intel?"

"No, I can't. He's here with Richard."

Michael paused. "William is here with Richard?" He blinked and turned around. Putting his balled up hand by his mouth, he frowned. "What is wrong?"

"I'm sure it's just time to give you another ultimatum," Geoff assured Michael. He patted his shoulder. "I'm sure it's fine. Why don't you go upstairs and get dressed? I'll wait for you."

Michael didn't trust it, but he agreed. "Hope and I aren't exactly presentable. She's in her studio working. Why don't you step outside and let me tell her what's going on and then I'll get ready."

"Whatever you need," Geoff said, headed to the door. "I'll just be outside on the porch, sir."

"Thanks," Michael said, turning on his heels to go and explain the situation to Hope.

Geoff stepped back outside in the sun just in time to see Sean's BMW come barreling into the driveway. His men quickly stopped him. They were parked at the low-end of the hill, blocking the drive. Stepping out of their Yukon in suits, guns and shades as well, they walked up to Sean's car and knocked on the glass.

"What in the hell do you want?" Sean asked, turning down his radio. "What is this?"

"I'm sorry, sir. Can we help you?" one of the men asked, eyes narrowed on Sean while two other men circled his car like hungry wolves.

"Nice accent, *asshole*," Sean said, purposefully provoking the bodyguard. "I'm here to see Hope. Who are you?"

"A friend," the guard lied. "And I'm sorry, but she's not available."

"Since when does she have fucking body guards outside of her home?" he asked, pulling out his cell phone. "I'm calling her. I don't believe you. For all I know, she could be held hostage in that place." As soon as he dialed Hope, her phone went to voice mail. He hung up quickly and hit *camera* on his screen. Snapping photos of the man in his face, he raised a suggestive brow as if to imply *now what*?

"Sir, I'm going to have to ask you to leave the property," the man said, tired of talking to Sean. "And I'm going to have to insist that you not return. Ms. Daniels doesn't want to see you."

"Let *her* tell me that," Sean said, snapping another photo of him. "Where are you from anyway? Definitely not from around here. London? Australia?"

The man looked at the phone and then at the other guard on the other side of the car as if he wanted to take it from Sean. He clenched down on his jaw and tried to stay as professional as possible. "Where I'm from is not important. I'll tell you one more time to please remove yourself and your vehicle from the property, and then after that I'm going to assist you," he said, moving his jacket where Sean could see the gun in its holster.

"I don't know if you've noticed, but I'm an American citizen," Sean sneered. "And you also happen to be on American soil, you piece of euro trash."

The bodyguard on the other side of the car laughed aloud.

Leaning closer, the guard closest to him lowered his voice and smiled, squinting as the sun shined in his green eyes. "Piss off, you fucking wanker, or I'll make a bloody mess of ya. How's that for an explanation?"

Reality was quick to set in with the threat. This was private property. Sean knew that he could be shot at any point once being told to leave no matter who Michael was or was not.

Happy with his initial proof, he nodded at the bodyguard as he noticed a menacingly wide man on the porch watching with his hands folded. On the side of the house were two more men in suits, standing still and watching their surroundings with ear pieces.

This was confirmation enough for him and a little too close for comfort.

As he pulled out in the road, he quickly picked his phone back up and sent the photos to Hannibal. Only seconds after he had hit send, the phone rang. Sean laughed as he answered. "Well, it's not a picture of Michael per se, but you can't tell me that you don't recognize the men on his detail."

Hannibal exhaled a deep sigh. "I've got the check for $100,000, and I'll be there in literally two and a half hours."

"I'll be waiting with an address," Sean said, hanging up the phone. "Thank you, Hope!"

Chapter 15

Exactly one hour from the time that Geoff relayed Prince Richard's message Michael was being transported via motorcade to the historic Peabody Hotel in downtown Memphis.

With bright blue skies and unseasonably cool weather, it seemed that even though it was morning there were tons of people milling about outside. All it would take was just one tourist with a good eye or a good phone to spot him, and blast this entire project to smithereens. That was why Michael thought this meeting to be uncalled for and in extremely poor taste for a man so concerned about his family's appearance, but that was Richard – the *do as I say and not as I do* prince.

Their drive from Hernando, Mississippi 20 miles north had been epic, especially for the town's folk. His cocktail of an entourage included DeSoto County Sheriffs with flashing lights and sirens until he crossed the state line where Memphis Police Department's Tact Unit took over and escorted him with his personal security, Prince Richard's extended security team, the State Department and God only knew who else through the city.

Hope had stood in the doorway watching with her mouth open as they all loaded in – all except the men he insisted stay with her to keep her safe. After all, she was his now, and he couldn't afford to have anything happen to her or anyone disturb her.

He was grateful that she didn't debate the issue. Instead, she simply raised a brow and grabbed her coffee mug. "If this is what it takes to keep you safe, then you have to do it," she said with understanding.

"I like her," Geoff said under his breath as he followed Michael off the porch.

Now, they were finally here.

Michael didn't particularly like having to possibly blow his cover to see his brother, but he did know foreign protocol. Traveling into a city as large as Memphis for an *official* meeting with all of these additional bodies and vehicles required taking the most security measures possible. A handful of very capable security men, Geoff included, had coordinated his small trip down to the last detail. Streets had been blocked off; snipers had been put in place on the top of the hotel, the perimeter had been secured and the entrances to the hotel had been shut down, all so he could spend a few minutes arguing with his sibling. He was certain that Richard would not have it any other way. He was a stickler about security, demanding the most elaborate precautions possible.

Michael slipped his sleek Aviator shades over his eyes as he stepped out of the back of his bulletproof SUV. He straightened his suit and then followed his men up the covered pathway to a secure entrance of the building.

Under his black Armani suit, he wore his custom-made slim fitting body armor and on his own accord, he always wore his own personal sidearm, just in case.

The extra layers of clothing and materials made him heat up a little bit under his clothes, and he was happy to be greeted by the cool blast of air as the doors opened.

Quickly, he was ushered through hollow hallways cleared by men in uniforms and wearing semi-automatic rifles to a large service elevator and with men standing in front of him and behind him, they loaded inside, sucking all the cool air out again.

By the time that he arrived to the Presidential Suite, he felt absolutely exhausted and reminded of why he was enjoying the simple life with Hope so much. He had never been allowed to just be a normal man before, but after getting a taste of it, he rather preferred it to the theatrics of the crown.

As soon as the doors opened to the luxury suite, the first person that he saw was Geoff's big brother, who was also Richard's best friend and confidant, William Becking. He was 10 years his brothers' senior, but his physical appearance made him look old enough to be Geoff's father. From years of late night strategies and worrying about the royal family's every detail, he had gone bald and what had not fallen out had turned gray. He had fine crow's feet at the corner of his ash gray eyes and a pale skin. However, just like his brother, he had a wide frame and a tall, bulking build.

He sat with a cup of tea, legs crossed in a $5,000 black suit speaking on his Bluetooth, but when the doors opened he abruptly ended his call. Standing slowly, he bowed to Michael and then nodded more informally at Geoff.

"Your Highness," William said with an air of arrogance that spoke of generations of service to the crown.

"William," Michael said simply. "Where is my brother?"

"Just being looked after by the doctor. He wasn't quite himself after the long trip over, sir."

"What doctor?" Michael said, walking toward the master bedroom. "Is Dudley here also?"

"Yes," William said, walking behind him. "It was the council's suggestion that he travel with a doctor from now on." There was only a short stutter in his words. "He is in his late 40s. A man needs constant attention after 25, especially a prince."

His light-hearted joke made Michael suspicious. William never joked, barely smirked and only smiled pleasantly once a year to make sure that the muscles in his mouth still worked.

As Michael was about to open the bedroom doors, they swung open and his brother emerged, fully dressed and as poised as ever. Standing taller than life, Richard looked his brother up and down and then offered his hand.

"Good of you to come," Richard said, shaking Michael's hand firmly.

"The message didn't sound like there was an alternative," Michael said, eyes narrowed on his brother. "What is this about? You fly thousands of miles to check on me now?" Even in his wildest years, his brother had never done such a thing.

"No," Richard said, sitting down in the chair furthest from the windows. He crossed his legs and rested his elbow on the arm rest. Wiping his face with his hand, he bit his lip. As he did so, his ring flashed in the sunlight. "I flew thousands of miles to retrieve you. This charade has ended as of..." he looked at his Patek watch. "Well, as of now."

Michael looked around the room. *So that is what this was about?* "Retrieve me," he repeated gravely. *He'd like one of them to try.* Shaking his head in defiance, he slipped his balled up fists in the pockets of his pants. "I'm not going anywhere."

Richard rolled his eyes. "Don't be a child. The story is out there. RQL received Intel that was confirmed by Hope's ex-lover that you are in Hernando, Mississippi. You can't expect to go back there now. This suite is simply your theatre holding area until you are escorted back to the plane."

"How do you know that RQL believes him? What did you do? Bribe an intern?"

Richard smirked. "Don't be stupid. I'm the Prince of England. I don't bribe anyone. William made a call to the editor who told him that Hannibal was on a flight from Los Angeles to Memphis."

"And why would she tell you that?" Michael asked, stepping closer to the door.

Richard smiled cleverly. "Because...I am the Prince of England." He released a sigh. "It's good to have favors occasionally from the crown when you visit England as much as that woman does. However, that is truly beside the point.

The *point* and the fact of the matter is that you're leaving for London now. Someone else can collect your things. I doubt that there is anything of real consequence."

"I'm not leaving here without Hope," Michael said sternly. His jaw clenched tighter.

Richard's aggravation grew apparent. "What is your problem? How do you continue to make these monumental mistakes? This woman, Hope Daniels, is not the type of woman you bring back to England and declare to the world as Thalia's replacement."

"Please don't tell me it's because she's black," Michael bit out.

"Don't be so ridiculous. It's not that she's black. It's that she's a commoner, a United States citizen, and..." Richard watched his brother's posture become more erect, "and her family is not desirable."

"Her mother." Michael knew that it would come up eventually, he was just glad that it could come up now where he could address it out of her presence.

"Yes," Richard said, glad that Michael already knew. "Her mother."

"Her mother is dead." Michael had heard enough. He turned to head to the door.

"Well, the scandal behind her life and her mother's death won't be, and we have no time for this. There are other responsibilities that you need to handle as the Prince of England. You have obligations to the crown, Michael."

Michael spun around. "No, that would be your obligation! Everyone knows you're going to be king, and I have no objections to that, brother. I truly do not. You're perfect for the job. But I want nothing to do with it."

William looked at Richard and then lowered his head. It was a small gesture, but one that Geoff quickly picked up on even though Michael – in a rage – had not.

Richard stood up from the chair. "I'll make you."

"You'll try," Michael said, legs planted firmly. "And you'll fail."

"Do you think this is a game?" Richard said, stalking up to his brother. He stared him in the eye.

It was then that Michael noticed that his brother looked peaked and pale. His eyes were darker than normal under his lids. "What's wrong? Where's mother?" Michael asked, feeling like something wasn't right. "Nearly two months ago you were chomping at the bit to get me out of the public eye, now you are demanding that I go back there?" he asked, fuming with anger. "To that place. Is she sick?"

"That *place* is your home," Richard reminded. "And nothing is wrong, but you being here. It was a mistake to suggest it, a mistake to see it through. I take full responsibility, but now it's time to remedy the situation."

"You're impossible," Michael snapped.

"This conversation is over. You are going back today, and that's final," Richard said, going back to his chair to have a seat. He seemed out of breath.

"I will not," Michael said low and serious. "Not without Hope."

"Because you love her?" Richard asked mockingly. "In two days, you've fallen in love?"

"It's been longer than two days and you know it," Michael argued.

"It's closer to two days than the years you invested in Thalia and look how that ended up. Don't you see that you're worse than an impulse shopper when it comes to love? You see a girl. You like the girl. You suddenly love the girl. Normally, it all happens in the same blink of your pretty little blue eyes. And in the next blink there is someone else."

"Don't patronize me," Michael growled. "I won't stand for it."

William walked over to the chair and bent to Richard. Whispering something quickly in his ear that made Richard nod in agreement, he looked back up at Michael and calmed himself.

"Very well. Go prove my point, you insolent child. Go back to her, try and retrieve her. If she won't agree, then my point is proven. I've heard various reports that she might have more sense than you anyway." He shook his head in disgust. "In three hours, the Royal Family is leaving the United States. And if I have to drug you and have you put on that plane in a coma, I will. I swear it on God and Country."

Michael knew his brother too well to doubt him. Turning on his heels, he stalked out of the suite and headed for the elevators. The men with him quickly followed.

"Something is going on," Michael said to Geoff. "Find out what it is for me."

Nodding, Geoff got onto the elevator with him. "We have to hurry, Your Highness."

"I know," Michael said, looking down at his watch. He only prayed that Hope would follow him.

Chapter 16

Before Michael could arrive back at Hope's house, the story had already broken and a complete media frenzy had quickly ensued. RQL had released not only the location of Michael's whereabouts but also Hope's name and photo.

Her face was plastered all over the front of RQL's webpage and had been picked up by 25 other national outlets, not to mention the story being shared over 100,000 times on Facebook and Twitter.

Radio stations were reporting on it as well as blogs.

Hope Daniels' name was on the lips of everyone who had a phone or a computer. She was being discussed in office buildings, gyms, hair salons, gas stations, homes and dorms across continents.

On top of what was going on in the media, her cellphone was blowing up every few seconds. Text after text came in from random people that she had not talked to in years. They wanted her to know that they had seen the story on her, and her photo, her story.

As soon as the madness began, the first thing she did was go online and cancel all of her social media pages. She couldn't take one more friend request. On top of that, she had received at least 600 friend requests in the last few minutes. Madness.

She was holding it together as well as she could, but when she turned on the television and saw her photo as the news broke on local media, she had to sit down. Photo after photo of her popped up on the screen as people literally gave commentary about her life.

"Oh, my, Lord!" she exclaimed. "Do these people have no respect for people's private lives?"

Her five seconds of fame had begun and she couldn't wait for it to be over. She knew that being with Michael would be a battle, but she did not expect it to hit so abruptly. Is this what he had to deal with every day of his life? It was pure chaos. No wonder the man was hiding out in Mississippi. This was enough to drive someone insane.

Seeing Bree's number cross her phone, she picked it up quickly and stalked out of the den where Michael's bodyguard stood by the window watching her every move.

"Hello," Hope said, running a frustrated hand through her hair. She didn't drink but she felt like she could use one at the moment.

"What the hell is going on?" Bree asked, closing the door to her office so no one could hear her.

"They found out," Hope said, shaking her head. "It's all over everywhere."

Bree plopped down in her chair and looked at her computer screen. "I know. I read the RQL article online. They interviewed that son of bitch, Sean. He spilled the beans. Told them everything." She took a deep hesitant breath. "They called me too."

Hope froze in her tracks. "They called you?" She frowned in confusion. "How did they get your number?"

"Girl, it's the media. They can find you if they want to. I just told them I didn't know what the hell they were talking about. My question is, what are you going to do?" Bree knew that her best friend was not a very public person. So while this would blow some girls' skirts right up, this would only make Hope back off.

"I don't know what to do," Hope said, frantic. "I'm waiting for Michael to get back. He text me and said he was on the way from seeing his brother." She paced in the hallway. "My face is all over the damn television. And people are literally trying to get in my driveway." She walked back to the living room and looked out of the window at the security guards cutting off media trucks as they lined up down the road.

"Do you need to come here for a while?" Bree asked sincerely. "You can hide out for a while until this dies down."

The idea of leaving Michael scared her. Plus, she had her work to finish. "I don't know," Hope said, hearing her phone beep. She looked at it and saw another blocked number. "Girl, I may have to change my number. So, I'll text you if I do."

"Okay." Bree sounded defeated for Hope. "If you need me, I'm here."

"Thanks," Hope said, closing her blinds. "For now, I'm just going to wait for Michael. He'll know what to do."

"Okay, call me later. Love you."

"Love you too," Hope said, hanging up her phone. She turned to see the guard standing behind her. That was another thing that she was not used to – someone lurking around like a ninja-but maybe he could be useful. "How far away is he?" she asked, throwing her phone on the sofa table. She was done with that thing for the day too. It was annoying hearing it ding every few seconds.

The suited man tried to provide her as much comfort as he could. Touching his earpiece and listening, he stoically answered Hope. "He's on his way momentarily, ma'am."

Hope blinked. "What does that mean?" she asked, voice strained. "Is he five minutes away? Ten?" She hunched her shoulders waiting for a real answer this time.

He repeated the same answer as before in the same monotone British accent. "He will be here shortly," the man answered, going to the window. "I need you stay away from the windows and doors."

"Why?" she asked, as he physically guided her away from the large bay windows. She snatched away.

"For your safety," he answered, even though he knew she was frustrated. He couldn't say in her situation that he blamed her.

That was a new one for Hope- her safety. Was she in danger now? Moving out of the view of the windows, she threw her hands up in the air, suppressing her rising nervousness. "You know what, I'm going to my room. When Michael gets here, tell him to meet me there, please. I need to talk to him about my face being all over the news."

"Yes ma'am," the man answered like a robot. Standing by the door with this hands resting in front of him, he quietly stood his post. He had learned from many years of training and serving Prince Michael to keep his answers short, concise and keep all of his opinions to himself.

Confounded, she turned and stalked toward the stairs, exhausted mentally by the media combat she had experienced. "I don't know how you people deal with this day in and day out."

The man smirked as he watched her make her way up the stairs. "You'll find out soon enough," he said under his breath.

***

Getting Michael onto the property undetected was going to be tricky, especially with his security detail. As they approached the property on the narrow road, the police literally had to go before them and clear the way. Reporters ran alongside of his SUV, trying to get a shot of Michael in the back seat, or the man that they thought was him. Others stood out in the weedy vacant lot across from Hope's home giving reports and pointing toward the convoy.

Used to the media bedlam, Michael had jumped in an unmarked police car with tinted windows. He slipped on a Memphis Grizzlies baseball hat, taken off his suit jacket and rode with one of his personal guards. While everyone was looking for him to jump out of the Yukon, he had slipped right pass them in the long convoy and was pulled around to the back of the house.

Running in with Geoff quickly to get out of the madness, Michael pulled off his hat and called out for Hope.

"Where is she?" he asked the guard.

"She's upstairs, sir," the man answered quickly. "She asked for you to meet her up there - alone."

Geoff grabbed Michael by the arm, making the other guards tense up. He swallowed hard. "You don't have much time. You need to get her to decide."

He nodded in understanding. "I will," Michael said, looking at his watch. "Have one of the men grab my things."

"They already have," Geoff assured Michael. "We just need her."

"Well tell them to stand by and be ready to grab her things," he said while running up the stairs.

Normally, Hope kept the bay windows of the bedroom open this time of year to soak up all the natural light and enjoy the fresh clean air, but with media outlets doing live shots from only a hundred feet away, she opted to close her windows and pull the curtains. She wanted privacy. For two seconds, she wanted to be left alone.

Perched on the end of her bed, she slumped over and held her head in her hands. This was a bit much. Only, she didn't want to scare off Michael by looking as worried as she actually was.

"Hope!" Michael screamed out as he rounded the corner into the bedroom.

Hope quickly stood to her feet. "Hey," she said, wiping the grimace from her lips before he kissed her.

Holding her tight, he rubbed her back. "Are you alright?"

"This is crazy," Hope said in a huff. "They've basically splashed my entire life on the screen in a matter of hours."

He tried to make light of their situation. "Yeah, the 24-hour news cycle can be vicious. I'm sorry about that." The look on his face confirmed his sincerity. "Look, we need to talk."

"Okay," she said, as he led her back to the bed. Sitting down with her, he took a deep breath. How did he say this in a thoughtful way?

"This *situation* has become a security concern for my family and as an indirect result, a concern for my country. I've been..." He bit his lip in frustration, still breathing hard from his run up the stairs. Pausing, he realized that he didn't have time to go into full detail. The men were waiting. "I have to go back." Staring at the floor, he shook his head. "I'd stay here for the rest of my life if I could, but..."

Hope stopped him, eyes watering at the sides. "I understand. You have to leave." She shook her head and fiddled with her fingers. "It couldn't last forever, right?"

Michael looked up and frowned. "Wait. No, I'm stuttering. My apologies. I don't think that I'm making myself clear. I want you to come with me." He turned to her and grabbed her soft hands, holding them in his own. If she only knew how much this meant to him, it might scare her.

"Go with you?" Hope was lost for words. She wasn't expecting this. A break up maybe, but not this. She swallowed hard, trying to hide her complete awe.

He smiled. "I can't leave you here."

"Because of the media attention?"

His eye lashes fluttered. "That's only one reason, yes. The biggest reason is that I don't want to be alone without you again." Moving a strand of hair from her face, he rubbed her cheek with his thumb. "I have some things to take care of back in London. Come with me. Please."

She could barely process his request. "What about my work?"

"I'll have it flown to us."

She tilted her head. "What about my house?"

"I'll have a security team watch it until we return?"

The word *we* had never sounded so sweet as coming from his lips.

Her voice grew softer but her eyes more serious. "What about my life?"

He lifted her chin with his finger. "It's with me."

She couldn't help but blush. "Do you have an answer for everything?"

"No, but I want to protect you. I want to keep you near me. Unless..."

"Unless what?" she asked, back rigid.

"Was this just a fling for you?" His heart nearly stopped beating.

Hope bucked her eyes. "No. God no! Was this a fling for you?"

"No," he said softly. "Not at all."

Resting her shoulders slightly, she looked around her room. "London, huh?"

"Yes."

"I've never been to London."

He could tell she was close to saying yes. "I know. But you'll love it."

"When?"

"Now," he said, standing up. "Right now," he clarified.

"Now?" her nervousness peeked.

"It's sudden. I know, and I'm sorry. But we have to leave now."

Hope had always been a smart woman. She had chosen her life path very carefully. And very deliberately, she had come to live in this home instead of selling it and jetting off to a city that would be more adequately suited for her profession like New York or Los Angeles. She had not had children out of wedlock, although at times she considered artificial insemination or adoption, simply to keep from being alone. She had kept her finances in order, never taking out unneeded loans or indulging in credit cards.

She had worked out religiously and gone to annual doctor visits on time to make sure that she was healthy as possible, and she had resisted temptation, especially when times were hard. These had been the tenants formed by the parenting of her grandparents. Their teachings through the years had kept her safe from many of the pitfalls of being young and spontaneous.

And because of that, she had become spontaneous-adverse. It was an odd thing to call it, but that was what she had coined as being safe.

Until she met Michael.

After meeting Michael, she had never felt so free and alive, and it wasn't because he believed in jumping out of airplanes or climbing mountains or any other crazy things. In fact, he was a pretty mellow man in all. It was because of how he made her heart feel. It was because he made her feel like she was the only woman in the room.

And she'd never had low self-esteem about herself.

She'd never second-guessed herself...much.

But here she was in this room, trying to decide if she should leave her home and jet off to another country with the Prince of England.

Michael took her silence as a bad sign. "Hope," he said, bringing her attention back to him.

She raised a brow and slowly pulled her gaze from the wall up to his beautiful face, bright with eagerness and determination. "Hmm?"

His blue eyes burned through her. "Are you going with me?" he asked again.

She let out a sigh and gave a tight smile. "Michael, I realize that you don't want to leave me with the impression that you don't care. And I don't think that at all, but you don't have to throw me on your back and carry me across the world like some newly acquired baggage because you slept with me. I'm not that fragile. I'll be okay. I promise."

"You think I'm doing this to keep from hurting your feelings?" he asked.

Hope had to be honest with him. She might not ever see him again. "Yes."

He raked a hand across his face and settled it at his chin. *Women.* "I'm doing this because I want to be with you." He walked to the window and looked out the curtains. More camera men unloaded from their vans and trucks by the minute. By nightfall, the house would be turned into a complete media circus with him as the ring master.

"This is a gamble," he admitted.

Hope didn't answer but agreed.

"On top of asking you to leave your country, I'm asking you to do it in the next hour," he said, watching as her head snapped toward him. He nodded at her. "Yes, it's rushed. Yes, it's sudden. Yes, it's crazy," he said, turning toward her.

Hope shook her head. "With that many omissions, your *but* statement better be good."

He smiled despite himself. She could always bring the humor out of him. "But..." he began walking back over to her. He grabbed her hands and pulled her off the bed. Looking into her eyes, he held her close. "But I love you."

Hope's breath caught in her chest and she had to force herself to blink. Did he just say what she thought he said...what she felt? Mouth flying open, she nearly buckled at the knees.

"Do you love me?" Michael asked, hoping that unlike Thalia, this woman who seemed to be so good and so pure, would actually tell him the truth.

Hope clenched his back. "Yes, I love you very much," she said, fighting tears again.

"Then come with me," he whispered on her lips. He kissed her gently. "Let's go on a little adventure."

Hope felt herself saying the words, but she couldn't believe that she was saying them. "Okay."

***

In all her years, Hope had never been packed so quickly. Michael's men were all given directions with Geoff leading the charge and within 30 minutes, she was downstairs with Michael full-packed and waiting for the helicopter to arrive in her backyard.

The idea sounded preposterous to Hope at first. She was literally awaiting an aircraft to land in her three-acre backyard. The game plan was for it to take them to the Memphis International Airport where she would board a private jet with Michael and return to London.

It sounded simple enough in theory, but the truth of the matter was that she was quietly shaking in her boots.

Literally, she had put on some of her low-heeled, brown boots to trek through the grass in the backyard, along with dark blue jeans and comfortable red fitted t-shirt that stopped at her hips. With a brown leather backpack thrown over her shoulder and shades over her eyes, she had pulled back her hair into a wispy ponytail, slipped on her grandmother's watch and her grandfather's dog tags, sprayed on perfume and slipped on gloss.

Michael on the other hand, looked like a million dollars in his tailor-made suit. He stood beside her on his cell phone talking to his brother in a low monotone voice while the guards made sure the perimeter was secure.

Unable to help herself, she left his side and went and turned on the television in the living room. Shocked, she saw none other than Sean Pritchard giving an interview on a local affiliate station of Fox.

"You've got to be kidding me?" she bit out, perching on the end of her sofa.

"What?" Michael asked, hanging up with Richard. He hadn't meant for her to see the television at all until they arrived safely in London.

"Sean," Hope said, pointing at the television. "I guess we know now who turned you in. It just doesn't seem fair that he be allowed to cash in on this."

Only a few feet away from Hope's house, a bandaged-up Sean Pritchard stood talking to a reporter about being assaulted by the prince all while pretending to be such a saint himself.

"He's got a very hot temper," Sean said, rolling his eyes. "I mean, look at my nose. This guy, out of nowhere, sucker punched me for no reason at all. I guess he didn't think that he could take me in any other way."

Michael snarled. "I hope that I broke his nose."

"How well do you know Hope Daniels?" the reporter asked. "Reports say that you were lovers."

"She and I were in love until recently. Things went downhill. I think it was simply because we just were working so hard. Our competing schedules caused us to drift apart, but she still means the world to me."

"Liar!" Hope turned from the television. "Turn it off," she said, holding her head.

The guard quickly turned off the television for her.

"He cheated on me with another woman and accused me of it being my fault because I was black.   That hardly qualifies as competing schedules. Can you believe him? "

"Yes," Michael said, looking at his watch. It had happened to him for most of his adult life. *Half-truths. Whole lies.* It was all the same.

"And he's just going to get away with it?" Hope put her hand on her hip, disgusted by Sean just a little more than before, which wasn't hard to do.

Michael shrugged. "They often do. It sells gossip magazines.   So lies will continue to trump truth." Seeing the frustration in her face, he went over and rubbed her back. "Now, now. I'm sure that everything will be okay. Sean Pritchard is in your past. You just have to move past him and his lies."

"He's making you look like a monster," Hope reminded.

"He won't be the first," Michael said soothingly, hiding his frustration with her ex-boyfriend.

Geoff walked through the back screen door with wind picking up behind him. His men were in place and the aircraft had landed, which was causing the media across the street to go crazy. They knew in just a moment, Prince Michael would again be out of their reach. Motioning toward Michael and Hope, Geoff stood in front of the opening with his ear piece in and his gun visible.   "Helicopter's here, Your Highness. We're ready for you."

Michael turned to Hope and smiled. "Are you ready for some fun?"

Hope didn't know what to say. She'd never been in a helicopter before, never been in a private jet, never been chased by the paparazzi, and never had one of these experiences. Shrugging her slim shoulders, she smiled. "Guess so."

Knowing that this was all new to Hope, Geoff raised his palm suddenly. "A few things, Ms. Daniels. Stay away from the rear of the helicopter. Crouch low before getting to and going under the main rotor. Approach the helicopter from the side or front, but never out of the pilot's line of vision. Hold firmly to loose articles. Never reach up or dart after a hat or other object that might be blown off or away. Protect your eyes by shielding with a hand or by squinting, even though you have on shades. And if suddenly blinded by dust or a blowing object, stop and crouch lower or, better yet, sit down and wait for help." He looked between Hope and Michael. "You got all of that."

"No," Hope said, having second thoughts.

Grabbing her hand, Michael kissed her cheek. "In other words, stay by me."

She nodded. "Will do."

Michael's excitement showed in his wide grin. "Good." He looked over at Geoff. "Did you take care of that thing I asked you to?"

"It's done," he said, opening the door for them. "Alright. Let's get you loaded and the hell out of Hernando, Mississippi."

As they came out of the house, they were covered on both sides and in the front and back by body guards. Making their way quickly to the helicopter, Geoff loaded Hope on first and then Michael, despite obvious protocols. Michael had already briefed him prior to the arrival of the plane that Hope was to be completely taken care of during her entire stay with him – no matter what.

When they were both on the plane, Hope noticed a woman she'd seen on CNC news outlet a thousand times. Looking over at Michael, she whispered. "What is going on?"

Michael pulled off his shades and shook the reporter's hand as she offered.

"Thanks for giving me five minutes, Your Highness."

"My pleasure," Michael said, buttoning his suit jacket.

"Ready to go live?"

"I am," he said, holding Hope's hand.

"We're live with Prince Michael and his girlfriend Hope Daniels. They are on their way out of the country. However, exclusive to CNC, he has agreed to give us one statement on his relationship and on the allegations against him by Sean Pritchard," the woman said into the camera that the man was holding beside her. Turning to Michael, she put the microphone up to him.

"It's a shame that we have to deal with this type of behavior in the 21st century. But I will say that Sean Prichard is worse than a liar. He's an opportunist and a bigot. The altercation that did not happen the way that he said, but did happen, was a result of his constant harassment of her, his belittlement of her as a woman and his attack on her race. Evidently, her being African-American was the source of their breakup and the source of his feelings of control over her life. I do not believe in those bigoted attitudes toward women or races. Quite frankly I'm utterly disgusted by the man."

"Any other things that you'd like to add, Ms. Daniels?" the woman asked Hope.

Squeezing Michael's hand, Hope pulled off her shades and looked into the camera. "Sean Prichard and I were never in love. He's obviously capitalizing off this situation and he's angry that he was emasculated by Michael, even before he knew who he was. This is simply another case of someone trying to cash in on lies.   I just hope the American public can see right through him."

"Thank you for your time," the woman said with a smug grin. "Safe travels to London."

"Thank you," Michael said as the reporter was escorted off the helicopter and Geoff loaded in. "Well, that handles that. I never respond to this kind of rubbish. But I promise you this, whatever he financially hoped to gain from coming out publicly; he will lose in professional circles of influence."

Hope was astounded. "You did that for me?" she asked.

"Yes. Anything to make you happy," he said as they felt themselves begin to make their ascent in the air. "You have no idea how happy I'm going to make you."

Chapter 17

The Matsworth House
The Dowager Duchess of Matsworth

No matter how Nathaniel tried, he couldn't get enough of Thalia. Even after three times of making love back-to-back to her that afternoon, he still could not ravage her enough. It was the way that her silky skin felt under between his fingers, the way that her hair spilled like oil against the nude-colored silk sheets. As the sun began to roll behind the vast green hills of the historic manor home, he hid his body from the rays of setting sun coming in from across the room under twisted sheets and pillows. Rolling around in the comforter as she giggled and kissed his neck, he buried his head in her lushness and drove himself deeper in between her succulent thighs.

"Harder!" she whispered in his ear right before she tugged at his lobe with her perfect white teeth.

He closed his eyes, trying to gain more self-control, and grabbed the end of the mattress for better positioning, then arched his back and thrust into her as she commanded.

They both let out a gasp of pure unadulterated pleasure.

"Is that hard enough, love?" he asked, sucking her spear-like tongue.

"Not nearly," she said, running her hands down the length of his slim back and grabbing his adorable bare backside. Opening her legs wider, she undulated under him, driving him insane with the motion of her hips. "There," she moaned.

"Right there?" he asked, raising up to see her tan angelic face.

Her blue eyes flashed open and gazed at him under heavy black lashes. "Yes," she panted.

Moving faster, he pumped into her body, making the headboard slam loudly into the wall. Grunting, he licked the sweat off her neck.

Feeling her tight womb pulsate with pleasure, she looked up at him as her climax began to surface.

"Yes," she said again, this time with much more base in her throaty moan.

"Thalia," he said, clenching his jaw.

"I'm so close," she panted. "So fucking close!"

Her father couldn't have timed his entrance any more perfectly. Right before she rushed full on into her orgasm, the doors to her bedroom burst open and a well-dressed man and his son came barging in.

Hitting the light switch, he startled both of them.

Quickly, they began to scramble to hide from their new uninvited audience.

Nathaniel tried to cover himself as he quickly rolled over on his back and snatched the comforter. "Shit!" he exclaimed, wiping his brow. "What is this?"

"Father! What the hell are you doing?" Thalia asked, panting still. "Get out!" Pushing her back up against the headboard, she looked up at her father, stern and rigid, as he walked casually over and stood over them with his arms folded across his chest.

"Just what do you think that you are doing?" he asked as his son, Mitchell went to the other side of the bed and literally pulled Nathaniel out of the bed by his blonde mop of hair.

"Grab your clothes and get the fuck out of here," Mitchell ordered, pushing Nathaniel towards the butler and the door.

Thalia screamed in anger. "What are you doing in my room invading my privacy?"

Picking up the remote, he turned on the television and changed the channel to the news. The breaking story was Prince Michael loading into a helicopter in Hernando, Mississippi with Hope Daniels. Throwing the remote on the bed, he looked down at his daughter as she tried to cover herself up.

"Do you know why I made you stay here at the family house instead of your flat in London?" he asked, ignoring Mitchell as he shoved Nathaniel out of the door and closed it behind him.

Thalia tried to process what she was seeing on the television. "To make me miserable. To punish me," she said, frowning at the sight of Hope.

"I brought you here to keep you under lock and key until Prince Richard had time to deal with Michael on his own and make him see his error. I brought you here to keep you out of the newspapers and off the television and to honor the contract that we have with the royal family to keep our business out of the social pages. Do you know why I did that?"

Thalia could barely turn from the television. *Did her eyes deceive her?* "To protect your name," she said smugly.

Her father's frustration ramped higher. "To ensure that your virtue would not be in question when the Prince came to his senses," her father snapped.

"My virtue?" Thalia said with a smirk.

Her father ignored her less than noble reply. "But what Prince will want you if he finds out that you're sleeping with your lowly tennis instructor?" He bent to her, close enough for her to see the dirt on his gold-rimmed glasses. "Stupid girl. Do you know how long it took me to make you favorable enough for the Queen's son? I spend hundreds of thousands of pounds to make you into the most logical, obvious choice out of the other women vying for his attention. I paid off families. I ruined reputations. I spent a third of my fortune investing in your lifestyle."

She leaned into her father and sneered at him. "I'm not stupid. I'm tired!" she screamed, hitting the mattress with her balled up fist. "I'm tired of pretending. I'm tired of waiting. I'm tired of placating."

"I will say so. You ruined your engagement by telling the Prince of England that you didn't love him."

"It's true."

"It's irrelevant!" he said, throwing up his hands. "An idiot could have known better than to admit to something so..."

"So true?" Thalia pulled the covers tighter over her breasts and raised up slightly in the bed. "I have done everything that you have asked of me. I offered myself on a platter to a man I do not love so I could protect this family's name and financial future. I've laughed at his ridiculous jokes, listened to his God-awful music, kept my peace on his far-fetched domestic and foreign policies and agreed to marry him and give him more ridiculous children. I've done all of it for the sake of this family. I hardly think that qualifies as idiotic or stupid. But finally he asked me very sincerely one question that I could not lie about and I answered him truthfully and it cost me everything. One question! Sue me!"

"We sued him, remember? For you, we took money from the crown, from our country to remedy your decision to be honest." Her father shook his head. "You made yourself lie for your entire courtship. What made it so hard to lie then?"

"He said he loved me, and I reciprocated by saying the same. He kissed me; I kissed him back. He desired me; I desired the crown. And I still desire it, but that has been my only focus – for you, for this family and for myself. When he asked if I would stand by him, love him even when he denounced his royal rights as a Prince to move off and be some godforsaken philanthropist toiling away in Africa with his charity organization, I answered truthfully because I thought that it would make him see that his place was here in England with *his* people."

"You said you didn't love him!" her father exclaimed, reiterating her betrayal to both the family and Michael.

"I said I wouldn't marry him if he were not the Prince of England. That I couldn't bear to think of leaving this country and being something other than what we were born to be...royal." She breathed hard, nostrils flared as she glared at him. "I told him the truth. I loved what we could become as a force of power for this country. Our two families joined would make England stronger."

"You told him that you didn't love him! You don't tell a man like that something like that and expect for him to simply brush it under his royal rug!" Her father swallowed down a breath of disbelief. "It was a test, Thalia. Pure and simple. He was testing you. The man would never denounce his royal birthright. It is what gives him the ability to fund his charity and do his work. He was testing you – testing your relationship."

"You don't know him like I do. You didn't put in the hours, the days, the weeks, the years. He *would* denounce his rightful place. He probably still will. I saved you the embarrassment of being associated with the first Prince of England to run off from his country with his tail tucked between his poor privileged legs because his family, or someone in it fed his mind with too much liberal thinking."

"There is talk," her father said, eye brow raised. He lowered his voice. "The Queen is nearly 70. Her husband is dead. The next in line is Prince Richard. And there is talk in secret that he is ill. This constitutional monarch requires a Sovereign. When the Queen passes away either from old age or sickness, if her elder son is already dead…"

Thalia couldn't blink though she tried.

Her father continued with a more even tone now that he had her full attention. "Even if Michael had plans to dishonor his family and denounce his thrown, which I seriously doubt all together, that time has come and passed. If Richard is truly sick, terminally so, then the next King of England is…"

"Michael," Thalia finished in nearly a whisper. "Oh my God." Rubbing the hair from her face, she pulled herself together. "How reliable is this talk, these rumors?"

Her father wouldn't give his source. "As reliable as it comes." He knew that she'd read between the lines. Standing back up straight, he pulled at his suit jacket.

"Right." Thalia said, looking back over at the anchor man still reporting on Michael's new girlfriend. A photo of Hope flashed on the

television, making her cringe. "Well that changes things dramatically. So what do you suggest
we do about her?"

Her father walked to the bedroom door. "We
will do what any self-respecting family would
do. We will discredit her entire existence and
make her completely unsuitable for the Prince.
I'll start making calls immediately to our friends
in the media and government to see what can
be dug up on her. By the time that he arrives
back in London with his little starving artist,
we'll have torn her apart. He'll have no choice
but to send her back and be done with whatever is between him."

Pulling herself out of bed, Thalia dragged
her sheet toward her bathroom. She had to get
ready – clean herself up and prepare to be as
beautiful and loving as possible when the
Prince returned from his exhausting travels.
And this time, she wouldn't get relaxed and
mess it up with being honest.

Pausing by the fireplace, she turned back to
her father with a deep breath. "Do me a favor,
daddy."

"Yes, dear. Anything," he said, ecstatic to
know that she was finally back on board.

Thalia smiled smugly. "Fire Nathaniel. Pay
him off and send him far away. I don't want him
to be a problem."

Her father smiled and opened the door. "He's already gone."

Chapter 18

Hope had never traveled out of the country, though for many years, she had her passport ready to be stamped. And never in a million years did she believe that she would travel to London. It wasn't exactly her ideal vacation destination. She had always imagined her first trip would be to Jamaica or Cozumel with the rest of the hordes of happy people going on cruises.

However, God seemed to laugh loudest at her plans.

Here she was in First Class on a British Airways flight landing on the tarmac of Heathrow Airport with the Prince of Wales. It was hard to believe, even as she looked down at his hand protectively over her own.

As if he could read her mind, he turned to her. "Are you nervous?" he asked, squeezing her hand gently.

His face made her smile involuntarily. "Yes. Is it that obvious?"

He shrugged. "I still get nervous sometimes with all the lights and madness. I guess that is why being in Hernando was so pleasant. For the first time in my life, I was left to just be myself."

"Well, being *yourself* is a wonderful thing," she said softly.

Looking over at Geoff, who was directly across the way, Hope raised a brow. "Does he ever sleep? I swear every time that I've looked over there, he's been awake – even after this long flight."

Michael sat up in his chair and smirked at Geoff, who was listening to them both. "He's a mean bastard. Military. Former MI6. A bit of a snake wrangler in my honest opinion. Nasty business...that Geoff."

Hope grinned. "I don't think he's mean. I just wondered if he sleeps."

"I do sleep, madam," Geoff answered gruffly. "Just not on planes when I'm escorting the Prince. After all, if I am a snake wrangler, the question is who am I wrangling?"

Michael pointed to Hope. "Her, of course."

Everyone laughed.

The British Airways staff, more formal than normal, quickly went to first assist the Prince and his entourage of eight, including Hope, who had booked up the entire First Class flight for security reasons. All smiles and perfectly applied make-up, they stood in waiting.

The head attendant came quickly to the in-
tercom and gave the current time and tempera-
ture in a chipper tone. "For your safety and
comfort, please remain seated with your seat
belt fastened until the Captain turns off the
Fasten Seat Belt sign. This will indicate that we
have parked at the gate and that it is safe for
you to move about." With a twinkle in her eye,
she kept her seductive gaze on Michael.

"Please check around your seat for
any personal belongings you may have brought
on board with you and please use caution when
opening the overhead bins, as heavy articles
may have shifted around during the flight," she
continued.

Hope had to giggle. Under her breath, she
nudged Michael slightly. "I think she has a crush
on you."

Michael blushed. "I thought she was looking
at you, my dear."

"If you require *deplaning assistance,* please
remain in your seat until all other passengers
have deplaned. One of our crew members will
then be pleased to assist you," the attendant
said even more directly to Michael.

"That was a bit much," Hope said with a
raised brow.

Geoff couldn't help his sudden growl. He
had seen the likes of the attendant a thousand

times on these trips, and it never ceased to amaze him how direct the women could be.

"We remind you to please wait until you are inside the terminal to use any electronic devices. On behalf of British Airways and the entire crew, I'd like to thank his Royal Highness, Prince of Wales and his esteemed guests as well as all of our other passengers for joining us on this trip, and we are looking forward to seeing you on board again in the near future. Have a nice evening."

As soon as the signal to move about the plane came on, Michael quickly unbuckled, glad to get that over with. Standing up, he offered Hope his hand. Slipping her little hand into his, she stood up just in time for him to plant a kiss on her full mouth. "Mmm," he said, pulling her close. "I can't wait to finally get you home, alone, away from all of these bloody people and into my bed."

The flight attendant immediately looked away. His sudden display of affection made it clear that he was not interested, and put to bed any discussion of him still being a playboy.

"I can't wait to be alone with you either," she said, as he bent and grabbed her purse from the floor.

"You'll be escorted off the plane first," Geoff informed Hope more than Michael. "After that, the rest of the plane will be allowed to disembark. Just remember to stay close and don't answer any questions."

Hope nodded but wondered who would have questions.

Quietly, she followed Michael and the rest of the entourage to the main cabin door. Shades covering her eyes, and baseball cap pulled down low over her face, she felt a surge of nervousness overcome her as the main cabin door opened. Michael grabbed her hand and they walked through the small port that had been completely emptied to the gate opening. As soon as they emerged out into the airport, flashing lights assailed them.

Reporters, cameramen and onlookers lined the sides of the roped off entry snapping pictures while fans screamed his name and professed how much they loved him.

Just as Geoff had suggested, Hope kept her head down and her hand locked in Michael's. She could feel a million eyes on her, crawling all over her, judging her. She nearly tripped until Michael slowed and turned to her. His bodyguards moved into the view of the cameras. "Hey," he said, with a gentle smile. "I won't let them get to you."

Hope nodded. She needed to hear that. Heart racing, she moved the backpack on her shoulder.   But Michael took it from her and passed it to one of his men.

"Are you ready?" he asked, looking toward the entrance.   "A few more hundred feet and we'll be in a car all alone again."

"I'll be fine," she said, hearing someone scream her name.   She was too afraid to turn and see who it was.   Walking with Michael again, she kept her eyes on the exit.

The   paparazzi   was   relentless.   They screamed questions out to them the entire time that they walked.   The camera flashed so many times until Hope was grateful for her dark shades.

"Turn around and give us one shot!" one of the photographers screamed.

Hope kept walking.

"Hope, give us a quote.   How did you meet the Prince?" another screamed.

She looked up at Michael, who kept his eyes on following his security, who pushed through the crowd and made a clear path for them.   *How does he survive this every day?* She asked herself inwardly.   The sight made her feel sorry for him and yet understanding of why he had run in the first place.

"Michael, what do you think Duchess Thalia will say when she finds out?" another reporter screamed.

"Is this just a fling?" another man screamed.

"Is she pregnant?" a woman screamed.

Hope and Michael were almost at the door to exit out into the light of day when the last of a barrage of questions came.

"How will the Queen react to Hope's mother's demise?   She's not exactly the type of woman that you vet to be in line for the throne," a louder reporter screamed.   "Hope are you suicidal as well?"

The question paralyzed Hope.   Stopping in her tracks, she began to turn toward the voice of the man when Michael wrapped his large arm around her and guided her out of the door. As the sun and the breeze blew through her hair and over her face, it carried with it a tear that slipped from the corner of her eye and down her cheek.

A large black Mercedes Benz was waiting for them at the door.   Geoff quickly opened the door for Hope and Michael and made sure that they got in without interruption. Hitting the top of the car to signal the driver to drive, he made his way to the car behind them and followed the motorcade out onto the roadway that had been blocked off for their exit off the premises.

Hope was speechless. Sitting back in the car, she snatched off her shades and finally took a deep breath. "What the hell?" she said, wiping her eyes. "Who told them about my mother?"

Michael sat back in the seat and shook his head. "I have a few ideas," he said, biting his lip. "I'm so sorry."

Hope folded her arms. "Is Thalia behind this?"

Michael clenched his jaw. "Funny, I was just asking the same question about that cock sucker, Sean." He caught himself. "Excuse my language."

"Excused," she smirked. "So what are we going to do about it? We can't just let them run over us?"

Pulling his cell phone out, he sneered. "I'll get Geoff on this."

Hope had other concerns. Putting her hand over his and his cell phone, she asked the question that was bothering her the most. "Am I going to be a problem for you?" she asked sincerely.

Michael gripped the phone in his hand and turned to her. "If you leave me, yes, you'll be a problem for me."

Hope knew that he was deflecting from the seriousness of the situation. "You know what I mean, Michael," she said, pressing him for an answer.

Suddenly, he was serious. "Did you mean what you said to me back in Hernando?"

"What part?" she asked, frowning.

"The part where you said you loved me too."

She shook her head. "Yes, I meant every word of it."

"Well, so did I. This isn't the 19th century or even the 20th century. No one is going to choose who I love and no one is going to be allowed to take you away from me. I may be a Prince to England, but with you I'm just a man. No one is going to get between the two of us."

His words soothed the deepest of her worries. "I'm just scared," she said, scooting over to lay her head on his shoulder.

Michael pulled off his jacket and pulled her into him. Kissing the top of her head, he looked out of the window and relaxed in the leather seats. "I'm scared too, but we'll just have to weather this together."

***

Kensington Palace
Apartment 1A

For years, Michael had fought the will of his family to live in the auspicious 1A Apartment on the historic grounds of Kensington Palace. This was the place of the extremely high born, where many of the royals and staff that supported the crown lived since the 17th century.

However, just like with many of his other protests, he had been silenced about wanting to live alone and was forced to move from his penthouse downtown to the Central London estate after a story surfaced on the news about how much he was paying in rent to live alone. Michael had to admit it was a pretty costly bill for security, the maid service, the entire top floor penthouse suite, access to helicopters, etc. But he would have gladly worked as an indentured servant to keep away from his brother's judgmental eye. So in order to appease the public and the taxpayers, he had moved begrudgingly back in the iron grip of his family's lair.

Richard lived in the well-known Apartment 1 with his wife and children, and from time-to-time demanded Michael's presence for dinner and clandestine conversations, especially regarding matters of state. However, where they were once strained, relations had gotten much better between the brothers when Michael started to see Duchess Thalia.

Now, here he was again, on the bad side of public opinion and his brother's approval. Home sweet home.

The motorcade pulled up to his apartment and the men quickly began to unload his few small bags. Standing outside in front of the entrance, Hope looked up at the darkening skies and pulled off her shades. She could smell the rain in the air.

Michael took her hand and led her up the stairs. His butler quickly opened the doors for him to his home and he moved out of the way and motioned for Hope to step inside. As she stepped across the threshold, a row of maids in formal staff attire, bent their heads and bowed out of respect.

Hope looked around the apartment in complete awe. It was so regal, so elaborate. Befitting a king, the home was a testament to his crown. Gold gilded doors, high ceilings, breathtaking art, and priceless statues, rich pewter colored walls, tall windows with expensive drapes, elegant furniture and the smell of unadulterated money.

She stood in the middle of the floor looking around in awe. "Michael," she said on bated breath. "This is…surreal."

He smiled, glad that she approved. "It's our home for now," he said, laying his jacket on the back of one of the chaise lounge chairs. "Shall I give you a tour?"

"Please," she said, pulling off her baseball cap. "I feel too underdressed to even be here." A nervous chuckle pushed out of her. "God, you must have thought my home was so shabby."

Michael frowned. "No, I did not. It was perfect." He walked up behind her and put his hands on her shoulders. Massaging her tight muscles until she began to relax, he bent and kissed her neck. "Shall we start with a tour of the bedroom?"

Hope blushed. Looking behind him for the staff, she realized that they had quietly excused themselves already from the room. "Where did they go?" she asked perplexed.

Michael shrugged. "Wherever they go," he laughed a little. "Let someone else take care of you for a little while. Trust me, they take great pride in their work. And they are well treated. I'm not the type of person that would allow anything less."

"It just feels weird to have a butler or maid tending to me," she said, turning to him. Her eyes were bright with excitement.

Michael was glad. Earlier, she had been so hurt by those hounds at the airport. He was hoping that being here might lighten her mood, although it had the opposite effect for him. He would have rather been back in Hernando in her bed making love.

Michael kissed her lips. "Let's get you a hot bath, a change of clothes and dinner. And we can talk about all the things we are going to do together now that you are here." The look in his eye said that he wasn't talking about things to do together outside of the bedroom. Slipping a hand behind her on her lower back, he escorted her to the spiral staircase that led upstairs to his master bedroom.

Hope felt like a fish out of water. This home was amazing and everything in it, but as soon as she walked into his apartment, the first thought that came to mind was did she belong here. However, Michael seemed to not have the same thought in his mind at all.

Leading her to the room at the end of the hall with white double doors, he grasped the gold-gilded knobs in his hand and pushed the doors open to a luxurious bedroom that seemed to minimize all the beauty outside of the room. A king-sized oak sleigh bed sat against a wall of art that span from the 18th century until today. In frames that probably cost more than her home under special lighting, the back wall was a sight that one would have more than likely seen in a Smithsonian. His bed, a vision of sex, was covered in dark thick comforters, huge body-sized pillows and a newspaper. On the opposite wall was an uncompromisingly large shelf of books in rows up to the vaulted ceiling and down to the floor. The only windows in the room were on the far right side of the opulent room and were covered by dark curtains with white linen drapes, pulled to the sides and hung against golden sconces. A simple wooden desk sat in front of the windows with a lamp, a photo of his mother in a beautiful frame and Michael's writing papers.

On the same wall was a large fireplace and to add a more modern touch to the room a television mounted over the mantle.

"It's very masculine," she said, trying to find the words. "And very stately."

"And very boring," Michael said, closing the doors behind them. "I wish that you could have seen my penthouse. It was more our style, you know. Very modern but at the same time a place that you enjoy without leaving for a month."

Hope smiled when he said our style. Her eyes flashed with promise. "So what did you have in mind in terms of a bath?" She dropped her purse on the floor.

Michael smirked. "I have the mind to give you one."

"Really?" she laughed. "You're going to give me a bath in the middle of the day."

Michael pulled at the buttons of his shirt. Slipping it off, he pulled off his undershirt to reveal his perfect muscular frame. "Do you have a problem with that, Ms. Daniels?"

Hope raised her palms. "Hey, you won't get an argument from me, Your Highness."

"Then why are you still clothed?" He asked, pulling at the buckle of his pants.

"I'm just enjoying the show," she said walking over to the bed.

Michael growled. "If you go over there and get on that, I'll be forced to move to DEF-CON 3."

Hope laughed as he threw his pants to her. "What is DEF-CON 3?" She looked out of the window and saw heavy raindrops hitting the window pane. It was a perfect day now. In the coziness of his private chambers, she felt suddenly as safe as she did back in her home.

He grabbed the remote and turned on his Bose system. "This is DEF-CON 3," he said, putting on a song. Pink Floyd's Marooned lit up the room. The hidden small speakers put out a crystal clear vision of sex.

"What is this?" Hope asked, listening to the song.

"Pink Floyd," he said, walking up to her naked. "And you're still clothed." Putting his palm in between her breasts, he playfully pushed her back on the bed. Grabbing her feet, he first pulled off her boots, then her socks, then made his way up to her jeans and pulled them off. Helping him out, she pulled off her shirt, but when she went for her bra, he stopped her.

"No, don't touch it," he ordered. "Sometimes, when you want something done right, you have to do it yourself."

Snickering, she laid back on the bed again. "Okay, Tiger."

His left eye twitched. "Why do you call me that, anyway?"

"Because you have a deadly gaze," she said, as she watched him slowly and seductively remove her powder blue lace panties. Massaging her inner thighs, he watched her give in to his demands.

Her mouth opened in pleasure.

"You like that?" he asked, as he grabbed her legs and turned her over on her stomach.

Her eyes closed as his fingers stroked gently over her backside. "Yes," she whispered.

His fingers flicked at her bra and unhooked it. Removing the article of clothing from her body, he kissed down the length of her long back to her ample bosom. Massaging her slowly, he kissed the round orbs with his tongue as he spread her legs further open.

Hope could feel his hot skin pressed against hers and smell his cologne all around her. She could feel his hardness pressing against her, aching to be buried inside of her body. She could feel his hands roaming all over her, stroking and massaging her muscles, easing the tension of a long day. And in that moment, she felt completely at ease. No more lights, no more questions, just the privacy they needed to do what they did best...love each other.

"I love you," he whispered.

"I love you," she answered.

Looking across the room at the rain beating heavily against the window, Hope closed her eyes as she felt her prince gently push deep inside of her.

Chapter 19

It had been ten days since the royal couple had been spotted at Heathrow Airport. And since their appearance, it was as if they had disappeared off the face of the earth. Instead of setting up interviews and coming out publicly the way that Michael had done with Thalia, he instead kept his mouth and his shutters closed. Holed up in the royal apartment on Kensington Palace grounds, he had ordered the best foods, wine and treats that money could buy and decided to stay completely out of the public's eye.

It wasn't that he was ashamed of her. In fact, he was prouder of her than he had ever been of any woman. It was simply that he had made a promise to protect her, and the only way that he could do so was to keep her away from prying eyes until he could train her in the art of public relations.

Every media outlet on both sides of the Atlantic Ocean had begged for an interview from the Royal Family, but just like Michael, Richard was happy to turn them down. So, the paparazzi was forced to do what they did best – stay outside of the property day and night in hopes of a glimpse of the now internationally known Hope Daniels.

Just to make sure that they were not interrupted, Michael changed the shifts of the staff to accommodate them when they needed help but to give them more privacy. After all, they liked *exploring* the rooms of the apartment alone and uninterrupted.

And while Hope and Michael had not left the house, he had ordered her beautiful clothes from some of the most expensive clothiers in London along with shoes, lingerie and jewelry – just in case they had to make an appearance somewhere. Only, Hope had not managed to wear much outside of the French lace panties and his t-shirts.

At near dusk on a dreary, rainy Wednesday, Michael and Hope cooked their dinner alone while watching one of Michael's favorite BBC shows, Copper, on the television mounted on the wall. The perfectly modern kitchen was made for a king with its stainless steel appliances, granite floors and countertops, beautifully designed oak cabinets and top-of-the-line appliances. It was Hope's dream kitchen. She couldn't cook enough. Every day, the staff brought more fresh vegetables, fruit and herbs. Every day, more wine and drinks and sweets.

She had to remember to pace herself, in case she gained more weight than she needed.

Preparing an eclectic meal of spring salad, bangers and mash and cottage pie, the two were scantily dressed as normal with Michael in his boxers and Hope in one of his most comfortable tailored Oxfords. With full glasses of wine and several cookbooks out, they laughed and talked over half-burned down fragrant candles and an island table full of ingredients.

"So, then I tell him the difference between the two is that she actually was once a man," Michael concludes his joke as he cut up the last of the onions and peppers on the cutting board. "So, it served him right with all of his woman hating."

Hope paused in shock. "Wait, really?"

He nodded. "Really." Popping a ripe cherry tomato in his heart-shaped mouth, he put the freshly cut vegetables in the bowl with the rest of the ingredients. Its fragrant mix wafted up to his nose and his mouth watered.

"But I thought she was a woman?" Hope frowned.

"She is a woman...now." He shrugged. "You know, after the change."

Hope's brows raised. "Oh...wow. How did he react?"

"He almost had a heart attack right there. Served the bastard right. She was more of a woman than he could ever handle and more of a man than he'd be."

Hope laughed. "Good for her."

Walking over to her side of the island, Michael grabbed her by the waist and pulled her to him. Nudging his head into her curly hair, he hugged her. "I have a surprise for you before we finish dinner."

She grinned, feeling him harden behind her. "Would that gift be about ten inches?"

Biting at her ear, he groaned. "That's on the dessert menu." Grabbing her hand, he led her out of the kitchen, through the hallway of historic paintings and up the back stairwell to the second level of the house.

"Where are we going?" she asked curiously.

"We're almost there," he said, so excited he wanted to burst.

Opening the door to one of the guest bedrooms, he stepped aside.

Hope walked in and put her hands to her mouth. In complete disbelief, she meandered up to her beautiful paintings all lined up with fresh new supplies to finish her work. The painting that she had left incomplete was sitting by the window with a beautiful little stool and a drop cloth draped below it. And beside it on a modest little table with fresh flowers were pictures of her mother and grandmother – the same photos she had on her nightstand at home.

"Michael," she said with tears in her eyes. "I can't thank you enough."

"I had them delivered while you were sleeping today. I'm sorry it took so long for me to collect them, but I knew you needed to get back to your work." He walked beside her and held her hand as he looked at the painting. "I just wanted you to know that what is important to you is important to me."

Turning to him quickly, she hugged him tightly. "Thank you, thank you," she said, wiping tears of joy.

Michael was happy that she was happy. It set the mood for what he wanted to ask her next. "So, with your work here, I was hoping that you might consider staying a little while longer."

She tilted her head. "How much longer?"

Forever, Michael thought to himself. Instead, he gave a more realistic timeline. "Until you decide otherwise," he said, eyes sparkling with promise. "I want you to live here with me."

Hope couldn't deny that she had thought about it, but broaching the subject might make this fairytale too real for him. So, she had simply allowed herself to live in the moment.

"How will your family react to us living together?" she asked, trying to keep everything in perspective. "You've seen the newspapers, and so have I. We're all that anyone can talk about over here or at home for that matter. I don't want to make your life any more complicated than I already have."

Michael huffed. "You don't make it complicated. You make it worth living. Since you've been here, since I've met you, I've been a changed man. I can think straight. I feel alive. I know what I want out of life. And I want you." He brushed through her brown locks. "You complete me, Hope."

Awash with emotion, she nodded. She believed his every word, because she felt it as well. She loved him more than any man she had ever loved before.

"So say yes," he said with a chuckle. "You have me in all sixes and sevens over here."

"Yes," she said, feeling like it was more of a proposal than an agreement. "I'll be your live-in girlfriend."

***

On the other side of Kensington Palace, the mood was not so amicable. Sitting among a room full of counselors, Richard listened as the men argued about his brother and what to do with him. He knew Michael well and he also knew that putting pressure on him to end his relationship with Hope would only push him further into her arms, but he was finally left with no choice.

"The public is demanding an answer," one of the counselors said, beating one hand into the other in a very dramatic fashion. "She's not even British."

"She's not noble. She didn't graduate from Oxford. She didn't even graduate from Harvard. She went to art school for goodness sake," another man argued.

"What if he gets her pregnant? A child would disrupt the very fabric of this country," William said as he stared out of the window at the rain. "This is a very volatile situation. She could bring the entire country down, Your Highness."

Richard had heard enough. Shifting in his chair by the fireplace, he rubbed the head of his Jack Russell, Porgie, waved his hand dismissively. "I've heard quite enough."

The men, all rumbling about, quickly quieted down, to hear what Richard had to say. He looked around at the men who were all conspiring against his brother and felt a sudden sense of regret for Michael. The boy had never truly been happy and he knew that whatever decision they came to tonight, would not make him any happier, but this was a matter of state, not of the heart.

"I am going to present him with everything that has been said," Richard said, picking up his glass of water to stop the tickle in the back of his throat. "I'm going to present him with Thalia's offer," he said, looking over at her father, who was conspiring more than any other in the room. "And I'm going to present Hope with the royal offer," he said looking at William.

"And what if they both deny all offers?" Thalia's father asked.

"This isn't a dictatorship," Richard said with a sneer. "And let me all remind you that my brother is still your soon-to-be-king. Keep your head about yourself with this plotting lest he find a way to figuratively take it off when he comes into power. Trust that any decision that is made, he will know who made it, because I will tell him. I will not leave this world a liar and a cheater of hearts. I will be persuasive and just, but the ultimate decision lies with him."

There was a tight stillness in the room. Most thought that Richard might be conversely heavy-handed about Michael's future, but it seemed that the hours and hours of conversation had only softened his position and sickened him with grief. Plus, the idea that Michael would know exactly who had a hand in this proposal might not bode well for everyone in the room.

Richard sank down in his chair, sick with not only physical pain but sorrow. "Leave me now," he ordered, looking into the fire. "And William."

"Yes, Your Highness," William answered quickly as he filed into a line to leave the study with the rest of the men.

Richard pursed his lips together. "Send Geoff in."

"Yes, Your Highness."

Geoff was standing outside with the rest of the various security details, waiting on direction. However, he knew, unlike the rest of the men around him, exactly what was going on behind those closed doors and that it would all come down to how far Richard was willing to push Michael. In order to actually get the desired outcome, however, that push would have to be off a cliff.

As Geoff eyed his older brother, William coming out of the study obviously exhausted from the conversation, he could tell by the worried look on his brother's face that things were not good.

"Prince Richard would like a word with you," William said, resting his hand on his brother's shoulder. "I need you to think of the crown and do exactly as he asks. It's no secret how close you and Michael are, but this is bigger than friendship."

Geoff hated that his brother felt the need to remind him. Without a word, he walked into the door and closed it behind him.

Richard had finally found his way up out of his chair and was making himself another stiff drink. From various quiet reports around the palace, it was being said that Richard, normally a very sober man, had taken to drinking more when he was alone – not that Geoff could blame him. When a man's mortality was nearing its end, one tended to numb the pain of the inevitable.

"Would you like one?" Richard asked, raising his crystal tumbler. It caught the light of the embers from the fire just across the way from him.

"Yes," Geoff said, politely. After all, why should the man be made to drink alone?

Richard gladly poured him a glass and then offered it to him.

Geoff took it and nodded. Quietly, he waited for instruction.

Richard, however, wasn't exactly ready to get to that. "You're the only one out of all these bastards who knows my brother and you're the only one who has met Hope Daniels."

Geoff wasn't sure if that was a question or not but answered. "Yes."

Richard raised a brow. "Well, what are your thoughts on their relationship?"

Now, he'd need the drink. Taking a gulp of the scotch, he relaxed his shoulders a bit "It's serious."

"As in love?"

Geoff's right eye twitched. "As in love."

"But so quickly," Richard said, scratching his brow in confusion. "You know he's never been the type to move quickly. What about this girl..." He corrected himself. "What about this woman, in your honest opinion, has changed him."

Geoff did feel that Michael had changed. He had seen him grow as a person in a few short weeks, but he didn't feel that it was all due to Hope. Michael had been hurt by Thalia's confession, but it had also opened his eyes to what he could be potentially missing in a relationship.

"She is real," Geoff said, following Richard as they walked, back to his chair.

"Go on," Richard said, truly intrigued. "In what way is she so real?"

That was such a fluid question until Geoff truly had to take pause. He took another gulp and licked his lips. "Michael has never felt good enough. And I say this with the utmost respect for you, sir."

"Of course you do. There are no airs here. We are just two men talking," Richard said sincerely. "Please, go on, Geoff. I value your opinion."

"And I appreciate it, sir," Geoff said, taking a seat beside him. Legs spread and elbows on his knees, he tried to find the best way to say what needed to be said. "I don't pretend to know how hard it is to be born to royal blood. While my family has always honorably been in service to your family, we are...commoners. That's never been a bad thing in my eyes, because it has allowed us to see the world in a different light and provide a different perspective for you. But Michael has always seemed different. He never desired the crown. He wanted to make his own way and do his own thing, and I think that he despised the idea that he was so close in line to be King, because with that responsibility came more attention from the media and the fans and the rest of the world."

Richard agreed. "Since he was a boy, I've noticed the same. But I'm inclined to believe that he will be a better king for it."

Geoff shrugged. "That could be. But growing up in your shadow was never easy for him. Sure, he got the girls and the popularity because of his looks, but you were so fucking put to-gether." He abruptly stopped and cringed. "Forgive my profanity."

Richard quipped. "Not a fucking problem."

Geoff exhaled and took another drink. "Hope doesn't seem to care at all about his title. I know for a fact that she couldn't see him, so she didn't even know he was handsome. She had no idea he had even a pound to his name. When she fell for him, it was instantaneous and it was genu-ine."

"Exactly what Michael was looking for," Richard said, finishing his drink. "Exactly what I told him wasn't possible."

"You said it," Geoff said, sitting back in the chair. "He loves her for her honesty and her ambition and how tough she is. She lost her family; he lost his father. They both have been hurt by the people that they thought loved them. They are sort of kindred spirits."

Richard understood perfectly. "And now here we are plotting like Brutus and his senate in the middle of the night to stab Caesar in the back." He put down his glass. "I'm not proud of it. And I'll not hide my hand. But have you seen the newspapers. Have you heard the public outcry? Because they have not given an inter-view or one explanation of their relationship, speculation is at the highest that I've ever seen."

"Maybe they should give an interview then?" Geoff said, knowing that was not the direction that the conversation was going.

Richard rubbed his hand over his smoothly shaven face. "I love my brother. I always have. After father passed, I swore to do my absolute best by him, and that's why it shames me to say this, but certain ties must be severed."

Geoff didn't answer. There was no need to answer. He wasn't here to make a final decision, just to deliver a message. Knowing his place, he settled for hiding his approval behind one final gulp of scotch. "What does Your Highness require of me," he said formally.

***

Hope had settled into the studio and began to work, so Michael excused himself and went to his study to handle some unattended responsibilities. It was strange. Although she was only a few rooms away, he felt she was too far. It was hard for him to concentrate as he tapped on his computer. He wanted to go back into the studio, grab a seat and watch her work. Better yet, he wanted to throw her on the floor and make love to her again.

He tried hard to get a grip on his emotions, but they grew exponentially by the day? Was this what love truly was? If so, he had been sorely misguided before. Hope was brilliant, funny and just. She was so incredibly honest until he found it hard not to ask her what she thought on all subjects in his life.

There was one subject in particular that was looming in the front of his thoughts. With Richard getting ready to take the seat when his mother passed, which would be a long while, based upon how well physically, she was. It left Michael with nothing but time to think of his own life. He had talked to Hope about his desire to return to Africa and continue with his work there. He wanted to continue his work at the village he had spent so much time in and work on further developing his infrastructure. He wanted to travel the continent to continue to talk with leaders about better schools and better global opportunities. He wanted to get the hell away from London.

And where Thalia had quickly tore down his idea, Hope found it to be a remarkable one. And when he had asked if she would travel with him, she had agreed.

There were a few other questions now that he wanted to ask. But he felt foolish about them. After all, while he was in love, he was still a sensible man. And Hope was a sensible wom-an. He didn't want to scare her away with too much at once. But maybe since he had convinced her to stay in London with him, he could also convince her of his other proposals.

Hearing the doorbell, he raised his head from his computer. Other people might very well receive unannounced guests, but he was a prince. Such a thing was not done. Making his way quickly and curiously downstairs to the front door, he opened it to find Geoff standing in the rain, just under the entryway.

"Shit, you gave me a start," Michael said, smiling. "Come on in."

Geoff did so quickly, leaving the guards, who were always there, alone in the rain to keep watch as normal.

Wiping the rain water from his face, Geoff looked around the apartment and smirked. "It's strange not having your staff here to greet me."

Michael ran a hand through his blonde curls. "Well, I didn't really want them to see me like this," he said, motioning down to his boxers. "Plus, Hope and I like our privacy."

"How is she?" Geoff asked, walking with Michael into the sitting room.

"She's great," Michael said, sniffing his friend. "Have you been drinking?"

"Just a couple of scotches," Geoff said, sitting down. His brow furrowed. "I need to talk to you. It's important. Otherwise, I would have rang first."

Michael's face tightened. Closing the doors behind him, he folded his arms across his chest. "What does he want?"

"He wants you and Hope to join him at Balmoral tomorrow evening," Geoff said, releasing a deep breath.

"Nothing good ever happens at fucking Balmoral." His blue eyes narrowed. "You didn't answer my question. What does he want when we get there?" Michael asked, lowering his voice just in case Hope came to the door.

"It's been run all the way to the top. This discussion is about Hope," he said, refusing to lie to his friend. "They believe that she is a liability to the entire country. Since the relationship has gone public, it's been a crisis. Even the stocks taken a significant dip."

Michael was well aware of the stocks. He had seen a drop in his own but didn't care. He focused on the thing he wanted to know the most. "The top?" Michael said, walking over to the window. "You mean my mother."

"She knows, yes."

"And just what did the queen mother say?" Michael asked sarcastically.

Geoff sucked his teeth. "To end it."

That made Michael laugh. Turning around, he shook his head. "Just like that, eh? End it. Send her packing. Who the fuck do these people think that they are? I'm not the fucking prime minister. I didn't sign up to run this country."

Geoff raised a hand. "Forgive me. I know you're angry, and I expected you to be, but I have to tell you based upon the number of men who were gathered at your brother's behest, this won't just go away because you choose to ignore it. I'd worry about more drastic measures later. You must face this head on for Hope's sake."

Michael silenced his rant. Breathing heavily, he put his hands over his mouth to keep from screaming aloud. A silent chaos was clawing at his insides as he took a deep breath.

"If they intend to push my hand, they won't like the outcome," he threatened.

Geoff nodded. "I know, Your Highness. But what say you? Will you attend the meeting with Hope?"

Michael got his wits about him and smiled. "Please tell Prince Richard that we will attend."

Standing up, Geoff debated if he should tell his friend the other part, the most important part, that Richard was dying, but he could tell by the redness in Michael's face that he had better stick to what he was charged to do.

"May I take my leave, sir?" Geoff asked formally. "You may," Michael said, turning from him.

Chapter 20

Hope could not make a decision. As she stared into the walk-in closet full of designer dresses that Michael had ordered and had delivered the night before, she was absolutely flabbergasted by the vast array of choices. He had already bought her so many clothes, but tonight was different. He wanted her to look special to meet his family – the Royal Family.

Just the idea of meeting Richard and his wife, his mother – the Queen of England and whoever else was invited was freaking her out. She didn't know anything about eating with 20 utensils. She didn't know how to properly greet a royal. She didn't know how to talk to one? She's be a complete fish out of water while making an utter fool of herself in a $10,000 designer dress.

As if there wasn't enough pressure on her, she couldn't quite figure out what was wrong with Michael. He seemed different after Geoff had stopped by yesterday, but he didn't say why. And she loved him too much to press him. It was probably something to do with country business, a thing that she had no business meddling in the first place. Besides, if it were that important, surely he would have told her.

A hairstylist, manicurist, make-up artist and personal assistant had been summoned before dawn to begin the royal prep for her, and it was now after 10:00 in the morning with a goal of being done by three. Plus, Michael had insisted on full breakfast, massage and facial for her, while he went off to handle some *things*.

This had been the first time since he had arrived back in London that he had actually left the apartment, and she was quite glad that she didn't have to go with him. Even though she'd been a ghost, she had seen all the news stories and read the blogs, articles and social media. It was enough to make any sane person crazy. So when he said that he'd be leaving alone, she nearly jumped for joy.

Still, this entire prep process was stomach wrenching. He wanted her perfect and ready when he arrived back to take a private plane to a place in Aberdeenshire, Scotland called Balmoral Castle. PERFECT. The thought was terrifying, especially since she'd never been perfect in her entire life.

Finally making her decision, she stood up from her chaise longue chair and pointed to the long black dress the assistant stood holding beside a shorter blue one. "I like that one," she said, scratching at her head, which was now covered in rollers.

"This one, ma'am?" the assistant asked, voice sounding questionable.

"What's wrong with it?" Hope asked, deflated. "Is it too revealing?"

The pudgy little woman in jeans, a green sweater and riding boots was flush with embarrassment. "No, ma'am. It's not that at all. I just think with such a beautiful figure, you might want to show it off more."

Hope shook her head. "Then help me, please. What would you pick?"

The assistant burst into a sudden and bright smile. "I have just the thing. Quickly ladies, pull out the Chanel dresses," she said running back into the closet.

***

Buckingham Palace
10:30 A.M.

The hordes of people surrounding the palace and screaming Michael's name was daunting. They had been there since the media first spotted him leaving Kensington Palace. All around the city, people gathered blindly hoping their destination might be where he ended up. And many assumed based upon the fact that he had been holed up in his apartment for two weeks that his first stop might be at the Royal Palace.

They were correct.

As security pushed their way through the crowds and into the gates of the palace, he ducked his head and hid behind shades to keep the flash from blinding him even through his tinted windows. It had to be hundreds of paparazzi out there all snapping their dreadful cameras at the same time.

Quickly escorted out by a large detail of security, he nearly ran to his mother's private quarters.

"Good morning, Your Highness," one of the Queen's closest assistants said as he approached the door of his mother's private chambers. She was obviously there to stop him, but such a thing would not be possible today.

"Is she available?" Michael asked, looking past her at the closed double doors.

"I apologize. The Queen is with someone," her assistant said, motioning toward the parlor. "If you would just have a seat, she'll be out…"

Michael had heard enough. This was no time for diplomacy. And to hell with anyone that thought they were going to keep him from seeing his mother for another moment.

Side-stepping past her, he pushed his way through the doors and past security to find his mother with the Duchess of Yorkshire. They both turned startled and looked at the man, visibly sweating.

Michael took a second to catch his breath. Dipping his head out of respect, he stilled his shaky voice. "I need a word with you," he said to his mother, ignoring the woman opposite her all together.

The queen, as graceful as possible, smiled at her son, and set down her porcelain cup of Earl Gray tea on the table. "Would you be so kind as to excuse yourself until I am done?"

"Forgive my abruptness and my rudeness, Mother, but no I will not," Michael said as security stood behind him, unsure of what to do. This was a first for them. Never had the prince been so direct. And if the Queen chose to have him escorted out, how would they be able to do so without creating a scene?

The Queen looked over at the Duchess, weighing all of her options quietly, and gave a smug smile of irritation. "I'll call on you later this week, and we can continue this intriguing conversation."

"It will be a pleasure Your Majesty," the Duchess said, putting her cup down on the table and standing. With a curtsy, she quickly excused herself and the doors were closed and security gone.

Michael walked up to the window and looked down at the people still crowding around waiting for a glimpse of him and shuddered in pure exhaustion. "Why would you not return my calls yesterday? I told them it was urgent," he asked, slipping his balled up fists into the pockets of his pants.

"I'm not here to serve you," she said simply. Her eyes followed him as he paced. "If I recall correctly, your phone has been unavailable for the last two weeks and for nearly a week while you were in the United States."

He turned to her and shook his head. "You know why?"

"Do I?" she asked softly. Wiping her mouth with the napkin, she placed it on the table.

"I knew what you would say? I knew what you all would do, what you're preparing to do in fact," Michael said, clenching his square jaw. His beating heart nearly leapt out of his chest. "And I won't give her up. I came here to tell you that."

The Queen, in an elegant pink suit, behind an elegant bouquet of carefully crafted pink roses, sighed. "You came here to beg me for intelligence about what is going to happen at Balmoral tonight. You came here to beg my allegiance in your quest to disrupt this country, but more importantly than that, my wishes. You came here to rant at me like a teenage boy the way that you did when I insisted that you return that horrible Maserati that was gifted to you by the Sheik."

"This isn't like that and she isn't an automobile!" He snapped.

The sternness of her tight face pulled her son back into a place of proper respect. Posture perfect, she motioned at the chair across from her. "Do you expect me to actually sit and look up at you while you berate me?" Her voice darkened. "Sit down."

Michael did what she asked reluctantly. "Why are you doing this? You have your King."

The queen's face seem to break as he said the words. "Your brother has important business that he would like to discuss with you tonight. He wants to be the one to discuss it with you. I will respect his wishes."

"You can just tell me what he wants *now*. And then I can tell you what I'm going to do *now*. I don't want to go to Balmoral and have him chastise me like a child. And I won't have him hurt Hope. I promised her that much. God, for what she has been through, I owe her that much."

The queen corrected him. "You're behaving like a child now."

"I am not a child," Michael said, trying to control his temper.

She shook her head. "Grow up, Michael. This world is bigger than you. And like it or not, after tonight, you will be required to be a child about your life no longer. These foolish ideas that you have about life and your place in it must end."

Michael placed his hand on the table. "I love her."

"You barely know her," she said, forgetting herself. "You are my son. And I love you, and a part of why you are so spoiled is because I have overindulged you, but this can be no more."

"I love her," Michael repeated more gravely. "And I won't be without her."

"You *will* be without her. You have a responsibility to this country and this family. And you *will* be without this woman."

"Her name is Hope Daniels," Michael nearly spit out.

"I don't care what her name is."

"You should," Michael said, eyes chaotic. "You should all care. And I love her, maybe not more than father loved you, but at least as much."

"You barely know her. How can you love her?"

Michael understood her disbelief. "I know enough about her to know that whatever happens and whatever is revealed about her in the future won't be enough to make me stop loving her. I know that she makes me feel better about myself than anyone ever has, and I know that it won't take years for me to know that she is who is best for me."

The queen reached for his hand and held it gently. Her eyes pleaded with him for under-standing. She loved her son dearly and what she had to say pained her to her core. Gripping his hand, she whispered the words. "You can-not marry her."

Michael looked at her withered, gentle hand and then lifted it to his mouth. Kissing it, he set it down on the table and stood up. Agony was evident on his face as he tried to formulate the words, but they would not come out.

"Michael," the queen said, worried for him. "Don't go. Let's talk about this calmly." She tapped the table and begged for her son to return.

Without a word, he ran a hand through his hair and looked up at the ceiling. Taking a deep breath, he looked at her and smiled. "It has been, as always a pleasure, Your Majesty," he said, turning his back to her, and then walked out of the room.

Chapter 21

Kensington Palace
Apartment 1A
1:00 P.M.

Hope could feel her anxiety building with every minute that passed. She knew that tonight was important for Michael, but she didn't understand why. She knew that she'd be meeting his family, but she didn't know exactly whom. She knew that the meeting had everything to do with their relationship, but she didn't understand what his family proposed to do about it. And to top off all the uncertainty, she felt completely alone.

And it had not been that Michael had not been a gracious host. In fact, every day, he found a way to make her feel just a little more special than the day before. He devoted all of his attention to her, and he opened up so much about his own desires in life.

He truly was an open book, and in her entire life, she had never had that with a man. Maybe it was because he had nothing to lose. After all, he was at the pinnacle of success. He was born the Prince of Wales...and gorgeous...and by all accounts of the life that he lived, extremely wealthy. Still, whatever allowed him to just be himself, she was grateful. Because just being himself, allowed him to be there for her.

And there was no doubt that Michael would be there for her tonight, but she would have liked to have Bree there as well. Such a thing, of course, could not be, but still in her mind, she fantasized about having someone at her side tonight to witness whatever might happen.

Just as she was about to pick up the phone and dial Bree, one of the staff knocked on the door and interrupted her.

"My lady?" the woman said in a mousy British accent.

Hope puts down her phone and looked toward the door. "Yes."

"The prince has arrived. He's just downstairs waiting for you," the woman said, stepping into the opening of the door. She smiled as she gazed upon Hope – fully dressed and ready.

Hope smiled back at the woman. "I'll be right down," she said, grabbing her clutch purse.

"If I'm not being too forward by saying, you look absolutely beautiful, ma'am," the lady said, moving out of the way as Hope passed.

"Thank you. Let's just hope that he feels the same," Hope said, taking a deep breath as she slowly made her way down the hall. Taking her time, she thought about what clever thing she might say to Michael when she saw him. After all, his team of assistants had dressed her up to the point that she hardly recognized herself.

As she made it to the long stairwell, she looked over the side to see Michael standing below with Geoff and his men. He was busy talking to them under his breath until her foot hit the top step. The echo silenced the room.

Then he turned to watch her descend toward him, completely paralyzed. Straightening his black suit, he walked to the base of the stairwell and waited. Looking up at her with a lusty gaze, he placed his hand on the banister, gripping it to keep himself under control.

Hope blushed incessantly. Her cheeks burned red as she realized that all eyes in the room were on her. Even Geoff smiled, which was something that she wasn't quite sure that she'd ever seen him do before.

"Your Highness" she said when she arrived one step away from Michael.

He gazed at her in sheer wonderment. *Was this an angel?*

Standing before him in a crimson red strapless Chanel gown that contrasted with her warm brown skin and fit her voluptuous form perfectly from bodice to her wide hip, down her long legs to her ankles, she presented herself with a small bow. Her long black hair flowed over her shoulders in a blanket of silken elegance. Her big brown eyes were bright with passion and desire. Her shapely lips outlined and glossed with shimmer. Her high cheek bones accentuated. Every single detail of her body had been catered to, every attribute highlighted.

"Hope," Michael said nearly in a whisper. "You are a vision," he said, taking her soft, delicate hand. Helping her to the floor, he whirled her around once. "A complete vision," he said with a proud laugh. "Isn't she, gentlemen."

"Absolutely," Geoff said proudly.

Hope leaned in and kissed his lips, despite the evidence that she knew it would leave. "Thank you. I'm very happy that you are pleased," she said, wiping his mouth.

Michael shook his head and inhaled her fragrance. She was too much. Everything about her at the moment was driving him insane. "I couldn't be more pleased." *Unless you were in my bed*, he thought to himself. The dark twinkle in his eyes told on him.

Seeing that his friend was happy and maybe a little more energized about tonight, Geoff opened the front door. "Are we ready, Your Highness?"

Michael winked at Hope. "Not just yet. One more thing." Walking over to the table nearest the stairs, he picked up a black velvet box. "While I was out, I found something for you."

Hope walked over and looked at the box with curious eyes. "For me?"

Michael opened it slowly. "From Bvlgari," he said, revealing a diamond necklace. The three-carat, flawless diamond sparkled across the room.

Her eyes beamed with joy. "Michael, it's beautiful."

He pulled the gold necklace from the box and stepped behind her. Placing the cold jewelry around her neck, he kissed her smooth skin. "Supposedly, it is inspired by the crown and the flower, two enduring symbols of glory and celebration since ancient times." He paused at her ear and hissed the words. "But when I saw it, it only made me think of you."

Hope placed her hands on the necklace and turned to him. "Thank you," she said sincerely. "I've never had anything so beautiful. It's...too much."

Michael held her gentle hands. "It's not nearly enough." Kissing her hands, he nodded.

"Now, we are ready," he said with a confident smile.

"Yes, sir," Geoff said, cueing the men to file out of the house.

As she walked beside him, she clutched his hand tightly. "I'm nervous," Hope confessed. "What if they don't like me," she asked, looking toward the open door that led out to the motorcade waiting for them.

Michael put one hand on her lower back to feel the curve that led to her well-formed backside. "You needn't worry, my dear. They will love you."

She smiled at his poor attempt to hide his own nervousness. "Liar."

"I love you," he said honestly. "And that's all that matters."

Nodding in agreement, she pursed her ruby red lips together. "Right," she exhaled. "Well, let's do this."

Out into the sunlight, they both walked together. Hand-in-hand, they were escorted to the limo and placed carefully inside. It was going to be quite a little day trip. They were going back to Heathrow Airport to a private hanger to get on a small jet that would take them on an hour's flight to Scotland and from their another motorcade would take them to

Balmoral Castle. And there Michael would present her for the first time to his family.

As the doors closed and they drove off, Michael pulled a bottle of champagne out of the side compartment and turned on the stereo. For the occasion, he picked John Coltrane's Blue Train record.

Slipping on her crimson shawl, Hope nestled down into the comfort of the leather seat. "What are we celebrating?" Hope asked, taking her eyes off the view outside of her window of Kensington Palace.

Michael's expression was calmly serene. "We are celebrating my decision to denounce the throne." Popping the cork from the bottle of expensive champagne, he poured her a hefty helping in a crystal flute and passed it to her.

Hope was suddenly confused. "Wait. What?" she said frowning. Did she hear him right? Was he kidding? Because if he was, it was a horrible joke.

Michael poured himself a glass as well. With a growl, he kicked back in his seat and put his feet up. "Tonight, my family plans to *admonish* me. My brother, who thinks he is already King of England, plans to do his usual song and dance and then present me with a shitload of ridiculous and childish ultimatums. But I'm tired of it. I'm tired of all of it. So, after a very stuffy dinner and a few drinks, I'll denounce my title as Prince of Wales, and we will leave and start our life together without any more people trying to ruin it." His blue eyes flashed at her with pure sincerity.

Lifting his flute in the air, he made a toast. "To freedom."

"Michael," Hope said, reaching out for him. "You can't do this."

"Why not?" he asked as he cocked his perfect chin up in a truly aristocratic fashion.

Hope didn't have an answer entirely. Shrugging, she ran her hands through her hair, "Because you…" She was lost for words. The music played in the background clouding out her thoughts. "Because you can't."

His head tilted. "Will you love me any less?" he asked sincerely.

"No," she said quickly. She blinked fast. "I will love you no matter what you decide. I will love you no matter what title you do or don't have."

And that was all that he needed to hear. "Then why should I worry about giving it up." He chuckled. "I don't want it."

Hope swallowed down sudden fear. "I don't want to come between you and your country. I don't want you to lose your family. Baby, you only get one – royal or not."

It was the look of concern on her face that moved him most. How she was always ready to put other people's priorities before her own. That was his comfort. "My country will be fine. They have my brother, and trust me once you meet him, you'll know exactly what I mean. He's what this country needs. And he has two beautiful children. *Heirs*." He smiled at her with all the cares now cast from his heart. "And I finally have you, and I won't just go throwing that away."

Hope's heart was heavy with despair. "I didn't mean to drive you to this."

He poured another glass. "You didn't, my love. I wanted this for so long. In fact, my desire to be alone is what tore me and Thalia apart. She was only with me for the crown so once I presented her with this outlandish idea of going to Africa to continue my work and denouncing the crown, she thought I was a complete waste."

Hope sat back in her chair and finally took a sip of her champagne. "So, you've wanted this long before me?"

Michael shook his head as he tried to recall when the idea had first come to him many years ago. "I've wanted it since I was a boy, since I buried my father. I just wanted to live. I wanted to be free."

Hope could understand that, as anyone could. After all, what was a life, if you were never truly free to live it? Plus, she had seen how hard it was to exist under the continual microscope of an entire country. Still, somehow, she felt sad to see him turn away from it, and mildly responsible for his decision.

"Don't be too hasty to decide because of me," she said, sitting up in her seat. "This isn't the kind of decision you make over dinner."

Michael moved from his seat over to hers and put down his bottle. Wrapping his arm around her, he rubbed his nose over hers. "My sweet little woman, I haven't been swift enough. I should have done this long ago."

She didn't understand. "You've been kind, and loving and honest. And I've never known anyone as noble as you. Honestly, if you were king, this world would be better because of it. The world needs leaders like you, Michael."

Michael whispered in her ear. "It's not that I don't love my country. I do. In truth, seeing my mother's standard flying high above the castle makes my heart swell, but my brother is the best king. And as long as he's around, there is no need for me."

"What about your counsel?" Hope asked. "Everyone needs good counsel. You could still be a help to your brother and your country as his counsel without giving up your birthright."

He ran a finger down her arm. "The parliament is very capable. The Prime Minister is a good man, a wonderful leader. They won't miss me," he said, laying his head on her shoulder. "I just want to go somewhere where I can make a real difference, Hope. My place is in Africa. It makes me happy. And I want you there with me. You could teach them so much."

Hearing the pleading in his voice, she could no longer argue the merits of his current position. She loved him too much to destroy his dream.

"Then, I'll stand with you," she said, holding his hand. "Whatever you decide, I'll be right there."

Michael pulled her chin up and looked into her eyes. "You are all that I'll ever need in this world."

***

Royal Deeside, Aberdeenshire, Scotland
Balmoral Castle

As the royal motorcade passed through the iron gates of Balmoral Castle with all its cars, motorcycles, pomp and circumstance, Hope sat erect in her seat utterly amazed at the sights around her. Hands planted on the leather interior of the door, she lit up like a Christmas tree as they entered the historic place where kings and queens had resided for over two centuries.

The air was thick and rich with elegance and grace.

Fresh open air. Lush green landscapes. Amazing gardens. High hanging trees and beautiful birds flying above. Even as they drove through the thickets of trees, blue skies and a triumphant sun peered down on them.

She had never seen such natural beauty. Excitement erupted inside of her, though she did a good job of hiding it. Inside, she felt like a little girl at Disneyland. She was all dressed up in a fine gown with a prince on her arm being escorted to the Royal Family.

Michael conversely became more and more physically ill as they approached the castle. His fingers clammed up and his heart raced. Opting not to have more champagne, he sat beside her quiet and stoic, going over what he was to say to his brother when the time came.

"Do I still look pretty?" Hope asked, checking her lipstick in her mirror.

"You look amazing," Michael said, pulling himself from his dismal thoughts. Sitting up, he wiped his tired eyes, ready to get this over with.

As the motorcade stopped at the front entrance of the castle, the doors to the Bentley state limousine were quickly opened. Michael and Hope stepped out and a crisp wind blew through the air. Hope looked up at the stone building in awe. Taking her hand, Michael led her toward the doorway, which was immediately opened by the head butler, Albert. Beside him stood a long line of staffers, waiting to assist the royal party.

"We are most honored to have you back in our presence, Your Highness," the butler said in his normal fashion. He bowed despite his curved fragile back. "Madam Daniels, welcome to Balmoral," he said to Hope. "We hope your stay is a truly pleasant one. Please let me know if I can be of assistance to you."

Michael stopped instead of proceeding into the foyer. "Albert, this is my girlfriend Hope," he said, looking at the other staff who stood stupefied by his introduction. "Hope this is our family's eldest and most trusted butler, Albert. He's like a great, great grandfather to me."

"Hello Albert," Hope said, offering her hand.

"My lady," Albert said, shaking as he took her hand in his own. "It's a true honor."

Michael smiled at Albert. "When I was six, he swatted me on my bottom for trying to sneak my pony into the house."

Albert smiled. "As I recall it did not stop you from trying, Your Highness."

"Nothing ever stops me," Michael said, guiding Hope inside.

While Balmoral's beauty was lost on Michael, Hope was completely transfixed. Every step she took echoed throughout the great halls. There were paintings and gold-gilded entryways, wooden doors, paintings of kings, and every imaginable beautiful thing.

William, Geoff's brother, emerged from the library in a somber dark suit and tired eyes. "Good afternoon, Your Highness," he said, offering his hand to Michael.

"William! What are you doing here?" Michael said, shaking William's hand.

"Just assisting for tonight, sir," William said, bowing toward Hope. "It's very nice to meet you, ma'am."

"This is William. Geoff's brother," Michael said, turning to Hope. He thought a more informal introduction was due. It was how he wanted the rest of the night to be. Simple and informal.

Hope's face lit up when Michael told her who William was. It was as if she was being introduced to Prince Richard. "Your brother is a charming man," she said, looking around for Geoff, who had suddenly disappeared from their side.

"We can't be talking about the same man," William joked. "Dinner has been prepared in the main eating hall for you both. Your brother and his family will join you shortly."

"How shortly," Michael asked, looking at his watch.

"Thirty minutes, sir," William answered quickly.

"Good, that gives me just enough time to show Hope the Castle Ballroom. She's going to love it." Removing her shawl from her arm, he placed it across his and took her hand. "Shall we?"

Hope nodded.

"Come and find me when it's time," Michael said, as he walked off with Hope. "I don't want to just sit around waiting on the old bugger."

***

The tour that Michael gave was absolutely breathtaking. There were so many gorgeous rooms, so much history. She tried to take it all in, but it was just overwhelming for a first visit. The paintings stuck out the most. So exquisite, so detailed. It lit her on fire with the desire to go back to Kensington Palace and begin immediately on her own work.

Michael gave his tour with true pleasure. He told her of the stories of old queens and kings, showed her private passages, allowed her to touch artifacts and opened up glass casings so that she could touch the fabric of historic garments. He took a picture of her inside of the electric car built in 1920 and took her to look at the beautiful breathtaking view from the veranda.

He was about to take her to the royal garden to get a little more intimate with her when William appeared again.

Clearing his throat, he stood in the doorway. His voice echoed throughout the veranda. "Prince Richard is ready to begin now, sir," he said, interrupting Michael giving Hope a kiss.

Michael pulled from her lips hesitantly. Looking over at William, he pursed his lips. "We'll be there momentarily."

Hope let out a sigh. "This is it," she said as the light from the windows shined down on her.

"This is it," Michael repeated. Taking her hand, he led her back to the main dining hall. Their walk was intentionally slow. Both of them wanting to take in the moment before the storm began. With no audible words shared between them, they still managed to say a lot through their emotion.

When they arrived at the main hall, the doors were opened for them by the royal staff and they were escorted inside where everyone was sitting.

The room was unlike any that Hope had ever seen. Tall ceilings with beautiful crown molding, walls painted in white and green, tall white Corinthian pillars, historic paintings of kings, cherry oak furniture, beautiful green and pink drapes, white sheers, regal chairs, crystal tableware, what seemed to be hundreds of candelabras lit with white tall candles, a table setting for a king, wine, food, drink and a table full of strangers.

The only person that Hope recognized with Prince Richard, who sat at the head of the table in a sensible black suit was his wife, Princess Madeline, who sat beside him to his left in a soft muted tan suit, black hair pulled back in a bun, diamond earrings sparkling in her ears.

Michael walked inside with Hope on his arm, looked around the room and cringed. He recognized everyone there. His brother, his sister-in-law, Richard's closest counselors, his mother's closest counselors and worse of all Thalia and her father.

"We're leaving," Michael said, turning to Hope. "We need to go now. This is an ambush."

Hope was confused. "What?"

Richard stood from his seat. All eyes on the two as they stared each other down, Richard, pressed his fingers against the table. "Sit down, Michael. We have much to discuss."

Chapter 22

It was as if someone had just stuck a red poker into Michael's eye when he saw Thalia sitting there among his family, friends and his rivals, with her chin up and her eyes blazing through him as though she had some major role in any of this. *How dare she*, he thought to himself. Sticking his chest out, he held Hope closer to him and gave a curt smile. "I'm sorry, brother, but we won't be staying," he said, eyes narrowing on Richard.

It was Hope to spoke reason to him, although she didn't understand fully what she had walked into. "Don't run from them," she whispered. "You're bigger than that."

He turned to Hope and looked down into her eyes. "I have you."

She nodded. "Yes, baby. You have me. But you need to handle this. I can deal with it, if you can," she said, pulling him gently forward.

"You don't know them. You can't handle them," he warned. He had seen them in action before, and they were nothing to trifle with.

"Listen to her," Richard said, walking over to the couple. "Have a seat. Talk with us."

Taller than his brother by a few inches, Richard stood over Hope and smiled gently. He bowed a little then offered his hand. "Very happy to have you in our presence. Michael has kept you all to himself. We haven't had the pleasure."

"Thank you," Hope said, shaking his hand. *This wasn't so bad.*

Richard turned and introduced everyone starting with his wife. When he got to Thalia, he looked over at Michael. "This is Duchess of Matsworth."

Hope recognized her face from the millions of photos and tabloids that she had read back at Kensington Palace. While beautiful, something about her face seemed sour. Hope raised a brow at the woman and smiled. "It's nice to meet you *all*," Hope said, following Michael to the seat at the end of the table.

Michael took his rightful place at the other end of the table and Hope sat across from him. Holding her hand, he tried to assure her that he'd be right here with her no matter what. Plus, seeing her in the same room as Hope made him realize how much he had settled before her. Thalia looked as bitter as ever and surely here for some great master plan.

"What vicious strategy have you been devising?" Michael asked as a servant with white gloves quickly came from the corner and poured him a glass of red wine.

"To the top," he told the servant.

"We are in discussion of the royal family," Richard said, taking his seat. He looked down at his brother and his beautiful girlfriend and felt ill. Never in a million years did he see himself having to do such a heinous thing, but here he was carrying out the wishes of his mother and his country.

"And by royal family, you mean me," Michael said in a matter-of-fact tone.

"Yes, Michael, *you*," Richard answered tersely. He let out an aggravated sigh. "There are people at this table that felt as though this conversation should have taken place between just the two of us, but I wanted you to know that everyone at this table has not only agreed to but devised the plan we are going to present to you this evening."

"Behind my back?" Michael seethed. He looked over the candlelight at his brother and around the room at the others at the table. "And why are you here?" he asked Thalia.

"I'm here because I love you, Michael," Thalia said, looking at Hope. She twisted the engagement ring that Michael had given her around on her finger. "And I don't want to see your future or this country's future in peril."

Hope bit her lip in frustration but kept a cool head. She was the one who suggested that they stay, she had to keep it together.

Michael's face was impassive to her plea. "You love the crown, Thalia. There is nothing more than that to you."

"That isn't true. You never gave me a chance to explain myself that night. You just barged out. I was overcome with worry and pain," she said, leaning into the table. "I just wanted you to understand that your place is with this country, with this family."

Madeline picked up her crystal glass and rolled her eyes at her husband. She was very much against the entire notion of forcing Michael to choose love over country or country over love, and she absolutely disliked Thalia with every fiber of her being. She found the woman vulgar and overly ambitious. In fact, she did well not to leave Richard alone with her, lest she try her best to tempt him.

Michael waved a dismissive hand. "Please stop with your lies, Thalia. They burn my ears."

"They are not lies," the Duke of Matsworth said with respect. He put on his most concerned face. "She has been in agony since you left her. My daughter loves you. Anything that she might have said that would give you reason to think otherwise was a mistake...too much wine." His words were desperate as he looked around the room for support.

"Michael, this relationship can go on no longer," Richard said, looking away briefly. "The crown needs you. This family needs you to take your rightful place. It's not that we do not respect your relationship with Ms. Daniels, which is why we brought her here. We completely respect her, but you have obligations."

Thalia looked away from Michael over to Richard. "I'm willing to forgive him. I'm willing to forgive this entire mess. We can start over. I just want him back. Would I be here making a fool of myself otherwise?"

"Things can go back to the way that they were. In actually, this relationship has proven to the British public that they will forgive you rather than push you away," William assured. "No offense to present company, but..."

"Offense taken," Hope spoke up. She held her head high and stared William in the eye. "Regardless of whether you mean it or not, offense is taken, sir. I'm not a Duchess, but I am a human being, and I won't be treated in this manner without sticking up for myself simply because you apologize first." Hope held his hand tighter. Looking around the room at the vultures, she released a breath from her parted mouth.

"Forgive me?" Michael laughed sardonically. His strong arm flexed as he pointed down the table. "You have to be fucking kidding me. *All of you.* And Hope is right. You are not excused; this is an offense, and I'll have no more of it. I don't want your forgiveness. I don't want your hand in marriage, Thalia. I'd rather be hung drawn and quartered first. I thought that I made that clear to you the last time your snakey little plan came to view." He threw down his napkin. His sneer became more pronounced. "I didn't come here for an ultimatum – to receive one or to give one. I came here to denounce my title as Prince of Wales."

Thalia looked over at her father with an I-Told-You-So glare.

Everyone else froze.

Michael continued, realizing that he had their attention. "And don't worry, I'll be making a formal statement tomorrow about it. I will not put up with this shit. Not from you, Richard, not from your gaggle of idiots, minus my loving sister-in-law, whom I deeply apologize to for having to bear witness to this atrocity, and not the crown. I love my mother, but I'm a grown man."

"There have been other developments," Richard interrupted with a physical pain now evident in his face as he wiped his sweaty brow.

"There far more important issues that have arisen outside of your relationship." Richard eyed his brother. "And they cannot be ignored any longer."

Madeline looked over at her husband and wiped a tear from the corner of her eyes. Looking down the table at Michael, she broke her silence. "Michael, you should speak with your brother in private," she pleaded.

"This can be said here," Richard said sternly.

"No," Michael said, standing up. His eye twitched. "This will be done in private, or not at all. I want to know what the hell is going on, and I don't want to hear it from this bunch."

"Please," Madeline begged her husband. "Talk to him alone."

Richard stood from the table. "We can step into the library alone," he said, looking at Hope. "I do apologize. This isn't about your caliber as a woman. This is a matter of state."

"Enough with the *state* shit," Michael said, offering his hand to Hope. "This is about a collective agenda of a very controlling family."

"We need to talk completely alone," Richard said, walking toward the door as the staff opened it for him.

"I'm not about to leave her here with these vultures," Michael said, looking at Thalia. "You especially. I bet you can't wait to be alone to say a bunch of bloody horrid things to her, but I won't allow it."

"Alone," Richard insisted louder.

"I'll be fine," Hope assured. "Just go. Talk to your brother," she said, letting go of his hand.

***

As soon as Michael and Richard left and were not in fear of returning soon, William turned to Hope awash in desperation. He only had a few minutes to present the last part of the proposal. He would have to suffer the wrath of his liege later, but for now, he had made a promise to this country and he planned to keep it.

Taking a deep breath, he smiled. "Prince Richard is sick, Thalia. He's dying of cancer. In his stead, who will run this country when the Queen Mother is gone? Richard and Michael have no other siblings and while there are others who can take up the seat, the point is that Michael is the rightful and true heir."

Hope frowned and looked over at Madeline. "Is this true?"

Madeline nodded. "He has three months *at most*. It's very aggressive. The doctors are doing all that they can, but it doesn't look good."

William got up from his seat and walked over to Hope. Sitting beside her, he ran a hand through is silver hair. "This troubles me. I've been around Michael and Richard my entire life. And the Queen has insisted that if it did not affect the state, we should do well to stay out of their personal affairs, but this is bigger than both of you. Would you not agree?"

Hope pushed back in her seat. She would not agree. "What do you want of me?"

William took the question as a sign of temporary neutrality. "The Queen would like to make you a very generous offer. She realizes that you love her son, and she has the most respect for you. But he must now begin to be prepared to be king. Within the year, Prince Michael will lose his brother. And the country will look to him to lead it sooner or later. This task is already difficult enough, but he if he is dating an *American* then it will only further impact the British community. They are looking for a British bride, ma'am."

"I love him," Hope said, tears running down her face. "And he loves me." She wiped her face. "He doesn't want this. He doesn't want any of it. You're all forcing this on him. And that woman over there is a manipulative viper. She doesn't love him, but you'd rather see him married to her than to see him happy and with me. It's senseless and archaic."

William turned toward Thalia and gave a look of contempt. That part of his plan had wilted just as he thought it might. Thalia's façade did little to entice the prince. Instead, she simply pissed him off. "If the Prince would be less burdened by being alone, then we will accept that. I speak for the Queen when I say that we won't push for a marriage to Thalia."

"He doesn't want her. Didn't you hear him? You can't make him marry her anyway." Hope finished.

Hearing enough, Thalia stood up appalled by the discussion about her like she wasn't there. "This is insane. We're placating to a black yank from Mississippi with the bloodline of a chimpanzee. Send her on her way, already."

Hope had heard enough. Before she could think, she charged straight for Thalia with intention of taking her pretty little head off her shoulders. One of the other counselors quickly caught her by her waist along with William who held her back despite her struggles.

"You bitch!" Hope exclaimed. "He hates you. And it infuriates you that he found a real woman, someone who makes you look as shabby as you are, hiding behind a title but not worth the paper it's written on. You're just a gold digging heartless social climber. It wouldn't matter if it was Michael or Satan, you'd marry anyone to be queen."

Thalia retreated behind her father. "Do you see? She's violent at the first thought of being offended. Is this what you want in your future queen? An irrational half-wit!"

Madeline stood up infuriated by Thalia's words and threw her full glass of red wine across the table onto Thalia's off-white dress. The glass landed on the floor and the staff quickly picked it up and moved out of the way. "Bitch!" Madeline sneered. "And what am I? Am I not Princess? My blood isn't as pure as yours either. As a matter of fact, it has black blood from the 18th century. I'm sure you'd be happy to sell that to the rags also. Well go sell it! None of us are good enough for your Arian bloodline. Get out! Get her out of here!" she yelled. "I want her out! I've heard enough from this tramp!"

"Your Highness," Thalia gasped. "I never meant to offend you. I had no idea. I apologize."

"Your presence offends me," Madeline said as the doors opened and Geoff waltzed in. She looked at Michael's security and wiped her hands of the wine. "Take these people off the property at once. I've heard enough."

"My apologies," the duke said, nearly push-ing his daughter out.

Hope pulled away from the men and straightened her dress. "One day, Thalia. You and I will finish this conversation," she said, pointing at her.

"I doubt it. You'll be out on your ass soon enough," Thalia said, grabbing her purse and pushing past Geoff toward the door with her father following behind her.

William quickly closed the doors, hoping that the ruckus had not breeched the library on the other side of the castle. He looked at his watch and pulled out an envelope from his pocket. Walking back over to Hope, who stood by the window, he offered it.

"This will take care of you for the rest of your life. You can paint, travel, explore...all the things that you've ever wanted to do," he said, opening the envelope.

Hope took the check and looked at it. "Twenty-five million pounds."

"We're not buying your silence. We're buying our kingdom back. Our prince is a symbol of this country. We will need him in these trying times. Your presence here prevents him from being able to do his job. Please, madam, I beg of you. Resist your temptation for him and leave."

Hope looked over at Madeline. "Is this what Richard and the Queen wants?"

Madeline fell back in her chair and rested her head in her hands. "Yes, it's what they all want." She wanted to say more but how could she go against her dying husband.

The room was rife with tension. Hope looked around in desperation. Who here was an ally? And would she ever have one if she chose to stay? Would they always be plotting against her – his Highness's ridiculous girl-friend.

William's voice was almost a whisper. "Richard is telling Michael the truth now. What do you think he will do when he finds out that his older brother is dying? Do you really think that he'll denounce his thrown then, and if he does, you always wonder would he have done it, if you hadn't been in the way?" He stepped closer to Hope. "Hate me if you must, but heed my word, you are an impairment to this king-dom. No good can come of it. Deep in your heart, you know that."

Hope felt the room began to swim. She re-membered in that moment every sweet word and promise that Michael had ever made to her, and she knew each of them to be true. She knew he would stand by her no matter what, loyal to a fault. She also knew that his true place was with this country, and if she loved him as much as she confessed, then she had to do what was best for him.

Maybe this was best.

"I'm not doing this for your money," Hope said, looking around the room with tears in her eyes. "I'm quite happy just the way that I am and with what I have. I'm doing this for him," she said, picking up her shawl. "It is apparent that if I stay, I will hurt him. And I can't bare that. I love him too much."

"The Queen insists that you take the check," William said, pushing it into her hand gently. "If you don't cash it, at least put it away. One day, you might change your mind."

Looking down at Madeline who was awash with tears and grief, Hope gestured toward her. "I'm so sorry for your loss. This must be killing you. Please accept my sincerest sympathies for your family and your loss."

Madeline wiped her face. "You're all a bunch of monsters for what you're doing to her," she said, standing up. "And I'll not have a second more of it." Leaving out of the room, she disappeared down the hallway.

Taking the check in her hand, Hope walked toward the doors with the men watching her carefully. Geoff met her and escorted her to the car.

"He will be furious that you've taken their offer," he said as they arrived at the front doors. The sun shined in on them both. She looked up into his eyes and smiled. Taking the check,

Hope tore it to pieces. Leaving it Albert's fragile hands, she sighed at Geoff. "I didn't accept their offer," she said as the doors opened to the motorcade. "I did what is best for him, because I'm just his girlfriend. And those are the wishes of his mother."

"He's a stubborn boy. Don't go too far, and don't be surprised, if he comes looking for you."

Nodding, Geoff took her hand and walked with her to the car. He helped her inside and slowly closed it securely behind her. "It's been a pleasure."

***

Michael stood in the library against the backdrop of a thousand historic books with a look of vengeance in his eyes. While he had imagined a lot from his brother, he had never truly imagined him trying to get between himself and someone he loved. His tone was bitter as he spoke.

"You disappoint me, brother," Michael said, hands in his pockets.

"I disappoint myself," Richard said, pouring a stronger drink. The wine was not nearly enough to satisfy him today. "But all that I can offer in the form of advice is to get simply get used to certain disappointments."

"I won't leave her," Michael said abruptly. "Nothing that you can say will make me."

"This isn't about the girl as much as it is about your country."

Michael cringed when he heard the words. It seemed to be the only line these people had memorized. "The people don't need me. They have you. You're the great hope. Everyone loves you. Everyone trusts you. What do they need with me anyway, Richard?"

Richard turned to his brother and took a big gulp of scotch. "There is no easy way to say this to you. I wish there were. You've been like a son to me instead of a brother and I feel completely responsible for you, but I'm dying. I've got four months before this thing they call pancreatic cancer takes me away from this place, and I need to whip you into shape."

Michael stood in shook. Unable to blink, he felt his heart pounding in his chest. "Is this some sick joke?"

"You'd have to ask the oncologist," Richard said, sitting down.

"There must be something that can be done," Michael started. He pulled his hands from his pockets and went over to the desk. Leaning on it, eyes away from his brother, he felt himself getting light-headed. Tears welded to the edges of his eyes. Damn it to hell. He had lost his father...not his brother too.

Richard pulled out his pill bottle and opened it. Taking three of the strong pain meds, he downed them with scotch. "There is nothing that can be done. And instead of staying in a hospital, I'm going to spend my final days with my beautiful wife and children."

Michael whispered. "This can't be happening."

"It's happening," Richard said in a matter-of-fact tone. "And it's happening now, which is why I've asked you to leave Hope and lead this country." He stared at his brother's wide back turned to him. "You can do this, Michael. You always could. The only person who didn't believe in you was you. It's always been that way."

"I don't want it."

"Most good kings don't want it. Most good kings have other ambitions. But another life is not what you've been given. You were given this one. Prince of Wales. And your mother and your country needs you. "

Even dying, Richard couldn't help but be a prick. Michael turned to him as he wiped the tears from his face and swallowed down his fear. "So this is why you think that it is best to run Hope off."

"Having a girlfriend is not going to help you in your current situation. You'll have enough critics as is. We need to get rid of some of your *royal* baggage and prepare you for the responsibilities that will be at hand as my cancer progresses to its full term. But I will agree that Thalia is a bad pick. I didn't see it until today. God only knows why or how I've missed it for so long." Richard set his glass down. "I want you to be happy. I've always wanted it. And I wouldn't be asking you this now, had I not just been informed in the last three weeks that I'm dying." He smiled sarcastically. "But the party is over." He meant that in more way than one, especially when it came to his own life.

"I love her," Michael said, feeling an overwhelming anger raging inside of him.

"So, I've heard." Richard folded his hands together and crossed his legs. "And I'm sorry about that. She seems like a truly lovely girl."

Michael wiped a hand over his face and drifted into the silence of the room for a minute. He would not allow himself to lose control, especially knowing that his brother was ill.

Smacking his lips, Michael looked at Richard. "I could give her up," he said, finally. "But I won't. The only reason why you are so resolute about dying is because Madeline has been the love of your life. You've had that and been allowed to keep your title. Love is what is keeping you going now. Are you really going to deny me the same thing? I'll do my job as prince, even as King, but I won't do it without her."

"You don't have a choice. You can't marry the woman," Richard said, sitting up. *Why was it so hard for Michael to see the complexities of such a thing?*

"Can't I," Michael said, pulling a box from his pocket. "I intend to, brother. I intend to just that."

"The country will not allow it," Richard warned. "They will turn against you."

"This country doesn't have a fucking choice," he said, walking to the door. "You're my brother and I love you. I'll see to it that everything that you want is done regarding this country, and I'll be there for your and my mother until the very end. I won't deny my responsibility to Britain, but I'll not deny my responsibility to myself either."

"Are you willing to live with grave the consequences of your actions? When the world turns on her, how will you feel then? " Richard asked, sitting at the edge of his chair. "I am thinking of her. Will you? For just one damn minute, will you stop thinking of yourself?"

"I am thinking of her, and every promise that I've made to her. If I cannot protect her, if I cannot love her, then I'm not fit to be king. More

than that, I'm not fit to call myself a man,"
Michael said, opening the door. "We'll talk
about this later. For now, go to your wife and…"

Madeline came barreling down the hall in
tears. Her feet echoed down the marble hall as
she ran with her hand covering her mouth.
"Where is he?" she asked Michael, nearly pushing him aside. She burst into the room and
looked at her husband. "I can't do this. That
God-awful woman, Thalia, cannot be a part of
this family. You can't leave me here alone on
this earth tied to her! This is wrong, Richard."

Michael looked down the hall. "Where is
Hope?" he asked, jaw clenched.

Madeline turned to him. "She was still in the
dining hall when I left."

Running down the hall as fast as his feet
would take him, Michael rushed toward the
dining hall after Hope, feeling as though something horrible had just transpired in his absence. When he came nearly sliding into the
room, he saw only the counselors there at the
table talking. His heart sank.

William stood as soon as he saw Michael.
"Your Highness."

"Cut the bullshit, William. Where is she?"
Michael asked, standing at the end of the table.

William looked around the room at the other
men. "We were ordered to encourage her to

leave," William answered. "By the Queen," he added. "She accepted our offer, and she is gone, sir."

Michael nearly doubled over. "What?" He hit the table with fist, knocking over the glasses of wine. "How long?"

The men jumped. "Only minutes, five at most," William answered.

"I will deal with all of you later," Michael said, belting out of the room. He ran as fast as he could, shedding his coat on the floor as he made his way toward the main hall.

Albert saw him coming and opened the door for his master.

"Where did she go, Albert?" Michael pleaded. "Where did they take her?"

"I don't know, Your Highness," the old man answered sincerely. "She left this." He offered the torn up check.

Michael saw Geoff outside sitting on the edge of the garden smoking a cigarette as he came out the front doors. "Which direction?" he asked.

Geoff stood and pointed. "She must be near the gate by now."

One of the men who had escorted them in still stood beside his bike. As soon as he saw Michael approach, he stood at attention.

"Give me your keys," Michael ordered.

"Sir?" the man asked, confused.

"Give me your fucking keys," Michael said, getting on the bike.

The man quickly gave Michael his keys.

"And your helmet," Geoff said, walking up to them.

"I have to catch her," Michael said, putting the helmet on. Turning the ignition switch on, he shifted the transmission into the neutral, pulled the clutch and pressed the start button. As soon as the engine fired, he shifted to first gear and applied the throttle. As he sped away, Geoff got on his earpiece to the front gate.

"Ms. Daniels should be approaching shortly. Stop her. I repeat. Stop her. The prince is on his way. She is not to leave out of the gates."

"Copy that," the security man answered.

It had been a while since Michael had been on a bike, but he rode it furiously. Hitting the curves and moving as fast as the bike would take him. He sped passed the confused grounds keepers and gardeners, rushed through the wiry lane, down through the thicket as fast as he could. At nearly sixty miles an hour as he approached the last stretch before the gate, he saw the car.

Flashing his lights and blowing the small horn, he tried to get her attention. "Stop the car," Geoff said into the earpiece of the driver.

"Sir, the queen has given strict orders," the driver answered.

"Tell that to your prince. He is behind you on a motorbike. If he maims or kills himself chasing you, I promise the Queen will have your head," Geoff warned gravely. "And I'll be the one to take it."

Slowing down the vehicle as they approached the gate, the driver looked back at Hope, who sat crying into her shawl. She had been crying the entire way.

From behind nearly thirty feet back, she could hear in a horn in the distance. She turned to look behind her and saw Michael on the bike.

"Stop the car," she said, turning back toward the driver. "Stop!"

The car stopped abruptly. Opening the door, she quickly jumped out. Kicking off her heels, she ran barefoot toward him. "Michael!" she called out, tears flowing down her cheeks. *She couldn't believe it. He had come for her.*

"Hope," Michael screamed. He knew that she couldn't hear him, but he still screamed anyway. Stopping the bike, he jumped off, nearly throwing it to the ground and ran to her. Catching her in his arms, he picked her up and held her close. "What are you doing, you silly girl?"

"I didn't take the money. I just heard about your brother and I know what is required of you, and I…" Her doubts pushed away as she saw his face, all red and flushed with life.

Michael stopped her mid-sentence with a kiss. Pulling away, he moved the hair from her face. "I know you didn't take the money. I wouldn't have cared if you did. I still would have come after you." He held her shoulders. "We made a promise, remember? We are not going to let anyone tear us apart."

"Michael, I love you. I love you more than words could ever explain. I just don't want to hinder you from running this country. It's such a huge responsibility." As she tried to find the words, he knelt on one knee.

"We made a promise," he said looking up at her. His blue eyes flashed with love and promise. Pulling the ring from his pocket, he smiled. "Worried that I lost it in the chase back there."

Hope's eyes bucked. Putting her hand over her mouth, she began to cry. "Michael," she said, shaking. "Baby, what are you doing?"

"Hope Daniels, will you do the honor of being my wife and…" he shrugged, "possibly the queen of England."

He opened the box to reveal a blue oval sapphire ring. It gleamed in the fading light as he waited for her answer.

Hope felt herself floating, even before she said the words. She almost had to pinch herself to make sure that it was real. "Yes," she said, swallowing down more tears of joy. "Yes, Michael, I will marry you."

Standing up, Michael slipped the ring on her finger and pulled her into him. Kissing her passionately, he held her close. "I'll never lose you again," he said with tears in his eyes. He laughed as he looked at her face still frozen in shock. "Come on. Let's get out of here and go celebrate."

"Somewhere private?" she asked as they loaded into the car.

"No," Michael said, putting his arm around her. "Somewhere where the entire world can see us."

TO BE CONTINUED
Fall of 2015

About the Author

Latrivia Nelson is proud mother of two bubbly kids, the President and CEO of RiverHouse Publishing, LLC and the Director of Communications & Marketing for a local non-profit.

When she's not working her 9-5, she happily writes interracial romance and romantic suspense novels for readers across the world. With 20 titles published to date and recognized as a national bestselling author, she has something for just about anyone.

In her downtime, she loves to have a strong Jack and Coke with fiancé, Bruce Welch, watch marathon 80's movies and order take out with her family.